The Brede Chronicles
Book 1

P.I. Barrington

Published by First Realm Publishing
Copyright © 2014 P.I. Barrington and Loni Emmert
Cover art by: Jared at Off the Wall Creations
Edited by: Gaele Hince

All rights reserved. Including the right to reproduce this book, or portions thereof, in any form without prior written consent of the author, except for brief quotes for use in reviews.
This is a work of fiction. All characters and events portrayed in this novel are fictitious or used fictitiously, and any resemblance to any actual persons, living or dead, events or locales is entirely coincidental.
ISBN 10: 1497340837
ISBN-13: 978-1497340831

DEDICATION

To my mother, Julia Anne and my sister Loni for their unwavering faith in my work.

CHAPTER ONE

The climax brought stinging tears to his eyes. The cry of the muezzin sounded out over the city calling the faithful to prayers as the new day came to life. Between dawn and early morning the flight traffic was at its slowest, giving relative quiet to the city for the brief time. Alekzander Brede rose and stood gazing out the window and then glanced back at the woman still lying in the bed.

"You know it might behoove you to know who you're sleeping with Mr. Brede," she said.

"I know who I am sleeping with…" He turned back to the window again.

"Then I presume this seals our deal?"

"It was sealed when you asked and offered to pay."

"So what was this?"

Brede shrugged.

"Your signature."

"It's not polite or helpful to insult your employer Alekzander. And I don't appreciate being dismissed like a common whore."

Rather than confirm her status, he remained staring down at the streets of New Cairo below him, watching one thief steal something from another, watched them scuffle until one ran away at full tilt. So engrossed with the scene, he barely ducked when the multi-rockets launched at him, blowing the top of the windowsill away. They exploded into tile and brick, shrapnel raining down and across the room. The woman in the bed squealed, pulling the blankets over her and screaming for servants. They came scurrying like mice, swarming the room and making obeisance to her.

Brede walked over, pulled the blankets down and inspected her briefly.

"You're fine," he told her in a dry voice. "If I leave now, they'll stop and follow me." He tugged his clothes on and eyed her one more time from her curtained doorway. Her hair and eyes were black and her body as curved and as sweet as her lips. He refused to let her know he'd have done the job for free. Unlike him she was all human, earthy and hot and passionate in all aspects.

Irresistible.

He'd be damned before he let her know that.

Brede left the room and walked down the steep stairwells and hallways of the ancient structure, emerging on the street. He walked down the middle, guns pointed sideways from his hips, occasionally blasting at ships and vehicles as he chose that might pose a threat to him, making them scatter among the crowded streets. The past existed alive and well, side by side in 2107 Cairo where hundreds of small craft jetted in and out of the huge new buildings towering a thousand stories above the edifices of the ancient city. Both space and land craft shared the narrow streets with citizens and camels, squeezing among them in the old city, scattering the screaming goats, donkeys, cattle and carts missing them by centimeters and leaving the citizens to try to gulp precious non-dusty breaths when they could. Howdahs swayed uneasily back and forth on the tops of the camels, the speed craft darting between their movements, close enough to lift their curtains from the engine breeze. They zipped over the souks barely high enough to miss entangling with the curtains and banners and flags of every color and design imaginable sending chickens, tables laden with baskets of fruit, vegetables, spices and bolts of silk flying across the narrow streets.

The city-states of New Cairo and Thebes Two and their combined 175 million citizens were two of the last bastions of civilization on Earth: both profited from the arrival of Midinium, brought by the Amphidians.

Brede didn't bother to check the damage he'd done as he walked, making sure his enemies were discombobulated. He'd added a few with his new association with Narita Sabbad as well as the myriad he already possessed.

People knew him; he was instantly recognizable with his impressive height and broad powerful body. They knew his dusky skin and glittering dark blue eyes with no pupils and box braids pulled back with a band. They knew him and they knew to stay away from him.

Brede turned down a side alley away from the crowds and followed its crooked path to the outskirts of the city where he kept his own vehicle, hovering in an archway, hidden by a thick heavy door that opened and rose into the wall.

"*Alekzander!* Hey! Wait! *Alekzaaander!*" The high voice followed him from the doorway he exited, through the streets and along the crooked road until he stopped and held the door open.

""Hey Alekzander! Didn't you hear me? I been calling you since Center Street," it was the thief he watched from the window just before it exploded. Brede rolled his eyes and shook his head.

"What do you want Elektra?" he sighed.

"I heard you just got a job!"

"How the hell do you know that?"

"I got my connections. Heard you literally just sealed the deal with a kiss. She payin' ya' big time Alekzander?"

"It's none of your business Elektra. Did you chase me down just to ask that?"

"No, I chased you down to ask if you need some help—on the job. I could do it—if you want me that is," she bobbed up and down, hopeful.

Brede sighed again.

"Elektra…"

"I got time Alekzander, that's all I got now. I helped you before Alekzander, remember? I was a good helper."

"No. I don't want or need a helper. And I don't want *you*." He pressed a hidden signature station on his gauntlet opening the faux wall completely to expose the Scythe the only ship of its kind and built to his exact specifications. By him.

"Get out-of-the-way Elektra."

"Wait Alekzander," she placed a hand on his forearm. "I'm not asking for a lot of money. If I could just eat every day—or every other day…I'll stay out of your way most of the time but I could really help you if you need back-up—" The words came out rapid fire to make her case.

"You stole your breakfast today." He gave her a pointed look. "You can steal it again tomorrow."

"Yeah, well," Electra looked at the ground and toed a dusty pebble.

"I can't afford it either monetarily or in taking care of you. Go find somebody else to annoy."

"Isn't she paying you much? With all that money? This is a bad deal Alekzander." She looked back up at him, the hot sirocco breeze tossing her blonde hair into her blue eyes. "I could re-negotiate this deal for you. I do it all the time on the street."

"No! You stay the hell away from my business Elektra." He leaned down and stuck a finger in her face. "You got that? *Stay the hell away.* I mean it." he growled.

She opened her mouth to respond but his expression made her reconsider. She stood still while he kicked on the hover rotors and backed the Scythe up silently. It waited for him to board it, the size of a small building large enough for him to travel alone comfortably, with a passenger very uncomfortably. Brede didn't bother warning her to back up again, but climbed aboard, locked down the doors and lifted it straight up kicking up dust and dirt into a whirlwind leaving Elektra Tate in the center of it all. She watched him go, hand shading her eyes from the scalding desert sun. He didn't bother to look back.

****

When the global Earth economy took its last dive, the country of Egypt with its newly created aluminum alloy Midinium gained stability and strength by virtue of its ability to create and manufacture new types of transport that could travel both on and off-planet: practical space craft.

The crippled government of Earth reacted to Midinium by doing what they did best: pandering shamelessly to the Amphidians who brought the economy metal to Earth at the expense of its own citizenry. Not only did the alien race bring financial resuscitation to the rapidly expiring Earth economy they also brought interstellar cross breeding with humans. Most similar to humans in physicality, those half-human and half Amphidian were also bestowed with rights that generally superseded those of complete human genetic make-up. The citizens with enough wealth or standing to buy their rights back lived relatively normal lives in much the same manner as before Midinium arrived on their planet. Humans who could not afford it lived in the filth and poverty on the ground instead of the megalithic buildings, scraping out livings along the trickling Nile River once so mighty and nurturing of human civilization. Those citizens, mostly proscribed, lived where and how they could no matter how uninhabitable or ghastly the locations and conditions. Egypt grew into a base and a center for the new alien life forms it met and intermingled with; like Alekzander Brede whose Earth father and Amphidian mother's marriage produced him with full citizen rights on each planet and most planets in between. Any other rights he did not have he merely took. There were others like him; perhaps not exactly the same mix but close enough to make them all humanoid, enhancing the economic state of New Cairo. It also gave him a taste for earth women, the more human the better. Like the woman, Narita Sabbad, who caused a lust in him he'd never experienced and he struggled to hide the fact that there was little she could ask of him that he could refuse. Unlike Elektra Tate who, abandoned, grew up in the streets of New Cairo, probably all human thereby reducing her to the lowest strata of society: the proscribed citizens. She lived as a child in Garbage City, the filthy area reserved for the poorest of the poor of New Cairo. Garbage City resulted as overpopulation of the country escalated unrestrained in recent centuries causing its citizens to take refuge anywhere they could. Her current abode was an ancient tomb in one of New Cairo's cemetery cities that even the residents of Garbage City avoided. The Cities of the Dead held people of the poorest levels, like Elektra, who possessed nothing. Brede had little use for Elektra and tried his best to avoid her though she somehow managed to zone in on his location wherever he might be and pop up behind or beside him at the most inconvenient times. Brede found himself cruel to her more often than not and found he enjoyed it almost as much. He only behaved truly evilly to her when she intruded on his business ventures or those that mixed business with lust and money, such as his job for Narita now. In one word Elektra Tate was a pest. He pulled out of orbit and headed toward his own planet to secure fuel and access his personal arsenal of weaponry. Brede kept several of them on both planets, hidden just as easily as the Scythe, right in the open. The laws on Amphidia were more lenient toward weapon possession, due to its population's tendency for aggression. That aggression served Brede well. It perfected his fighting skills; from hand to hand combat to being a crack shot. He experienced little remorse over those he killed, only killing when paid to do so…or when the kill was being particularly annoying. Both reasons were justified in his mind and Alekzander Brede rarely looked back. He made enemies of course; impossible not to. Not when your job was sometimes hunting down and killing the son or daughter of a corrupt major political player as a warning to other corrupt players. For some reason, those corrupt aghast parents blamed Brede himself and not his employers and more than a few swore vengeance upon him.

On his own planet, there were less of them and those that existed inclined a little more toward lenience for aggressive behavior. Amphidia a dark green planet, covered 90 percent with thick, evergreen trees that grew hundreds of meters into the air, and rivers that flowed ran wide and deep, eclipsing the biggest rivers of Earth by three times. They spread into giant fingers, rivulets gone awry, keeping the green growth of the planet deep and cool and healthy. Amphidia grew a violent, aggressive civilization that fought itself but never its planet's environment.

The Scythe hovered a moment and then aligned itself with the beams of the docking bay, almost parking on its own. All the buildings on the planet stood in stark white contrasting with the dark green of the forests, not unpleasantly, and none stood higher than fifty stories making distinguishing them from one another difficult at best.

Brede maneuvered the Scythe into the bay and into a half-hidden freight lift below ground level riding all the way down to the lowest final floor. He left it in the dark hangar, silently awaiting his return. The level was eerily empty triggering his alert mode as he walked along the hall that measured 20 meters high and wide. It curved around in a half-circle and then branched into a network of smaller hallways. Silence made his steps echo loud and he pulled out both guns shooting out to his sides as four doors ground open to show shooters with no opportunity to fire. He kept walking, waiting as groaning breaths that grew louder came abreast of him. When they did Brede flung out the gun in his left hand, touching it to the temple of the owner of the rattling breaths still looking forward as they walked.

"Brede," the rasping voice grated alongside him, dragging the name out. "You've just squandered four of my most expensive mercenaries."

"Why do you even try Qitarah?"

"One day I will have my revenge on you I swear it."

"You can barely breathe let alone swear oaths."

"Just like the death of my son, you are the cause of that."

"It was a job. *I* was the merc on that assignment. Go after the bastard who ordered it, not me."

"You took on the job."

"I was a hired gun. It wasn't personal. It never is."

"It was personal to me. You killed my son and maimed me when I tried to save him."

"You walked into the firestorm on your own Nikolai. I didn't push you."

"You might as well have. I couldn't let him die without trying to save him. You wouldn't understand that."

"I'm not paid to understand."

"No. But one day you will, I promise you that, Brede."

He stopped and stared at the man who dragged in breaths through various clear and metallic tubes running in and out of his nose, mouth, sinuses and ears and finally converged at the back of his skull. He cocked the gun still resting against the man's temple.

"You know, I could stop this harassment if I killed you right now. But that would end your misery and I am not paid to do that either. However," Brede squeezed the trigger slightly. "Should you come up with enough money, I would consider it."

"One day I hope you will find yourself happy to kill me for free. I will stay alive for that moment Alekzander Brede."

He let go the trigger and pulled the gun up and away from the man.

"I have things to do Nikolai."

"As have I," the man gazed into his eyes with intensity and then turned away dragging his bent and burnt body and his sonorous breath back down the hallway. Brede watched him for a moment, debating shooting him in the back. He decided against it, holstered his gun then turned back to the task at hand. Precious time wasted by the encounter with Nikolai gave any other violent enemies time to prepare for another assault on him. None appeared however and Brede loaded a forklift droid with enough firepower to blow apart the floors above him including the ground level. He keyed programs into the droid and walked along it as it floated toward the hangar where the Scythe hung waiting.

"Stop," he told the droid when they reached the door of the hangar. He walked past it and stopped at the side of the door, listening. Brede ran his fingertips along the edges of the door feeling without seeing until something caught his attention and he stopped, frozen in the action.

"Back," he hissed at the droid and it retreated at his word. "Three meters."

It rolled to a stop at the distance and hovered in silence.

Brede kept the fingers of his left hand on the spot that interested him and moved his right hand toward the outside pocket of this coat. He pulled out an alumina coil, running it along the edge of the door until it reached his fingers still pressed against the doorway. The coil thrummed in blue and he stuck the needled end of it into the crack of the doorway, pulling his fingers out at the same time. Brede leapt backward, landing almost beside the droid. Brede placed a hand on it, guiding it back even further from the expected blast. Luck joined him and the blast imploded into the hangar sending searing flames along the walls and ceiling. They were weaker than they appeared and only a slight singeing showed along their path when they burned out with weakened speed.

Brede kicked the lever with his boot and the activation sequence chugged into life. Violet lights flicked on one after another in two lines along the ceiling and the power burst on with a vacuuming suck before it exhaled and ignited the system. It also ignited the Scythe which lit up and raised itself into hover mode, rotors silently spinning.

"Proceed with alignment configuration," he told the droid. It moved steadily into the hangar, its infrared beams focusing and locking the Scythe's loading bay. "Load," he waited until the payload was transferred and then dismissed the droid. He boarded the Scythe, locked down the cockpit and glanced about the hangar one last time. Locking the exits Brede watched as the hover rotors sped up, grinding the lone assailant hiding in the shadows of the hangar, into slices and bits of flesh and bone spattered across the hangar floor, walls, and ceiling. It sprayed a light pattern on the side of the Scythe as well. He didn't recognize the assassin and didn't care. It would be just one more job left incomplete for whoever hired the killer to kill him and was killed. Brede breathed out a snicker at the human debris when the Scythe broke away as the roof separated like fan blades, giving it the briefest of windows to launch and he headed back toward New Cairo to undertake the assignment Narita Sabbad commissioned.

****

The slight flurry of excitement shivered through the residents of Garbage City when Bannar's wife gave birth to a boy child and he could not be located. The happy buzz ran throughout the city as people scrambled to find him. After twenty minutes they collected in a loose consortium in the city center asking each other where Bannar was last seen.

"I know where he is," Elektra strutted into the group from the side of a building where she'd watched the activity. They stopped talking and stared at her.

"Well, where is he then orphan?"

"I don't know if I should tell you." She made a line in the dirt with a toe. "I mean, he told me to come and tell him myself when his baby was born and that he would pay me..." she gave them a furtive glance. A long hesitation ensued until finally one of the men shrugged and pulled out a credit. He walked close to her and pressed the chip into her hand. She squeezed it tight and looked up at them debating whether to lie. At last she made her decision and spoke.

"He's below the souk having a drink because his baby is coming," she told them.

They looked at each other and gathered to exit the city at top speed. Drinking was mostly regarded as semi-taboo regardless the occasion and they headed toward the marketplace below the marketplace at full speed. When they arrived again he could not be found search though they might. The men returned furious at having been duped. The search now turned toward Elektra and when they found her, confronted her with the lie.

"Oh, well, I thought I saw him there." She explained with rounded eyes. "But I must have seen somebody else and got confused."

They knew she was lying and they knew they could do nothing about it. Her answer could have gone either way—truth or lie—and another taboo prevented them from punishing her physically. They finally turned away, conversing quietly between them planning to make sure their children stayed away from her for a good while to teach her a lesson about lying.

For her part, Elektra smiled to herself rubbing the credit in her pocket. She'd finagled it artfully she thought, wondering what other situations she might manipulate to gain more credits. When they ostracized her it hurt; couldn't any of them understand she had no other means to survive?

She played the same game several weeks later when she wrangled dinner from a family more kind to her than the others and received the same treatment for it. The city stayed fairly lenient toward her scams, fearing to harm her in any major way, including starving or beating her. Then Alekzander Brede came and took care of it for them.

****

The young man, in a turban and Djellaba, followed Brede closely, jumping into doorways and arches when he thought he got too close and Brede might see him. At length he scanned the sky to find a particular craft that would drop enough to pick him up and speed away through ground and air crowds. It found him seconds later and hovered low enough for him to leap aboard.

"Well?" the pilot asked once they gained altitude to skim the tops of the monolith buildings

"I know what he seeks and where he is headed to find that information. Who he is working for I have not learned yet."

"We must know. We must have the power of it now. We cannot rise to domination if we do not."

"Am I to follow him again then? Amongst the crowds I can easily blend."

"Yes, for now at any case."

"And what will you do?"

The pilot gave him a grin.

"Whatever is necessary," He shifted the craft into high gear and sped back to where he'd picked up the young man.

****

"Hanif I need this information immediately. I swore to find it if possible. Where is the object I seek?"

They sat in the marketplace that served the proscribed citizens, under the ancient arches below the ground level above the catacombs. In the dark of the entombed cavern the proscribed bought and sold everything from contraband fuel and weapons along with the highly prized coffee and tobacco or anything else that might have value on the street or to those who inhabited it. This souk sold the real thing; no counterfeit items passed hands there and only the true Cairene knew of it at all. The old man Hanif sat cross-legged on the floor before a small intricately carved ebony table, valuable beyond price for its history alone, sipping a cup of authentic espresso. He filled a tiny cup before Brede and handed it to him before responding. Brede squelched an impatient sigh.

"Are you aware of what it is that you are seeking?"

"I know it's an artifact of some antiquity. I know it's called the Vessel of Beket-Ra. What it holds is unknown to me."

"What it holds it something that certain people would kill for; have killed for my friend."

"Gold?" Brede asked. "It is still the most precious currency on Earth. As for other civilizations, perhaps not so precious."

"Do not make light of this Alekzander Brede. Many religions have powers—real powers—that they wield. Those are the quiet religions, those that do not harangue people in the streets, who have voices but no real power. Those who have this power truly believe." He took a large sip of espresso.

"Are you saying it holds power Hanif? My…employer is one who would seek that out. What type of power are you speaking of?"

"Each artifact carries its own type of power. It is up to you to find out, Alekzander Brede."

"In order to do that Hanif, I need information. I need to know where to find this vessel."

"I am coming to that Alekzander. There is more that you need to know before you find this piece of power—"

Brede heard no more. Hanif's head toppled off his body and landed right side up on the antique table, making Brede leap up weapons drawn, scanning. The laser blade had to have come from the outer corridors and he knew the culprits were long gone in that short moment. He'd wasted the trip and his oldest and favorite contact sat with his head on the table in front of him, the small coffee cup ironically near his lips. Before walking out of the marketplace, Brede reached out and closed Hanif's eyes.

****

The blast ricocheted off the left engine and its fire skidded across the windshield, surprising Brede who immediately pulled up the Scythe's volt guns. They disengaged from the flanks of the ship, spread like wings and began blasting from revolver barrels. Brede, forced to dip and roll the Scythe, steering the ship where he wanted the guns to fire since they did not have the ability to shoot in various directions; they only shot straight ahead. The two attacking fighters separated and brought themselves up at the rear of the Scythe that shuddered from five direct hits. Brede swore in Amphidian, rolling the ship one last time and dropping it straight down then bringing it up behind the two fighters themselves. He kicked up the speed of the blasts to maximum revolution and rolled the Scythe end over end trying to spread as much destruction as he could before they regrouped.

They surprised him again by stopping, spinning and heading directly at him, guns blazing. But before Brede could respond, the crow's nest gunnery disengaged itself and rose over him. It swung out in an arc, a battery of firepower searing the oncoming ships and then swung the opposite way repeating the damage disabling them both enough to send them limping away to whatever base they originated. Brede overrode the nest gunnery controls and spun it out and down to face him through the windshield.

"See Alekzander," Elektra grinned at him through her own windshield. "Aren't you glad I tagged along? I told you I could back you up."

"Get the fuck in here." He sent it back into hibernation mode and waited for her to join him in the cockpit. "What the fuck do you think you're doing? And how the *fuck* did you get onboard without me knowing?" He asked when she did.

"I live on the street Alekzander. How do you think I get around?" she still had the stupid smile plastered on her face. Brede clenched his fists to avoid hitting her.

"Why are you here? Didn't I tell you I didn't fucking want you?"

She shrugged and put her boots on the top of control console.

"I figured you needed help so I—"

"Did I not tell you to stay the fuck out of my business Elektra?" He said in an even voice designed to unsettle her and force him to control his temper.

"Well, yeah, Alekzander, but you know I just thought you might need the help and guess what—you did!" She laughed and let it fade as she watched his expression freeze. "I did help you Alekzander," she pointed out quietly.

"If you ever, *ever* do this again I will kill you Elektra. Don't make the mistake of thinking I won't. You will *never* come near my business again, do you understand?"

She nodded eyes wide as if the thought of being obnoxious or unwanted never seriously crossed her mind and that she finally understood he meant what he said.

"Okay Alekzander." She pressed her lips together and blinked.

Brede ignored her for the next five hours, and she sat in the navigator's seat without speaking.

At last he programmed the Scythe to autopilot and left the cockpit without saying a word. He crawled into his small sleeping space and lay on his back staring at nothing, too furious to think.

"Alekzander?" He heard her voice and turned his head eyeing her.

"What?"

"I—well, I don't have anywhere to sleep, just the jump seats up front."

He said nothing.

"So, um, I was wondering if…maybe I could climb in here with you…"

"Elektra."

"I'm not very big Alekzander I won't take up much space." She said quickly. "It's just that it's very cold up in the pit and…"

Brede closed his eyes and sighed through his nose, a habit that increased when Elektra Tate was around.

"Christ. Alright."

"Thanks!" Her boots were already off and she was up in a second. She lay on her back next to him silent for a long while. Finally she turned her head and looked at him. She reached out and ran a finger down the crease between his brows. "This is from too much frowning Alekzander," she said quietly. "You need to smile more. I bet I could make you smile." She ran her finger along his jaw. Brede said nothing, deciding she was human enough to be enjoyable and that she deserved whatever she got.

****

It wasn't her name but Narita's he called out in passion. When he finally awoke he found Elektra kicking off ice scales from the interior exhaust plates at the back of the pit.

"You know," she said, not looking at him. "You really should slick these down before you lift off. Otherwise the ice builds up like this."

He grunted in response and sat down in the pilot's seat inspecting the dashboard. Nothing unusual presented itself and he leaned back glancing at her again. She now sat behind and to the right of him in the navigator's seat again, feet pressed against the back of the co-pilot chair. She leaned forward and dusted ice particles from her boots.

"Alekzander," she said still refusing to look at him. "I been thinking. I know you didn't want me along on this job and I know that I pushed myself into it anyway," she inspected the toes of her boots again more closely. "But I'm thinking now that you were right. I'm not really helping you here—"

"Oh you're helping." He grinned at her.

Elektra chose to ignore the bait.

"Yeah, well, I also been thinking that I really don't have any skills on a job like this so…" she let the sentence hang.

"What are you saying Elektra?"

"I guess I was just thinking that maybe you could drop me off at the next station and I could catch a ride back to Cairo." She finally glanced up at him to see his reaction.

"Why would I do that now?"

"I mean, I'm telling you that you're right Alekzander. I'm more in the way here than helping so, you know if you could just drop me off—"

"I haven't given you any money yet. How are you going to pay the fare back?"

"There's other ways to pay Alekzander." She kept her eyes down this time.

He leaned back in his seat and clasped his hands behind his head, eyes closed.

What the hell was her problem now? She'd done everything possible and impossible to come along on the job including stowing away and now she suddenly wanted out. It didn't make sense at all; Elektra could never afford to pass up money and would never pass up the chance to tag along with him which Brede knew she used to enhance her status on the street. He looked down at the navigation bar. There were two more light cycles to the next station and then no more until the return trip. He looked at her again. She watched him warily, awaiting his decision.

"Alright," he sighed. "The next station is the last one out here—"

"I'll get my gear." She stood up before he even finished the sentence.

By the time the Scythe docked and began sequencing, Elektra stood at the doors waiting to disembark. She hit the airlock making the doors open with a hiss and the ramp drop enough for her to walk down.

"Elektra—"

"Goodbye Alekzander." She refused a third time to look at him, stepped off the ramp and into the station center. He sat watching her through the windshield as she disappeared with a small crowd into the interior of the station.

It didn't matter. He'd done thousands of jobs like this without her and he'd do a thousand more. And he didn't need her on this one either just like he'd told her. She'd probably be better off back in New Cairo where she could steal her living as she'd done all her life. She'd never be anything better than what she was: a street thief and proscribed citizen. Brede turned back to the Scythe, charging it back up and trying to shrug off the anger that came from nowhere and directed itself at Elektra. She really was the most irritating person he knew and he was better off without her altogether.

****

She didn't know much but she knew when someone was bad. And the man who carried her over his shoulder like a sack of garbage was bad. He scooped her up ignoring her terrified screams and slapping her face until she shut up as he ran through the piles of filth that lined the streets of Garbage City. She tried to resume screaming but her body bumped up and down on him so hard she could barely breathe and concentrated on that for the moment. At last he stopped running and flung her down at the end of an alley where she hit the ground with a lung shattering thump. For a moment everything went dark and when she could see again her clothes were ripped apart and his hands were touching her roughly everywhere. Too terrified to make noise she struggled to no avail and even biting him did not help. When he knelt over her undoing his pants fear gave way to fury and she glimpsed something protruding from one of his pockets. She quieted for a moment and she could smell and feel his rancid breathy laughing over her. She waited for the opportune moment and the grasped the only thing that might come to her rescue.

"*You are bad.*" *She said in a small angry voice.* "*You are very, very, bad.*"

He laughed again until she pointed the gun at his face. He tried to swat it out of her hand but wrath made her aim precise. She pulled the trigger making his hand and arm snap back and he screamed with pain, staring at the hole in his wrist.

"*You little—*" *He tried to lean over her again but she sat up and pointed the barrel at him again.*

"*No. You are bad.*" *She pursed her lips solemnly and aimed for his shoulder.*

When he screamed the second time people's heads appeared in their windows and by the fifth scream many ran into the alley to see what could make a grown man sound like that. None dared approach her as she stood over him gun still in her hand, frowning and breathing hard. He looked at the gathering his face imploring.

"*Catch this bitch! Look what she did to me! God damn it don't let her go! Look what she did!*"

No one moved.

"Catch her for God's sake! She—"

"No!" she cut him off. "He is bad. He tried to do bad things to me. He is bad." She never took her eyes off him and even took a step toward him. "If you ever do bad again I will do more bad to you."

He tried to sit up and she shot the ancient cobblestones near his knee. He screamed again and managed to scramble to his feet fast enough to avoid being shot at again. He looked around the crowd with wild eyes until he realized none there would help him. "She's a crazy little bitch! You'll be sorry you let her live." He backed out of the alley never taking his eyes off her and the gun. "You'll be sorry. You'll all be sorry! Bitch!" he spat at her feet and then turned and ran.

She faced them all, gun dangling in her hand waiting for reaction. None came. They slowly turned away and went back into their three room apartments silently until no one was left. No one said a word, no one berated her for bad behavior, all turned away silently as if she was a disease not to be discussed openly. At last she stood alone in the full nightfall; building high piles of trash giving off horrific stench as they cooled from the searing daytime heat. She gazed down at the weapon in her hand and knew it was her best friend. She shuffled among the filth until she found a niche carved into a wall and crawled down into it, covering herself with trash and cradling the gun in her arms.

****

The howdah sat still and silent in the florescent yellow light of the night streets, perched on the top of a camel sleeping and breathing in rhythmic beats. For some unknown reason the flight traffic was light, providing a small steady hum throughout the hot city making everything drowsy including her. The howdah proved irresistible to her and Elektra ran a hand along the animal's neck to keep it calm as she opened the thick curtains and peeked inside. The lush thick padding of piles of blankets and rugs beckoned her and she climbed with measured stealth into it. The camel snorted and gave a little rustling shake and for a moment Elektra didn't breathe. He settled back down and she snuggled down among the softness planning to awake and leave even before the muezzin's call in the dawn.

It didn't happen that way. Long after the muezzin's call to the faithful Elektra found herself being dragged from the howdah and flung to the floor before Narita Sabbad who sat holding court.

"Show obeisance!" One of the guards, armed with a laser sword brought down a boot on her spine, flattening her body against the tiles. Elektra grunted and rose to her knees.

"What level is this citizen of New Cairo?" Narita asked.

The same guard answered for Elektra.

"Proscribed petty outlaw Majesty."

"And what charges are brought against her?"

"She is accused of stealing Majesty's howdah."

"I wasn't stealing—"

"Silence!" he thundered knocking her down again and stepping on her left wrist for good measure. Elektra gasped as the bones crunched and held her hand to her chest.

"Are there any other charges?"

"None that we are aware of Majesty."

Narita waved away a bowl of dates and leaned forward.

"Then I shall bring my charge against you. Stand."

Elektra managed to push herself up still holding her left hand against her.

"You are charged with infidelity to this throne by seducing and stealing the current consort I have chosen."

When she didn't respond another guard stepped forward and jerked her head back laying his own laser sword against her throat. Elektra eyed Narita and said evenly, "I have already been punished for that."

"For that insolence you shall suffer." The guard threw her to the ground one last time, stomping on her wrist and hand, breaking whatever bones not crushed the first time. She screamed and with his boot on her neck he pressed the side of her face to the tiled floor once more.

"You may now plead for mercy from the court." He told her.

Elektra said nothing but whimpered from the pain.

"Throw yourself on the mercy of the throne!"

She breathed hard and then raised her eyes to Narita's.

"I did not steal from the throne," she managed, "on either count."

"How dare you?" A female servant sprinted from the dais and slapped Elektra. More would have followed but Narita raised a jeweled hand.

"No. For her disrespect she will spend seven days in the underworld prison. Perhaps then she will have learned respect for the royalty."

****

Very little spooked Elektra Tate but lying chained to a wall five stories below the ground did. Not that she believed in ghosts never having met one even living with the dead in her tomb house, but the rotting horror of those buried above seeped down through the ceiling in icy black liquid that ran down the walls. She twisted as far away as she could but the floor remained damp and without escape. By the time they brought her back up before Narita, Elektra did not have to be encouraged to beg for mercy. Narita drew out her verdict of pardon as long as she could to enjoy watching Elektra suffer. When she was satisfied the young woman learned her lesson to stay as far away as possible from Alekzander Brede, she pronounced the sentence served and allowed her guards to escort Elektra down and out of the building.

Elektra landed on her knees on the ancient stone cobbled sidewalks and used the wall of Narita's edifice to help herself stand. The pain, now near unbearable, shrieked when she touched the blackened and bruised flesh to anything including cloth and she struggled against the throbbing crowds to make her way toward the only place she thought to go for help.

"Please Mahmud I don't want to lose my arm. You have to help me," she stood before the self-appointed doctor of the proscribed citizens. He inspected it and then shook his head.

"I can do nothing for you," he said. "It is already too far gone by now. Even should you sit in the sun for five days it would be no help."

"I'll get you money. Whatever you want, I'll get it. Please, save my hand, please?"

He shook his head again sorrowfully.

"I can do nothing. This does not need my type of medicine. You must ask the mechanical doctors, those with science and not nature. I am sorry I cannot help you Elektra."

Crying she stood against the wall of the crooked street, thinking what she might pay to those who if they could build space machines, could build anything. She slid down the wall and sat on her haunches against it sobbing.

A shadow fell across her, changing the scorching temperature a degree. She opened her eyes and a man knelt before her. He took her arm and gently inspected it.

"I can give you a new arm and hand," he said. "But you must pay what I ask." He stared directly into her eyes. "You will have a new arm—a new hand—better than before. But you must pay the price."

"What is it you want?" Elektra asked, still gasping in pain.

"Alekzander Brede."

****

Somebody besides Narita wanted the Vessel of Beket-Re and wanted it more than she did. They wanted it enough to kill someone like Hanif, harmless but full of information. Whether they were aware that he did not get the information before Hanif was murdered Brede didn't know nor did he know the unknown enemy or enemies. Whoever they were they were just another addition to the long list of those who wanted his blood.

Screaming air brakes slid across the street filled with hundreds of people and the spitfire of Kalashnikov-4700s spattered bullets through the crowds. The throng scattered, diving into doorways, alleys or hitting the ground as the gunfire sought its mark. Three men screamed as the shots cut them down and the Cadillac Annihilator ground into high gear rose from the street and sped away. Brede walked amidst the bullets the shrieks and the falling dead, unperturbed by the violence. He didn't look around, didn't make a misstep, and didn't blink as he went. He stopped before the ancient building, glanced up at the mountain tall towers over the gateway doors. As they ground open and more throngs of people moved in and out, he joined those entering and disappeared inside.

"Brede," he said to the live guard standing tall, his Kalashnikov 908 at his side. The guard eyed him a moment and then stood aside, allowing him to pass into the floors through the metal skeleton that was left. He rode to the highest floor, the apex with clear glass walls to see the enormous courtyard one thousand floors below and the entire country on the outer side. The city began to awaken, dawn a tiny faint sliver over the horizon, too early for even the Muadhin to call for morning prayers.

"Ah, Alekzander, I see you've accepted my invitation." The fat ringed fingers rubbed tiny sands of incense into a brazier. They belonged to the man dressed in ridiculous sumptuous attire of a sultan even to the silk, multi-colored turban.

"I'm here." Alekzander Brede answered with shrug. "Do you realize it's no longer the dark ages on this planet?" He walked along the long table spread before the man, inspecting the objects that lay upon it.

"Why? Oh, because of my dress? I like it. Besides, it enhances the peoples' impression of me as overlord. Why shouldn't I wear it?"

Brede said nothing merely picked up various objects on the table, turning them about and setting them back down with care. He shook his head slightly at the irreverent treatment of the precious historical objects, their worth incalculable—to humans at least.

"You're no one to talk about fashion Brede. You look like a refugee of the last century with a bit of early millennium style thrown into the mix."

"It's functional. I'm here so what do you want from me?"

"For starters call me Ashur Dabi. That is who I am now."

"Hah. You're no more Arabic than I am Colin."

"And only you and I are aware of that. As far as anyone and everyone else I am Ashur Dabi, not Colin Factor. That is who I've become. For all practical purposes, Colin Factor is dead."

Brede refrained from adding his own wish for that reality and hid a small smirk. He folded his arms across his chest and waited. Colin Factor sat up a little straighter and rubbed the tips of his fingers on a maroon silk handkerchief removing traces of the incense. He tossed it aside and a young man scurried forth from his place behind him, snatched it and scurried back. Colin looked at Brede and smiled.

"I've found that notion saying good help is hard to find completely untrue. If you instill enough fear in them, you can have a top-notch staff of servants more than eager to do your every bidding. Now, as for you, Alekzander, I consider you almost an equal if not a friend per se." He pointed his finger out and the entire staff vacated the room immediately. "And that brings me to your part. I understand you are seeking something of tremendous value," he paused. "There is a recent rumor— that it is an artifact of incalculable value—and I want you to find it and bring it back to me."

"What is it Colin?"

Colin leaned forward chest against the table.

"*Ashur* please! My interest is purely as a collector and historian."

"Is your collection not comprehensive enough?"

"This is...*special* Alekzander."

"In what way?"

"That is my concern Alekzander; yours is to find it and bring it to me at any cost. Those are the terms. Do we have an agreement?

"Not yet. What do I get out of it? I'm no archaeologist, in it for sheer intellectual glory."

"If you bring this back to me, you can almost name your own price."

"It's that special?"

"To me, yes. Now do we have an agreement?"

"I already have an employer for this job," Brede dropped his arms and turned to go.

"This is more precious than gold Alekzander."

"Then why aren't you going after this precious artifact yourself?"

"Be realistic Alekzander. I'm the overlord of Thebes Two—I cannot spare one second away from my rule. You are in better shape than I in any case. There! I believe I've covered everything you need to know. Now, will you agree to do this job for me?"

Brede hesitated. He knew he would never abandon anything Narita Sabbad asked but he needed more information to even begin the search in earnest.

"I'll be back tonight."

"Fine," Dabi leaned back. He leaned back in his plush seat and watched Brede leave.

CHAPTER TWO

Brede stopped at a crosswalk where two teens were engaged in a game of slash tag; circling each other to close in for the kill. They held laser hooks powered by light energy, deadly if they sliced through vital organs, major arteries or eyeballs. The teen boys were mismatched: one obviously older, stronger and bigger threatened the smaller, weaker one who wore an angry but frightened expression. Half-functional addicts sat against the walls of an ancient ruin betting on the fight with all they possessed, namely miniscule amounts of counterfeit tobacco mixed with espresso. What the fight was about no one seemed to know except the two engaged in it, and Brede glanced at the scene for a moment without interest. He debated stepping in to even the fighting field especially since police on levitating cycles passed ignoring the fight as if something more pressing might be occurring elsewhere. In reality they possessed absolutely no power whatsoever on the streets of Thebes Two. Only the military minions of Ashur Dabi held any real power and that ranged from brutality and incarceration to out-and-out assassination either by order of Colin or their own evaluation of the person's life worth. Still, he'd seen more violence on Amphidia with fewer police present. Out of the two hundred lights at the intersection, fifty lit up on Brede's curb and he crossed the street forgetting the scene immediately. The Amphidian in him took pleasure in letting the weakest die without interference.

Colin Factor never counted as one of Brede's friends, as if Brede possessed any, and just as he murdered his way into the title of Overlord, he could murder Alekzander just as easily and with the same lack of conscience. But Brede wanted information and so far Colin gave him more information than even Hanif; he might finagle even where the artifact might lay hidden, if he maneuvered the foppish ruler correctly.

Colossal buildings towered over and between the ancient wonders of Egypt, making them appear insect sized. Most of the surviving cities on Earth shared the same design and size in buildings, three-mile tall towers dwarfing the ancient monuments once considered monolithic. In Thebes Two as in New Cairo only the dregs of society lived at street level and Elektra Tate entered into Brede's thoughts as he moved along the streets of Thebes, eyeing the pathetic, uneducated, and mostly violent residents. Not that he cared but he wondered briefly what she'd been bred down from; what ill-considered non-earthling parents or grandparents caused her to be abandoned on the streets as an infant to live or die as she would. Oddly enough, he realized, she possessed entirely human features unlike most of the unlucky cross-breeds who roamed the streets on Earth. He also wondered what she'd learned on the streets that kept her alive as a child amidst the thieves and killers that haunted them. No matter how or how long she lived there he still considered her stupid, childish and annoying as hell. She hadn't learned enough if she thought it safe to pester him relentlessly. Why he never killed her remained a mystery even to him, anyone else would have been summarily dispatched to death after a week. At times he fantasized that when she gave him her stupid lopsided grin that he blew it right off her face. Brede shrugged again, meandering down the streets seeking out a way of contacting

Narita to keep her informed of his progress. He found a communications shop shut down for the night and pounded on the door without response. He gazed into the window until he found what he wanted and pulled out one of smaller guns he carried. He shot the window and part of the frame and reached into to grasp the small air writer and scribbled the name and number of the Pyramid in the space in front of him. "Narita," he said when the room materialized. "Calling to give you an update on what's happening with the job."

"What? Oh, right. The job," She said mouth full of something.

"I'm updating you on what's happening," Brede didn't realize he sighed.

"Okay, so what's happening?" Her image shimmered like a desert mirage.

"I'm still suppressed by lack of information. My contacts are eliminated before I can get it."

"Well make it happen faster, Alekzander. I need and want that Biscuit of Ra immediately."

"Vessel of Beket Ra Narita not biscuit, do you even know what it is?"

"I don't care what it is I just want it. I will reward you handsomely for it Alekzander."

"Alright but it better be good Narita."

"Oh, it will be. It will be Alekzander."

He cut the call and tossed the writer back in through the window to its scowling owner and then turned to face the open air souks of Thebes Two to seek food he rarely needed but did now. By the time he found something actually edible half the day was gone.

Brede headed back toward Colin's lushly absurd residence at the top of the highest building, nine hundred stories up. After identifying himself again he rode the express lift, a lit-from-within tube circling the outside of the massive building, to the penthouse where the Overlord of Thebes Two resided.

"Have you decided to accept my offer?" the Overlord asked when Brede entered the main room.

"Since I am searching for the Vessel of Beket-Re anyway, if I bring it to you first, I assume you will pay the most," he said.

"I will pay what you want. Just bring it to me. You can use whatever means you consider necessary Alekzander."

"I would ask if any of your rumors concern locating this vessel. I'm sure that along with me many others are seeking it as well," Brede said.

"That's why I'm hiring you Mr. Brede." Colin said.

"Then I shall do my best to find it."

Brede hid another small smile by bowing slightly. He knew Colin well enough to know that it would appeal to his immense vanity but that he would never realize the mockery of it.

"Thank you Alekzander," Colin said. "You are a true friend. Now, be off with you. The Overlord has many responsibilities to attend."

Brede exited, frowning on the ride down to the docking bays on the five hundredth floor. Colin might be murderous but he was also weak, a quality Alekzander found as cause for elimination; one that he hated intensely. On Amphidia weakness in any form was cause for allowing the weak ones to die on their own once cast out to the mercy of the streets or forest predators...if they didn't eliminate them themselves. Amphidians let their weak ones die as they deserved. Colin Factor was one of those.

****

With Hanif gone, Brede needed to find another source of information, yet he hesitated returning to the proscribed citizens' underground marketplace. Hanif's assassins now knew Brede haunted the underground on occasion and no doubt kept watch for his return and the opportunity to eliminate him. If Hanif was 150 years old another might have the same age and perhaps even more knowledge than the murdered informant and Brede stopped during the Scythe's undocking process, thinking. He instructed the Scythe to re-dock itself and walked out into the still warm night of Thebes Two, gazing at the edge of the city where the desert blew its sirocco across and between ancient wonders that stood half buried and abandoned in the rush of developing Thebes Two into a megalopolis. Thebes Two's proscribed citizens took the form of Bedouins and wandered the desert moving in the earliest light when air traffic lessened and those that flew exhibited no interest for their existence whatsoever. The New Bedouins revived the eons old edifices and tradition of the caravansary but maintained a permanent collective outside the city where they kept their own marketplace. There they traded only with their kind, selling the best of the goods they collected on their journeys back and forth across the burning dunes and the rare traverse on the millennia old Silk Road to the east. The rest they sold to the indiscriminate tourist customers and unethical business owners inside the walls of the city. Once the Earth economy permanently tanked the roads that had been developed returned to their original state due to abandonment except by those like the New Bedouins. The irony of human evolution never ceased to amuse Brede; the more humanity evolved, the more the oldest ways of life emerged and stubbornly clung to the edges.

It also did not escape him that those who lived the oldest ways knew the most about their own societies and the supposed progress of the society of the cities. If anyone knew about the Vessel of Beket-Re, it would be the New Bedouins. He left the Scythe docked and headed out to the edge of Thebes Two on foot, easier to find them in the encroaching dark; easier to approach their hospitality and trust. He hoped.

Like a modified Arabian Nights, turbaned guards stood watch over what the locals called the Suradeq Sea, inviting tents much more glorious inside than outside, waiting until just before dawn to escort their caravans and howdahs on their perennial trek. Brede approached openly stopping before the first two guards and identifying himself. He allowed them to scan him; one holding a Glock 950 against the back of his head. When they determined he posed no threat they could not handle they asked his purpose in visiting their community.

"I seek an artifact that remains hidden to this day." He told them.

"What artifact would that be?" The first guard said.

"I am bound to speak of it only with one who knows."

That apparently satisfied them.

"Come then," one said, holding a hand toward the center of the Suradeq Sea where the most important, elderly and young stayed in the caravansary. He led Brede to the building, bidding him to stay until approval was given. Brede entertained himself by memorizing the layout of the caravansary, rooms in a rectangle around a large courtyard, a stopping place for weary day travelers, safe and secure. A handful of camels sat in sleep, howdahs removed for the night. He turned and looked back at the titanic city in the distance, huge and blinking even that far out, and if the Vessel of Beket-Re might lie somewhere there, its possessor might be unaware of the power it contained.

"Come with me," the guard returned and led him into the caravansary proper. The corner room behind the sleeping group of camels served as the host for the eldest member of the caravan, a more than wizened old man wearing a white small turban, the same color as his thin linen Djellaba. He too, like Hanif, sat at a small ebony table inlaid with gold and ivory and from what Brede knew of human history, the table's worth probably ten times that of Hanif's. The old man did not sip espresso but smoked a long, dirty white hand rolled cigarette that gave off a luscious fragrant scent and he waved it at Brede as he ducked under the doorway and entered the room.

"Come, come in my friend," he smiled at Brede with shocking white teeth that shone out against his brown skin. "I am told you are seeking something of value."

That was an understatement. Brede pushed aside the heavy curtains and knelt on one knee across the table. "What I seek is the Vessel of Beket-Re." he said. The old man laughed silently as if Brede joked.

"Forgive me my friend," he said. "I do no laugh at you but at the foolishness of those who pay you." He shifted a little and indicated for Brede to sit. "Besides, we do not even know one another's names. I like to call my friends by their names. What is yours?"

"I am Alekzander Brede." He sat cross-legged.

"Alekzander Brede," the old man pronounced it as if tasting the sound. "I am Anhur. By the look of you Alekzander Brede you are not entirely human. Is this not so?"

"It is so Anhur. I regret disturbing you while you rest but I must find this object as soon as possible. I am not the only one seeking it. I'm told that it possesses great power. My employer highly desires it."

"Mmmm," Anhur said inhaling a long drag from the cigarette. "Please, have one." He opened the lid of a box with the same design as the table and held out a cigarette to Brede. He took it from the old man, lighting it off the cherry of Anhur's and inhaling deeply. He found he liked it and made a note to find more if he could. Anhur continued. "Alekzander Brede, the Vessel does not possess power of itself but rather bestows power on whoever possesses *it*."

Brede briefly wondered if all old Arabic men used both first and surnames when they spoke with friends then focused on Anhur's words.

"So that is the urgency and ruthlessness of those who want it," he said, imagining Narita's face when he presented her with it. He imagined his reward when he did. Her ruthlessness bothered him less than the thought of displeasing her, cutting off their sexual and social relationship. Besides, there were others even more ruthless and reckless than her, those who could and would kill him without a second thought to get possession of it. He looked back at Anhur whose expression made him think of a mildly amused baby. The baby spoke again.

"Yes. All of those who seek it are precisely the ones who should not own it. Those desirous of it are inevitably destroyed by the power they lust after. You would be better to find it for yourself since it is not something you personally covet." He stopped simpering and stared into Brede's eyes. "Is it?"

Brede met his gaze.

"No. I believe in my own power not some glamorous trinket of antiquity."

"Do not speak so arrogantly of this artifact, Mr. Brede. You have the opposite problem than those who want it. You dismiss the power it conveys. I foresee you regretting that attitude."

"I rarely regret anything I do Anhur. Now may I ask again where I might find this object of power?"

"I must apologize for keeping you so long when I have so little information that could help you. However, you came to me I did not come to you," Anhur pressed his lips to the tiny butt of his cigarette and sucked hard. "The reason I have no information is that nearly all the valuable artifacts of this historically rich area have been discovered and excavated the Vessel of Beket-Re as well. The difference is that it is not in any governmental warehouse or private collection as are all the others. The Vessel of Beket-Re has been hidden—or possibly taken off this planet—to hide and to protect it. I can however, give you a clue that was left to me by the last sheikh. He said merely that it is hidden 'with the dead.' Whether that is on the Earth or another planet he did not say. I believe that he did not know."

"Are you telling me a necropolis?" Brede asked, crushing his own cigarette butt into a primitive clay ashtray.

"I am telling you nothing Alekzander Brede. I do not know."

"There is more than one necropolis on Earth Anhur. Are you sure you can recall no more details?"

"Nothing. I am sorry."

"No," Brede said, not rising all the way to avoid hitting the ceiling. "Do not be. You have given me more information than anyone else—and lived for doing it. I would advise you and your entire caravan to take care. Several other vessel seekers follow me and will not hesitate to cut off my lines of information meaning any or all of you. They have already done so once. I thank you Anhur and hope that we may meet again at some time in the future. I enjoyed your choice of tobacco."

"We shall meet again Mr. Brede." Anhur smiled again in earnest. "I shall have a large bundle of it waiting for you."

Brede opened the curtains and nodded to the guard. They walked out of the caravansary and to the edge of the tents. The guard turned to Brede.

"I hope you have what you came for," he said.

"Not exactly but enough."

"Take care Brede."

So he'd been eavesdropping just as Brede suspected. It was a good thing too; he could now mobilize the others to enhance their protection of the caravan. Brede wanted those cigarettes.

****

He headed for the most logical place to look first: Thebes Two's Valley of the Queens. Beket was a goddess and the Vessel of Beket-Re was a feminine object; perhaps the Pharaoh Queen Hatshepsut might still hold it somewhere near her. The necropolis of Thebes the ancient sat on the west bank of the Nile, now no more than a thin shallow stream, evaporated by two centuries of abuse and development and now only a handful of self-appointed holy men stood watch over The City of the Dead with fanatical violence. Unnamed, no one knew whence they came or why, only that they devoted every fiber of their being to protecting the ancient religion and its temples, funerary marvels, and its gods and did not hesitate to destroy anyone who posed a threat real or imagined.

Brede didn't know either. In fact he did not know the holy men soldiers existed at all and walked to the entrance to Hatshepsut's Luxor funerary monument unaware. They nearly picked him off in the dark, missing his head and body by increments so small he knew the misses were intentional. He stopped where he stood and waited for them to approach, weapons ready for physical attack.

"You!" one shouted in a thick accent Brede didn't recognize. "What are you doing here?" His weapon pointed up, a good sign. "What do you want with the tomb of the Queen?"

"To look around," Brede tried to sound friendly.

"No one comes here to 'look around' my friend. Now, what do you really want?"

"Alright, to look around for something that might be here."

"No one looks for anything here either. The temples and tombs have been raided and stripped. There is nothing here you could want. Now, again, what trouble do you bring to the dead?"

"Well, if you let me look, no trouble."

"And if we do not?"

"Probably trouble."

"Hah! You are a funny man I see. What exactly is it that you seek here among the dead?"

"I am bound by my employer and those who have given me information."

The man stopped and peered into Brede's face in the dark. He stood almost as tall as Brede himself.

"Ah, an honorable man as well. That is good for you."

Brede said nothing.

"We are honorable men too. We protect the last vestige of the ancient holy religion and its Pharaohs." He pressed the barrel of his gun against Brede's jaw. "We are only violent when necessary."

"And how often is that?"

"Every day my friend."

Brede grinned at the gun thrust against his throat. It was the same thing he would do. "If you do this to your friends, it's not surprising that you have many enemies. Now do I get to look around or not?"

"We will escort you. Do you have quarrel with that?"

"No," Brede told him. "In fact you might be able to help me."

"We will not allow anything to be removed from the Pharaoh Queen's Temple. Enough has been taken."

"I may not need to. What I seek may not be here. But information might and if it is, I will be satisfied."

"Then I will escort you myself."

He waved off the other guards and walked Brede to the entrance. Brede stopped a moment and gazed about the edifice once considered immense, looking for anything that might give a clue or hide something. He saw nothing but flickering flames in the shadows of the darkened temple. An ancient copper tripod with a large copper bowl resting on its top, burned incense in the center of the temple. Brede inhaled enjoying the scent almost as much as the tobacco of Anhur's. He gazed up at the walls covered in art and pictographs, still astoundingly beautiful after millennia. Enormous statues still kept watch over the magnificent building. Brede wondered if the old architects of Earth were better than the new. He certainly preferred the ancient ones to the current. The priest-warrior stopped beside him and then turned to face him directly. He could see the beauty of the man's face in the shadows; long and elegantly boned with dark silky skin akin to his own.

"I am Aarif. What is your name?"

"Brede, Alekzander Brede. But I'd appreciate it if you don't spread it around."

"I will not, Alekzander Brede. I like your attitude. You are casual but not ignorant. I do not like those who show too much respect. We are men like yourself—" Aarif stopped and glanced at him. "As much as you are a man," He grinned at Brede. "No disrespect intended."

"None taken," Brede shook his head. "Aarif, there is another reason I do not want my name spoken and it is not for my convenience. There are others who will not hesitate to kill you all if they think you have given me information or the object I seek and they cannot get it out of you too. I suggest you let no one else in regardless what they may say. They often believe I am ahead of them in this race although they are mostly wrong. As I say, be more vigilant than you already are—much more vigilant."

"Hah! You are a good man Alekzander Brede!" Aarif clapped a hand against his back. "As much as you are a man," He added again laughing out loud at his own joke.

"Is there anything left in the temple that you protect as well, other than the temple itself?"

"Alas, not much of any worth," Aarif's attitude changed to sorrowful. "As I said, much has been taken. We now guard merely small items of little worth other than the Pharaoh Queen touched them herself. You know she is a god, do you not?"

"I've heard something of the religion. Hatshepsut is known to most Earth societies. I confess I do not know much of her or the religion. I am not a convert or a believer. I hope that does not bar me from being in her presence."

"Not at all, Alekzander," Aarif said quietly. "We would rather share our pride and religion to those unfamiliar than those familiar enough to destroy them."

They walked into what was left of the interior, carvings and art still glorious under the stress and destruction of modern man. Brede shook his head over it once again, thinking that mankind apparently would never evolve to the level of not destroying himself. He looked at the walls, the art, the writing, inspecting closely the cracks or crevices that might be loose enough to hide something. He did not have the time to decipher the hieroglyphics and turned to Aarif.

"I will tell you now what it is I seek. It is the Vessel of Beket-Re. Do you know if it is here or not? Is it possible that it is still hidden even from you?"

Aarif's expression turned to one of fear.

"Alekzander, this is no toy for you to bring to your woman. You do not understand what you are after, what power this holy object can bring. If it is here we do not know of it and if it is I cannot give it to you."

"As I told you Aarif, it may not even be here. You can read this language as I do not have time to; does it mention anything like the Vessel or where it could be?"

"I have studied these walls and paintings and writing both what is written openly and what is written veiled for all of my life. The Vessel of Beket-Re has never been written or spoken of openly though all those who guard the cities of the dead know of it."

As if mentioning the Vessel brought on vengeance from the god queen herself several barrages of gunfire sounded outside and shouts and cries of the guards could be heard. Brede pulled both guns and ran out of the temple alongside Aarif. He did not recognize the small on-planet craft or their origin but shot several of them, killing the pilots and causing them to crash dangerously near the temple. Several guards lay along the steps as the others shot from hiding places among the temple statues and hidden stair steps. They put up a good fight of their own, making his defense a bit easier and upping his estimation of their prowess as real warriors. Between them they managed to destroy all but one craft and its pilot. The small ship screamed into a turn and retreated back to the city as Brede and Aarif stood to count the casualties. Three of the nine guards lay dead and the others rushed to carry their bodies away for purification and mummification as Aarif directed. He turned back to Brede.

"You are a good friend to us Alekzander Brede. You have told us the truth and we will not forget it. Although we have lost some, we have learned of the enemies we now face and how to prepare for them in the future."

"To be a better friend I will leave you now. I ask only if you learn of the vessel to contact me in New Cairo. There is a young woman there by the name of Elektra Tate. She can always find me." He tried not to roll his eyes to go along with his dry tone. Now he'd have to let her hang around.

"We will do so my friend. Please do not forget us and please visit again in more peaceful times."

Aarif shook his hand and clapped his back again.

"I will Aarif. I thank you for your trust in me. Goodbye for now." Brede took a few steps and then stopped and turned back to Aarif. "How did you know my employer was a woman?"

"The part of you that is a man told me." Aarif laughed yet again the sound echoing around the tomb and retreated into the temple where he could guard the Pharaoh Queen from inside the dark.

****

Dawn broke over Thebes Two, rays splintered between the massive buildings, making morning shadows cast themselves even over The City of the Dead. Brede headed back toward New Cairo thinking about the time needed to explore the many necropolises in the New Middle East and various other places on Earth. He didn't have that time with his enemy-competitors tailing him, destroying anything he left, be it things, information or people. Brede couldn't worry about any of it; he needed to haul ass back to Cairo and find Elektra as soon as possible.

He pushed through the crowds that gathered and filled the streets after morning prayers, the sun now raised. He tossed them aside like dolls but few dared to give him even a resentful glance. When he approached the pyramid Brede debated whether to check in with Narita, hesitating only because he knew it would end with sex, robbing him of even more time. Though he wanted it he decided to find Elektra first. He needed the information more than he needed Narita. Ironically, it was Elektra he needed the most.

"Hey. Here I am," someone tapped the back of his shoulder.

He didn't jump. Years of Elektra popping up unexpectedly killed any surprise. The difference now was that he was actually looking for her.

"How do you know I'm even looking for you?" he stopped and turned to her.

"You're looking for me alright Alekzander. In fact it's the first time. I'd remember *that*." She didn't smile. "I'll let you know if anybody passes information to me." She turned away from him and took a few steps. Brede stared at her surprised. Even with the speed of the Scythe the information he'd given to Aarif arrived before him.

"You don't know what I want or why," He fell into step with her.

"I don't know what but I do know why. What else is there?" Her voice was bitter and she gazed straight ahead.

"Why are you giving *me* attitude Elektra? It's not like I won't pay you."

"I said I would do it didn't I?" she snapped but kept walking.

"What is your problem?" Brede grasped her shoulder and turned her to face him. She winced hard and grunted making him glance at her arm in a metal sling. "You've been giving me a hell of a lot of attitude lately. What the fuck is wrong with you?"

"Look, I have a de—lot of stuff to think about. Okay?" She glanced at him with an odd expression and then tried to resume walking. He grasped her shoulder again stopping her and turning her back once more.

"No, it is not okay. I'm relying on you to relay information that is critical to me. I don't need any of your fuck-ups Elektra. Understand?"

"I under*stand*." She hissed through gritted teeth and wrenched her shoulder out of his grip, winced again and walked away at a fast clip.

Brede stood still and watched her go. The attitude now was even more dramatic than when she'd left the Scythe mid-job for no reason he could discern. Was she pissed that he was looking for her or that he never had before? Brede closed his eyes. If she fucked this up he'd kill her for sure. He decided that it *was* time to check in with Narita.

****

"Follow the girl. She will lead us directly to him."

"How can you be sure?"

"She protects him. She has done so since a child. He doesn't even realize it and it makes him that much more vulnerable. If it is done correctly, he'll be delivered almost directly into our hands."

"How will we find her? What if she does not do what we expect?"

"There are plans in place for any contingencies, do not worry yourself."

"I am paying you through the nose to have him. Remember who finances your 'research'. I can cut you off faster than I can kill him. I want him and I want complete control over him. Is that understood?"

"Yes. We are always aware of your generosity never fear. You shall have him one way or another."

"One way—alive, bring him to me alive and well."

"Yes. He will be."

"He'd better be."

They parted ways, each pondering his own plans in his own mind.

****

She was eleven when they first saw one another. Brede glanced at her as he passed by Garbage City where she stood atop a two story pile of trash, sorting out the trash at the command of one of the men supervising her. Her mouth opened a little and she stood up straight, flinging the cigarette dangling from it and abandoning the man and the mountain of filth to run and walk along his side.

"Hi. I'm Elektra Tate. What's your name?"

"There's no need for you to know that," he said looking down at her.

"Well, maybe I could help you some time, like if you need information. I know everything that happens on the streets or almost everything. And what I don't know I can find out. I know lots of people and lots of them are important too." She inhaled before every phrase and the words shot out rapid fire.

Brede kept walking.

"So like if you ever need anything you could ask for me Elektra Tate, everybody knows me." She skipped a step to keep up with him. "So, what's your name?"

"Alekzander Brede."

"Alekzander Brede. I'll remember that. Just remember if you ever need help my name is—"

"Elektra Tate."

"Right, everybody knows me."

Brede grunted and quickened his pace leaving her behind at the intersection. What she did after that, he didn't give a damn.

****

"How did you get to Garbage City Elektra?" He asked inspecting the Scythe. She'd appeared again and stood watching him. "Where's your family?"

"My family…" she thought a moment and then inhaled "…got lost from me. I know they looked for me but could never find me in all the crowds of people. I live here in Garbage City on this street 'cause this is where they got lost. They'll prob'ly find me soon."

"But how do you live? Where do you sleep? How do you eat?"

"Most of the time I sleep in the door—" she stopped and glanced at him. "I mean…most of the time I stay with my friends at their houses. They like me and ask me to stay for supper."

"Ah, so you're a leech."

"What's a leech?"

"They're indigenous to Earth and are little worms that survive by sucking the blood of others."

If she got the insult she gave no sign.

"No, my friends like me and they invite me. And I don't drink blood, ever." Her eyes rounded.

He sighed over her ignorance.

"It's not meant literally Elektra. It's a metaphor for someone who lives off other people, like you."

"I don't live off other people!" She thrust out a lower lip. "I told you. They're my friends and they invite me!"

"Because they feel sorry for you,"

"That is a lie Alekzander! They—they like me! That's why they ask!"

He found it so easy to hurt her. He also found he liked to do it; so much it grew into amusement to him and it didn't help her that she could not lie to him either. He always called her out on it.

"You're mean Alekzander."

"No I'm truthful. I don't need to lie."

"Well, I'm not lying either!" She snorted and folded her arms across her non-existent chest.

It was cruel but so enjoyable he knew he'd never stop. Besides, she made herself an easy target. And she never gave up. No matter what insult he threw at her or awful truth he pointed out, she always came back for more. Perhaps it was the perfect sadomasochistic relationship. Whatever it was Brede truly enjoyed it, even if Elektra did not. In fact he found that he almost loved it.

Six months later, she popped up at his side again, taller and better able to keep pace with his stride.

"Do you need anything Alekzander? I could get it for you quick. Everybody knows me," she said for the thirty thousandth time. Brede saw the weak spot and decided to attack. He stopped walking and she did the same.

"Everybody knows you're full of shit Elektra. You don't know anyone or anything of any worth. Everybody knows you're running a line of crap and everyone laughs at you."

Her face fell a bit and she forced the tears to stay back.

"That's not true Alekzander. I have friends. Maybe they're not as important as yours but I have them."

"You know I have connections on the street too and word is that you've pretty much worn out your welcome and are beginning to be…slightly…unwanted. I think everyone is tired of your little scams."

He watched her mouth twist in a bitter frown and her eyes shone with tears she still refused to shed. She turned and walked away from him in the opposite direction. Brede watched her go, a satisfied expression on his own face. Only part of what he said was true.

He didn't see her again for a year and a half, subconsciously counting the time. When he did she was low-key and tried mostly to avoid him, disappearing into the throngs of people on the crowded streets of New Cairo when they glimpsed each other and eventually he did lose track of how much time passed until he saw her next.

He also never saw the Cadillac Annihilator flying low toward him through the scattering crowds of screaming people and animals, guns trained on him, nor the moment Elektra stepped out in front of it, causing its driver a knee-jerk reaction that tipped the vehicle sideways and slammed it into the second story of a nearby wall.

****

She no longer had any choice. When you lived on the streets you couldn't afford to lose anything that assisted survival and Elektra's left arm and hand was something that did. She needed it for self-defense if nothing else. She knew it was wrong, knew it was the worst decision she could make and tried everything she could think of to rationalize it away, to make the choice justified. She stopped walking and turned around in time to see Brede enter the "pyramid" where Narita Sabbad held court and made her decision.

"You have made your choice?" the doctor, she didn't know his name, asked when she stood before him again.

"Yes," she squeezed her eyes once to press back tears. "I guess I don't need any more time to think about it."

"You don't have it anyway Miss Tate. In order to save that arm and hand we cannot wait any longer. It is a long procedure; long and delicate. But you will be satisfied with the results. Do you have any further hesitation Miss Tate?"

Elektra shook her head.

"No, no more."

"Are you ready now?"

"I guess I am."

"Good then let us begin."

Her last conscious thought was the hope that Alekzander would forgive her.

****

This time the rocket launcher hit its mark and the half dome blew apart. For once Brede was unprepared and when the mercenaries blew the door off its hinges and stomped into the room, he was pulling up his pants.

"Shit!" was all he managed.

CHAPTER THREE

She sat on the edge of the table, legs and feet swinging, flexing and turning her new left arm and hand unable to discern what was natural and what was not. The doctor who'd found her on the street stood before her smiling.

"It looks exactly like my own," she said, still holding it aloft and forming a fist, "Right down to my fingerprints. How did you—"

"We took everything from the original, everything. We saved what we could but that was next to nothing so most of it was destr—discarded. The bones were almost crushed. What I have done is replace them with a metal polymer alloy of Midinium. You should feel thankful toward your Amphidian friend for that! Flexible but almost indestructible yet allowing me to reconstruct the billions of nerve cells again from the original. But I doubt you will be able to notice the difference once you are used to it."

"How long will it take?" Elektra looked at him.

"It varies. Depending on how concentrated your efforts are, long or short time."

She gazed at her hand again but did not look at him.

"And the payment?" she asked.

"You have paid your debt entirely. You paid for your arm during the surgery. I hope you're not having second thoughts my dear. It's far too late for that."

Elektra swallowed.

"And when you have him?"

"We have him now. Would you like to see?"

She nodded.

He led her through a hall and down into the bowels of the building. They rode the elevator to the basement and he guided her into the one-way glass walled room where she could see Alekzander sitting at a table wrists cuffed to the top of it. She grasped the back of a chair watching him. Alekzander was alone in the room, questions being asked by a disembodied male voice.

"Once again Mr. Brede will you name your employer and the job?"

"Same answer for both—no."

A shock of some sort twisted him into a spasm and then stopped, leaving him gasping for breath.

Elektra jerked and moved toward the window.

"You're hurting him," she looked at the doctor. "That wasn't part of the deal."

"I think you should reserve judgment for the moment my dear."

"Who gave up the information?" Alekzander asked, breathing hard.

"It came from an acquaintance yours—one proscribed outlaw citizen, Elektra Tate."

Alekzander snorted.

'Elektra's only worth is what she can steal on any given day."

The thick metal bent like thin wire in Elektra's hand and she did not take her eyes from him.

"I suggest you double-check any further information you receive from her."

She dropped her hand and the doctor stared at the twisted metal. He wondered what would happen when she realized what she could do with it.

"I'm done here." She looked at the doctor. "Take me back."

****

He would never give up Narita. No matter what, no matter anything they could do he would never do it. He cursed Elektra and swore that he would punish her one way or another for the ultimate betrayal for no apparent reason. As much as he suffered so would she. If Narita suffered for one instant Elektra Tate would wish she'd died on the streets as an infant.

"So, have you decided to change your answers?" The voice did not emanate disembodied from somewhere overhead but from a real human who entered and stood across the table.

"No. Have you decided to change your attitude and release me?"

"We are at an impasse then Mr. Brede. The only way I know to intervene in an impasse is to literally shock one of the participants until they agree. It's time-consuming Brede, and I don't like to waste time. All you have to do is tell me who pays you and confirm what you are looking for. It's a simple thing."

"If I give you a name, will you release me and whomever I ask?"

"If you give me a name I'll give you anything you want...pretty much anyway." He smiled at Alekzander.

Brede gazed at the unnamed man until he dropped the smile and looked away.

"You're lying."

"Think what you like Brede. It's your choice to suffer or not."

"Can I ask you a question? Why would you or anyone of science be interested in something that's...vaguely hinted at having magical powers? I would think you'd debunk that once you opened it. So why is it so important to you?"

"I'm just the wingman Alekzander. I follow orders."

"And who is it that *you* work for?"

The man stared at him either in anger or fear. Brede laughed out loud and shook his head. "What is it they used to say…the gun is in the other hand now?" It was all he got out before the screaming pain seared through his body again.

"Shoe," the man said. "The shoe is on the other foot now."

Brede screamed again.

"What the fuck ever," he gasped when it stopped. "If you think I'm going to give you a fucking thing, you're wrong. I won't give it up alive or dead. And you're going to have to kill me because once I get out of here, you don't exist."

"You'll never get out Brede so stop hoping for the impossible. You and anyone else with you; don't doubt it."

"I'm tired of this fucking conversation. Either kill me or let me go. You'll get nothing either way."

"Suit yourself." He left the room and rounds of pain ran through Brede at irregular intervals exhausting him as well as ripping his skin apart.

****

Narita sat in another room, the one below her bedroom that now served as the new one, sipping a glass of contraband wine—not contraband for her—and waiting for Brede to extricate himself from whatever predicament he'd gotten them into and return to her. Whoever abducted Alekzander placed guards all around her and the lower levels of the pyramid, in every room; at every door. Not that she stepped outside very often it was the point that now she couldn't if she wanted to; so far they'd done nothing to her except house arrest and she planned to let Alekzander know just how unhappy she was when he returned. She'd managed to convince them that she had no part in the search for the Vessel of Beket-Re, something easy to do since she had no real idea what it was or what it contained. A female she'd given a duchy to and who claimed to be her friend had spoken of it, indicating it had great value and anyone who possessed it would be incredibly impressive and Narita took the bait. She dispatched Brede to find it and he acquiesced just as fast. She could do that to men when she wanted and she knew Brede would never, could never refuse her and that he had no idea she knew that. He was a major conquest both sexually and socially among those whom she appointed as semi-royalty and she loved parading him about under their noses. As soon as he brought back the trinket of value she planned to reward him and herself with a permanent union.

"Bring me something to eat," she said to the room in general. "I'm bored being stuck inside all the time."

Her sentence brought them scampering to her with pastries and honey to dip them. She picked over them delicately with a long fingernail finally choosing four and a handful of the dates she adored then sat back and waited with growing impatience for Alekzander.

****

"It wasn't part of the agreement," Elektra insisted. "You said you wanted to question him. You said nothing about torture damn you!" She frowned at the doctor whose name she still did not know. He was no longer the kind, sympathetic man who offered her a new arm for a price. He stared back without sympathy now.

"You agreed to the terms, my dear." He said. "Why do you care what happens to him?"

"He—he's a…a friend of mine. I didn't give him to you to make him suffer."

"First of all, if he's a friend to you, you haven't been one back. Second, you did give him up to make him suffer. Don't tell me seeing what he really thinks of you made you reconsider your decision, it didn't. Are you going to tell me after he insulted you that you weren't upset? I saw your face. In any case it is too late to renege, Elektra."

"Will you release him after you've finished questioning him?"

"No one said anything about releasing him."

"But—but you have to!" Her eyes widened. "You can't keep him forever—he'll tell you what you want eventually and then you can let him go."

"My dear you are mistaken. Did you understand the terms? You gave us Alekzander Brede and we gave you a new arm and hand. There were no specifications about details such as letting him go or giving him spa treatment. I'm afraid we cannot do that now or ever."

"What does that mean?"

"It means whatever we want it to mean. It could mean permanent incarceration or permanent elimination. Right now it's the latter. As soon as he talks that is," the doctor didn't smile.

"No. You can't do that. He's done nothing to you for you to murder him. Once you have your information, it doesn't matter if you let him go. You can do what you want with it. He's no threat to you once he tells you."

"What happens to him is no longer your concern Miss Tate. You've received your part of the bargain and have we received ours. That means the deal is done. It is over. Goodbye Miss Tate." He grasped her right arm and led her to the door. He pressed the keypad to slide it open, shoved her quickly through it and then locked her out. If he heard her pounding on the door he gave no sign. Elektra finally gave up and headed toward the marketplace on the ground floor above the catacombs and the under prison. She didn't look back to see the indentations in the metal door left by her newly acquired left limb.

She wandered the marketplace, appearing distracted but in reality seeking someone who could help her. She moved casually, walking from stall to stall, until she spotted the ones she sought. Stopping at the makeshift stall selling ancient religious items, statues of ancient gods and goddesses, she picked up a statuette of Hatshepsut and turned it about inspecting it. Two men came to the table and stood waiting for her.

"I'll take this," she said setting it down on the table. "It's for a friend of mine. I think he'd really like to have it now." Elektra raised her eyes to them and then slid them sideways, checking who might overhear.

"Of course, please let me wrap it for you," one said.

"No, thank you, there isn't time."

"Ah, I understand."

"He's with a doctor now, he's not feeling well *at all* and I know he'd like to have it right away."

"Perhaps we can deliver it to him personally?"

"Yes, please. Let me give you the address."

****

Brede sat on a metal bench protruding from the wall, residual shock waves still wracking his body with small seizures. When it reached his lungs it pulled coughs from him making him double over with pain. With every hideous breath he swore to punish Elektra and it kept him alive. Whoever the hell they were they knew how to hurt him and not just his human side either. They'd done their homework and dispatched a medical droid with a hypodermic dripping with an unidentified compound—they didn't bother to tell him and he couldn't be bothered to ask—and when injected it sent rivers of fire through his veins and giant gagging seizures through the rest of him. By the third injection he was unconscious, on his back, sprawled out on the floor.

****

She didn't join them on the operation she had other things to do. Elektra left the marketplace and the center of the city heading outside it altogether and into the open air toward the filthy bay of Cairo. Bright hot daylight gave into mellowed sunset as the desert landscape changed slowly into the image of blinking diamonds in the lengthening dark. One or two obvious slums lined the rusted and decrepit docks where the most violent corrupt of the poor still took shelter, but Elektra passed them by and walked farther out to the skeletal remnants of the hotel where the dissident fighters convened and conducted their business in the night. They knew her by sight if not by name and knew her association with Alekzander Brede, enough that she would not venture out to them unless she meant serious business. The conversations were hushed and short, buying and selling in minutes. Whatever they asked she paid and then turned back the way she'd come, skirting the poverty camps that populated the abandoned areas of the New Middle East. Night came fast and she moved between the monoliths on the way back until she reached the slums in the city center and stopped just outside the pyramid, sitting in a doorway, assuming the disheartened slump of the proscribed citizens who still begged outside the buildings as they'd done for millennia. Then she waited.

****

They left no calling card, nothing traceable, when they fried open the front door and melted the monitor system that no one else could find or identify, let alone disable without leaving their images or time stamp. They moved throughout the glass walled lobby with views of nearby super monolithic buildings their own lights blinking in the black night. They walked through the interior offices and surgery where Elektra received her new arm and hand, and exchanged looks as they found the first floor guard engrossed in personal business in his private restroom. His business concluded early when they fried that door and stood, weapons drawn upon him.

"Tell us where is Alekzander Brede and you will live to finish your personal activities," one of them told him. "And do not press the button on the paper roll, lest you lose the finger that does."

He trembled as he told them and when they left he realized it was a good thing they did not ask him to stand up from the toilet. He also realized that he was in luck that they did not rip out his tongue when they broke his jaw and instructed him to never speak of them again unless he desired a painful and slow death. He never did.

Before they rode the elevator, they located the central monitori and video station in the center of the first floor designed in an octagon, surrounded by the interior wall. Changing weaponry they sprayed semi-combustible gel on the entire console. Designed to both flood and melt down the equipment; if one didn't complete the destructive job the other one would. It self-ignited, sending a ring of flame that snaked a trail around the console, singeing melting and fusing the control board keys before dying out and liquefying to seep into the interior as acid to obliterate anything operable left.

The first man silently indicated to his partner to use the stairwell and not the elevator, preserving silence for their surprise entrance. They slipped through the always open outer stairwell that ran down along the outer wall and continued down to the third level and cased the hallways until they came upon the green chroma-lit glass walled doctors' station. Two doctors in blue moved back and forth peering through a window that showed Brede still lying on the floor, unmoving, a medical droid standing over him needle feeds piercing his body in several critical locations and transmitting the information back into the station. The door left unlocked due to the late hour and the business day over; no unexpected guests due…their mistake. The intruders slid it open silently and by the time the doctors looked up the barrels of the guns touched their temples.

"Wake him up," the lead gunman said. "Bring him here unharmed."

"We can't do that. He's heavily sedated—"

"Liar," the gunman said. "You put him out you can bring him awake. Now do it."

One doctor glanced at the other who nodded.

"I have to get to the console to instruct the droid," he told the men.

"Do not try to kill him or any tricks. You will die the moment he does."

The doctor moved to the keyboard console and looked through the glass wall at Brede. He typed rapid fire instructions to the droid that awoke and whirred, extracting all the needles except one. It hovered next to Brede awaiting further instruction.

"I have to give him a stimulant to bring him back to consciousness," the doctor twisted his head a little to look at the gunman.

"Then do so."

Turning back he keyed another sequence and pastel blue liquid bubbled and gurgled up through a tube and into the needle feed. Several minutes passed before the body on the floor moved slightly. Brede sat up coughing and grunting a moment before standing and looking at the glass wall he could not see through.

"Well?" he said to it. "I am not dead. What's next?"

"Let us speak with him," the gunman told the doctor. He pressed a key and nodded.

"Your release is next Alekzander Brede," the gunman said.

Brede's expression changed from resentment to surprise.

"I recognize that accent and voice, Effia. Did Aarif send you?"

"That I cannot tell you Alekzander Brede," Effia said. "I am sworn to both who sent us and our own need for safety and secrecy. You will be out momentarily."
Effia looked again at the doctor. "Open it up now."

The doctor pressed his hand on the sig station and leaned to speak into the microphone again.

"You need to turn left and then right—"

"I remember the way," Brede cut off his sentence. He walked out to the lobby with his saviors and then stopped and frowned. "I forgot something," he told them. They nodded and waited while he re-entered the offices and remained even after they heard the blasts of his own guns. Then they looked at each other and laughed.

****

"We don't have time, Narita," Brede watched her put on gown after gown before rotating mirrors that showed her image from every possible angle. "We can do this later."

"No Alekzander! What good is a union ceremony if there's no one to witness it? Besides, it will only take a day or so to arrange it," she gazed at her reflection. "Now, how do I look? I'm torn between the blue one and the gold. Which do you think?" She spun around before him.

"I don't give damn Narita. We have four days to get our asses out of here. You can only take what's necessary. I don't know how long we'll be gone or if we can come back."

Narita frowned in earnest.

"Why do we have to leave at all? I am the royalty here, Alekzander. I should be able to do what I like."

"Narita, do you have any concept of what danger is? Do you understand that your life along with mine is in danger of ending…entirely?"

She remained frowning but with anger.

"How did this come about? Who is responsible for this?"

Brede sighed.

"Someone I—trusted betrayed me…and you. Now we have a very short window of opportunity to escape with our lives, so—"

"Who has done this?" Her attitude changed to imperious. "I shall have them punished!"

"It doesn't matter Narita—"

"It does! Tell me who did this?"

"She is—was—someone I thought was a friend."

"Who?" Narita insisted.

"Electra Tate," Brede said finally. "And I can assure you Narita she will be punished. I promise you that."

"Well, then, if you can promise me that you can promise me yourself in the union ceremony. It will take place tomorrow and then we can leave. Will that suit you?"

Brede thought for a moment and then smiled.

"Yes."

"Then I shall wear the gold and you shall wear gold too. Now I must get the invitations out." she turned to the mirrors and her attendants, tossing the blue gown aside and left the room reeling off the innumerable guests she wanted to impress.

Brede left her there and walked the streets of the City of the Dead, toward the crooked streets where the proscribed citizens lived in the tombs with the deceased, once more pushing through the crowds or weaving through them when necessary. If Elektra held true to her obnoxious personality he could expect a tap on the shoulder at any moment. But she did not appear beside him, behind him, or anywhere at all and that annoyed him more. He turned at the crooked street and walked along it, among the slums of the city-state, worse than they even were in the last century. The buildings stood taller and yet still crumbled like dried out wheat cakes.

She was not to be found any place that she usually haunted not even in the tiny hovel she called home. Normally, she could be found stealing or hustling scams on the streets during the day and that she wasn't around made the streets slightly eerie. He glanced at the lowering sun, halfway below the horizon, telling him night was on its way to the city soon, ending the first full day of his—and Narita's—remaining freedom. He sped up, needing to find her as soon as possible before it was time to lift off Earth, possibly permanently.

Finally he stopped at a group of men and women gathered around a fire, even in the heat of the early night, preparing a group dinner. They stopped talking and looked up at him, dark faces suspicious even in the fading light.

"Elektra Tate," he said. "Where can I find her?"

"Not here," one of the women said.

"Will she be here later?"

"Don't know," another woman said. "Haven't seen her since yesterday why?"

"Can you give her a message—if I pay you?"

"We can try," a man said. "What is the message?"

"It is urgent. Give her this before sunrise tomorrow." He handed the man a small vial with a sealed top. The man took it and looked down at it. "Do not open it upon pain of death. She will know what it is when she receives it."

The unnamed man's eyes rounded in slight fear. He nodded.

"Before sunrise," Brede said to him. The man nodded again and Brede turned and left the slums heading for the pyramid and Narita's bed for the night.

****

He meandered through the streets of the City of the Dead; through the crumbling tombs that they transformed into houses, windows without permaglass or Plexiglas and frames without doors, open to the air. The walls and doorways crumbled, growing more and more decrepit and empty as he walked and for a while Brede moved with uncertainty that Elektra even slept there let alone made it her home. He reached the far end of the cemetery mausoleums that held the poor and poverty-stricken over many centuries. When he reached the last sector he arrived at the empty one-room tomb that she probably haunted he went inside and gazed about wondering how the hell she managed to wrangle a single tomb she didn't have to share. A ragged cloth lay on the floor near the wall and another wad of material lay at the end of it.

Her bed.

A tiny table sat in the corner, small objects arranged on top of it. He leaned down and picked one up. It opened on hinges showing a tiny doll house scene in pastel colors. Brede shook his head and set it back down, picking up another. It was a locket on a chain, something unfamiliar to him but he began to open it anyway.

"Alekzander," Elektra stood in the doorway. "What are you doing here?"

"What are these things?" He dangled the unopened locket.

"That's mine!" she snatched it from his hand and clutched it at her chest. She backed away from him a few steps.

"Where did you steal them?" He gave her a sardonic smile.

"I didn't steal them—"

"Elektra you can't lie worth a damn especially to me. Why the hell do you want them anyway? They're worthless."

She drew her brows down like a resentful child.

"Not to me," she said in a small accusing voice. "You shouldn't be looking at other people's things Alekzander."

For a moment he thought she might cry but she didn't. He'd never really thought of her as a girl before; just some sort of androgynous female; he would have called her a skinny tomboy had he ever heard the antiquated term and known what it meant. He looked back down at the doll house trinket and held it up for her to see.

"Why the hell would you want this?"

"It's—it's pretty." Her voice changed to defensive.

He snorted.

"You stole this because you thought it was pretty?"

Elektra frowned deeper.

"And what the hell is that?" He pointed at the locket she held in her fist.

"It's mine. I found it."

"Right,"

"I did! I found it."

"Where?"

"I found it when I moved here. It was in the dirt. I kept it."

He raised his eyebrows and closed his eyes for a moment. She was beyond stupid, she was crazy. He could never have guessed she'd have another side, a feminine one, a silly one if she thought the useless little objects had value.

"Why are you here Alekzander? What do you want?"

"Well first I didn't know that you actually lived anywhere after Garbage City,"

"How did you find me?"

"I asked your neighbors—well, your closest living neighbors. Why are you living in the last inhabitable house—if it can be called that," he said.

"I like to be private."

"You certainly are that. The real reason I'm here is because I want you to deliver something to someone for me."

"Like a messenger?"

"Exactly."

"What am I taking?"

"This." Brede held out his palm. In it sat a tree of his own planet composed of Amphidyte its brilliance outshining diamonds by twenty.

"Oh, it's beautiful," Elektra breathed. She tried to touch it with her fingers but he pulled it away.

"I'm hoping she'll like it," Brede said.

Elektra kept her eyes down.

"She?"

"Narita Sabbad. That's where you're delivering it."

After a long moment Elektra looked up with a plaintive expression.

"Yes, I will pay you," he said.

"When do I take it?"

"Tomorrow morning and take good fucking care of it Elektra," he said. *"It's not one of your worthless trinkets. This has real value."* He turned and walked out the door without looking back to see her holding the Amphidyte tree in one hand and her ancient locket in the other.

"They're not worthless to me Alekzander," she said. *"Not worthless to me."*

****

Colin Factor smiled at the group of three treasure hunters standing before him. They were about to become bounty hunters as well though they knew it not. He also smiled at the thought of Alekzander Brede's carcass being dragged and dropped in front of him like the prey of a cat bringing a gift to its master. Brede had no idea of just how devious and deceptive Factor had grown over the years or just how much Colin despised him now. Of course he could never know what he'd taken from Colin and that made the concept of revenge even sweeter than the thousands-of-centuries old honey cakes that originated in the first Thebes. If the death of Alekzander Brede invoked joy in him, Brede suffering as he watched Colin take back what was his flooded his entire countenance with unrestrained bliss. He focused again on his would-be bounty hunters and presented them with the tools of their new trade and the treasure they would fetch: Alekzander Brede alive enough to know suffering.

****

She walked to the main door of the pyramid where the outside guards crossed laser guided 4700s to prevent her entry.

"I—I have a message and a gift for Narita Sabbad," Elektra said.

"No one enters unless referred. Who is the message from?"

"Alekzander Brede."

Immediately the weapons rose and both resumed their stance. She entered the building where another man approached her and asked her the same questions. She repeated what she'd told the guards and waited for him to confirm her permission to enter the inner sanctum. Once the voice in the comlink embedded in his jaw squealed out an answer, he escorted her all the way to the top of the pyramid and left her standing before Narita Sabbad, seated upon a large throne-like chair on a small dais. She stared at Elektra and the man returned to give Elektra a small shove. She resisted a little and took two forced steps toward Narita.

"I—I have a gift and a message for you," Elektra cleared her throat. She'd never been inside the pyramid and found its luxury daunting.

"Well, what is it and who is it from?"

Elektra swallowed again before answering.

"It's this," she held out the Amphidyte tree sitting on her palm. She ignored the 'court' that sucked in a collective gasp at its beauty.

"I can't see it from there," Narita said and a servant scampered forward, snatched it from Elektra and brought it to Narita's waiting hand. She inspected it closely and then looked at Elektra.

"And who is it from?"
It took Elektra a moment to respond.
"Alekzander Brede," she said at last.
Narita narrowed her eyes at Elektra and then smiled.
"What is the message?"
"He—he hopes you like it." She kept her eyes down as she spoke to the throne.
"You may tell him that I do like it very much and find it an acceptable gift for our royalty. You may thank him for me." She watched Elektra's face closely and then turned to the same servant and whispered something. The audience was over.

****

She stood in the back, peeking through gauze curtains, watching the event that would take Alekzander Brede away from her forever, even as a friend. Elektra took refuge against the wall behind the curtains that hid a side door. She knew if Narita glimpsed her, she faced arrest and imprisonment again and so peeked from behind them waiting for Narita and Alekzander to enter and for him to swear permanent allegiance to her in every aspect of their lives. The gigantic room filled beyond capacity, standing room filled with bodies pressed together and no one noticed her, all focusing only on the ceremony to begin.

Dancers entered to a flourish of ancient music enhanced to deafening levels, original instruments of millennia past, invaluable and only used for momentous occasions such as this. The musicians paraded behind the dancers until they reached the thrones also as old and valuable as the musical instruments and stopped, lining along either side of the throne. They began a low steady drumming as Narita made her entrance with more flourish and pomp than even her dancers. She walked to the front of the throne, faced the audience, and then climbed the short dais to sit on the seat. She waved an arm, jeweled from fingers and wrist to elbow and simpered at the crowd. They responded by sitting down themselves after a long collective breath.

Alekzander entered without fanfare, walking silently to the dais and stopping before Narita, back to the crowd. She'd had a breastplate made for him, fashioned after ancient design as well and made of gold. He wore nothing beneath it exposing his broad shoulders and his customary pants and boots and Elektra guessed he refused to go any further to please Narita's insatiable lust for ostentation. He stood silently waiting for her, for the officiator, whom Narita referred to as "vizier" to begin.

"Do you Alekzander Brede swear allegiance to Narita Sabbad, sovereign of New Cairo?"

"Yes." Alekzander said.

"Do you swear to protect her with your life?"

"Yes."

"Do you foreswear any other women as long as she lives?"

"Yes."

Elektra swallowed a sob and coughed to hide it. A few heads turned her way and then back to the service.

"Do you accept your place as 'sworn consort' of Narita Sabbad?"

"Yes."

The vizier turned to Narita still seated.

"Do you accept Alekzander Brede as your sworn consort?"

Narita smiled widely showing bright white teeth.

"Yes. Yes I do.' She rose and held out her arm toward Brede, stepping down the dais to place her hand on his forearm.

'Then it is done." The vizier bowed to them and retreated behind the throne. They turned to face the audience who stood and applauded as they walked slowly and regally down the center aisle. Elektra blinked back tears and stared at them as they neared her. As they passed where she hid, Alekzander turned his head, gazing as if he could see her and Narita followed his gaze. Elektra dropped the curtain held open less than an inch and vanished through the door behind her.

****

The night shift doctors' parts lay flung across the control room and the night watchman refused to speak, terrified out of his mind, only capable of shaking his head in the negative. However the doctor attending to Elektra remained alive, if not happy with the circumstances of his hard work. His benefactor could pull the massive amounts of financing for anything he wanted to experiment with, including her arm, in return for Alekzander Brede who somehow got out of his drug induced prison and spread destruction and fear in his wake. He ran a hand over his tired face and walked back out into the lobby and sat in a guest chair, resting not only his body but his mind while he could before he needed an explanation and solution to what happened overnight. It was a short respite. He already placed more than one fail safe should any contingency like this occur and he chuckled, thought himself quite clever. He stood again, watching the sun rays burst and reflect against the glass walls of all the buildings in the complex to make complicated patterns on the rubberized carpet in his offices and surgery. Brede would not get away in the end, difficult as it might be to re-apprehend him, there would be no escape and his employer would be more than satisfied at last.

****

She couldn't do it. She couldn't abandon Alekzander to whomever his new enemies were no matter how much she needed her new appendage to survive. If there was no Alekzander Brede there might as well be no Elektra Tate, even if he left her life entirely she needed to know he was alive, or at least free from what she'd done. Elektra didn't need the pyramid…just yet. She carefully skirted the front and outside of the building now surrounded by pseudo-military guards that were no longer at Narita's command. They surrounded the first floor and intimidated anyone wanting to enter for selling, royal business, or passing information of critical nature. The building was old, nearly a skeleton of its original self when it stood magnificently housing the adjudicators of religious conflicts. Now it stood half empty, used mostly for Narita and whatever contingent she declared royal along with herself, ignored mostly by the legitimate government rule except when the royalty accused and punished those it deemed as committing crimes against itself. Most of the time Elektra stayed away, being one of those criminals punished and because Alekzander frequented it. The last thing she wanted to imagine was what happened there when he did.

 This time it didn't matter. What mattered was getting them both out safely and uninjured and alive. Circling the building twice seeking unnoticed entry ports, she carried the one thing that could fix it all one way or another in her pocket, its warning system disabled and undetectable. She stayed far enough from the new militia to raise no suspicion and in random paths to keep her intentions unnoticed. The night before Elektra visited the outer rim of the poverty-stricken wharf, underneath the pilings in the nearly complete dark of the moonless sky and inky sea to complete the transaction rapidly and then made her way back to New Cairo proper where she abandoned her regular hangouts, waiting for the dawn to break and the usual disruption of downtown by the religious marches and their anticipated clashes clogging the streets to hide her entry and activities.

 As if on schedule, two opposing religious factions did clash on Center Street still the main road in New Cairo and the ensuing fracas distracted the guards who snapped to fighting stance while Zonal Enforcement Craft responded humming like furious wasps in large numbers and with more firepower than usual. They did indeed zone in on the offenders spitting out stinging fire beams intermittently at each group. It provided enough time for Elektra to climb a half-hidden entry hallway that slanted up to a back door used by ancient peoples and re-constructed during the modifications to the pyramids. Now hidden behind native plants and trees the entry was virtually unseen unless one knew it was there. And now she knew.

She walked the ramp casually as if she belonged there and slipped an alumacoil between the door and its jamb, an unnecessary action. The door swung open silently on recently greased hinges. Suspicious Elektra pocketed the coil and went inside. Pale light from tiny square windows illuminated the stairwell, she climbed until the stairs ended at a solid door, locked this time. Again she pulled out the alumacoil and slid it between the lock and its dead bolt. Small yellow fire seared itself along the outline of the door, ending at the bolt with a small puff of smoke and the door popped open. All good signs so far, making her plans easier and more effective in the near future. Her next problem was getting inside the pyramid itself. The door led to hallway doors placed randomly but with no sign where they might lead. Elektra stopped, thinking. Any use of the alumacoil would create smoke that, while faint, might alert whatever alarm system in place. She walked counting the doors from the one she entered and tried a door. It opened without resistance and she walked through it without sound. Across the room stood the slit doors of an elevator, and Elektra sprang toward it. It creaked a bit as it opened, shut and then climbed slowly and she waited, rocking on her heels in nervous bobs. This time she counted the doorways and picked one at random. She opened it an inch and heard voices. A group of Narita's servants sat around the kitchen discussing whatever servants discussed and Elektra, shocked, dropped the door with a loud clunk. She ran halfway down the hall and flung herself against a side wall, waiting. Someone opened the door after her and she heard two male voices moving toward her. When they stopped no one stood in her place.

"Huh," said one. "Just a gust of wind I guess."

The other gave no response and Elektra stood waiting without breathing. When she heard the door open and shut again, she crept out of the first doorway she'd found and inhaled deep with relief that didn't last long. As she crouched against the wall a red light in her left palm began pulsing brightly. Stunned she held it up in front of her face, the light from it highlighting her face and then shading it in the dark hallway. She tucked it under a thigh to hide it but at that same moment, a beeping noise emanated from it as well. She squeezed her eyes shut and she banged the back of her head against the wall.

A tracking device—I should have known.

"A gust of wind doesn't blink red and sure as hell doesn't beep," one of the men said.

From behind one of them caught her, lifting her off the ground and clapping a hand over her mouth. She kicked her feet in the air wildly, trying to make her capture as difficult as possible.

"You!" the other man said. "I remember you. You're the one sent down to the under prison! What the hell are you doing creeping around here?"

"I was just..." she hesitated, trying to think of a plausible lie.

"Just what?" he repeated.

"Look, this is going to sound crazy but I'm here to help Alekzander Brede and Narita Sabbad."

"What? What kind of bullshit story is that?" the man who held her laughed in her ear.

"I told you, it sounds crazy but I have to get them out of here without the guards or anyone else for that matter, knowing it."

The men looked at each other a long moment.

"Why would you do that? What's in it for you?"

"I—Alekzander is a—friend of mine. At least he was, and I got them both a death sentence and now I have to fix it. Please believe me." She stopped kicking.

"Hah, Narita Sabbad has a contract on her head?" The man across from her laughed out loud. "I'd pay to see that happen."

"Seven days in a black hole doesn't make me a fan either," Elektra said. "But she also issues your pay chip. And if Alekzander likes her...either way, it doesn't matter. Neither one deserves murder. And I'm the only one who can stop it. Please let me go.'

"How do you plan to do that?"

Elektra managed to pull the small object out of her pocket and held out her palm. Both men back away from her, letting her drop to the floor.

"Sweet God woman! You can destroy this whole building!"

"The whole fucking city block," the one who'd held her corrected.

"Please get everyone outside through whatever exit you can. I don't want to hurt anyone that doesn't deserve it. Just get them out of here now without letting the guards know. There are people coming in after me who mean business and won't hesitate to ignite this, me still holding on. I'm trying to save Alekzander and Narita and all of you as well."

The man grabbed her again.

"I don't believe it. You're lying."

In desperation, Elektra raised her left hand and squeezed his chin. They all heard a small snap and he dropped to the floor himself, grasping his throat and neck as he landed on his knees. She stared at her hand for a shocked moment and then faced the other man whose skin paled.

"Get everyone out," she said.

He nodded, lifted his co-worker and headed for the door she'd peeked through, dragging the man who still could not speak. They ran back down the hall as she ran the opposite way seeking the stairwell that would take her to the top. She stopped only once to pull out a razor strip and slice the artificial flesh around the pulsing light to no effect. In the end she stabbed at it viciously without success. She found a set of doors opening into the bedroom where she found them asleep beside each other. She inhaled deeply and slowly and tried not to think about the scene.

"Alekzander," Elektra whispered, kneeling beside the bed so close to him she could feel his breathing. "Alekzander, wake up!" She shook him a little and he sat up, gun pressed against her jaw.

"Elektra?" he blinked in sleepy shock. "What the *fuck* are you doing *here*?"

"Shut up and listen to me for once. You and Narita have to get out of here *now*—"

He gazed at her wide awake.

"Why?"

"People are coming to kill you both. You don't have time for me to explain. I can hold them off until you launch if you get out right now. Don't take anything just get into the Scythe and go. Buzz the apex when you lift off so I'll know you're safe."

"Why are you doing this now?"

"I don't have time to—okay, look I got you into this and now I'm getting you out of it. Please Alekzander just wake her up and go."

He glanced at Narita who slept with her mouth open drooling and snoring loudly. "Hey," he said, giving her a shove. She moved a little, snorted and then resumed all actions.

"Just get her up and get your asses out of here. I'm going to wait for them in the main chamber. I'll intercept them to give you a little more time. Hurry," Elektra stood up and ran back to the outer hallway. No one arrived yet and she looked down through the window, sighting the trio of men and a cadre of armed guards flanking them heading toward the pyramid. Trying to estimate their time of arrival she watched them advance praying silently that she'd warned Alekzander in time.

****

Narita was already in the Scythe waiting when Alekzander turned to Elektra one more time.

"You need to go Alekzander," she said and held up her left palm. The pulsing red ball still throbbed at the heel of it, exposed by torn artificial flesh. "I tried to cut it out but I couldn't," she said. "They've been tracking me. They know where I am you'll be. Just buzz the window so I'll know you're safe when I—" she licked her lips. "When I finish this."

Brede stood silent.

"You know Alekzander, you never knew but the real reason I stowed away on the Scythe was because…well, because I just wanted to you know, have an outside chance with you." Elektra said the words speeding up as she spoke. "I know that I annoyed you and I pushed my way into your life. I guess I thought that if I pushed hard enough you'd finally let me in and if I just had a chance—that you'd *have* to see how much I *lo*—" She caught herself and stopped, blinking in search of another phrase. "…wanted to be…around you. It wasn't me you wanted though, it was Narita—I'm not sorry Alekzander, I'm not sorry at all!" She shook her head then gave him a small sheepish shrug. "I just wanted to tell you that."

He continued staring at her. Elektra looked back at the doors and then at him.

"You need to go," she repeated and at last he turned toward the door, "Alekzander."

He stopped in the doorway and turned halfway toward her.

"I just—I just wanted to say…thanks for inviting me to the ceremony. At least we could still be friends, huh?" She let out a small wobbly laugh and then tried to compose herself. "Go—I hear them coming. Remember buzz the apex."

Brede walked out without any response, leaving her to whatever fate she drew herself into when she sold him out for the traitor hand that now betrayed her. He did buzz the Scythe past the large window, close enough for her to see and then ripped the ship out of Cairo's atmosphere and out of orbit completely. The last thing he saw was the explosion visible even from the edge of the ozone layer and he turned the Scythe away to whatever future without Elektra Tate awaited him.

CHAPTER FOUR

Aedificer Industrial Port Station was the largest and most excellent installation shipyard in the galaxy with huge maintenance facilities for star ship construction and overhaul and Brede headed straight for it. The megalithic station stood so large it was visible from beyond its atmosphere and was the only thing providing light on the planet moon where its platform rested. He maneuvered the Scythe and touched down on the main landing strip and left Narita to sleep while he walked to the Operations Center. He skirted the manned and droid vehicles as they skittered about delivering and picking up parts for the hundreds of hangars filled with partially overhauled ships and their weapons. Occasionally a driver and passenger rode past him, beeping and calling out warning tones or voices that he ignored for the most part. On the way to the Op Center he glanced at the hangars filled with ships surrounded by giant apparatus and machinery that dismantled and reassembled them with efficiency and speed to the specifications of their pilots. He planned his own reconstruction of the Scythe as he passed them. Brede constructed the Scythe on the Aedificer Station and frequented it when he upgraded the ship usually with weaponry and speed modifications rather than comfort and convenience.

"Hello, how may I help you?" The small squat square droid addressed him from just above the rim of the counter.

"Need a hangar for major overhaul and reconstruction," he said to it, just one of the fifty counter windows manned by droids and supervised by humans from a second level.

"Name?"

"Brede Alekzander."

"Do you have an account?"

"AED Port eighteen Scythe."

"Identification signature please."

He moved to the Iridentifier and when it found no iris or pupil a small alarm sounded. He pressed a palm on the sig station and the squealing stopped.

"Identification accepted. Thank you Alekzander Brede, your receipt for the hangar and facilities' use will be issued at the end of your lease. Thank you very much."

Brede returned to the hanger where he'd left the Scythe and woke an unhappy Narita to lodge her in the best and safest room in the Port's hotel levels convincing her at last that no fancier digs existed there. She pouted as he left the room, glancing back to see her pick up the room service keyboard.

He stood watching and supervising the enormous machinery that tore out the fuselage on the Scythe and broke apart the ship's framing as easily as it would break desiccated skeleton's bones and he experienced a momentary regret over the destruction and reconstruction of his beloved ship. Brede designed the new Scythe himself, quadrupling the size and installing eight times the firepower and speed.

Knowing Narita's obsession with being royal, he chose the most sumptuous, most richly colored textile materials, ignoring the cost that racked up with every choice he made. The price of the new firepower and speed could have paid for his ship to orbit the station five times over despite the fact that the Scythe's new power generators took longer than usual to fire themselves up enough to arm the volt guns. Brede also installed a new alarm system to give him early warning of attacking fighters. He did retain one feature of the old Scythe however: the gunner's nest at the top. Whether he kept it as a major surprise weapon or as a memory of all that was left of Elektra that Brede carefully refused to think about.

It took five months for the total reconstruction and most of the upgrades and specifications he paid for on credit, planning on other jobs that could bring in enough money to cover the bills spent to continue to make Narita a happy and sexually available woman. Feeding her and maintaining her lifestyle created another cost paid on credit which Brede reluctantly did as well. He said nothing to her, but kept a running tally that gave him a vague estimate of just how much he owed. It didn't matter; he could make it up with three or four jobs in a row…if he got lucky. If she didn't eat him right out of ownership of the Scythe with her addiction to Middle Eastern dates that he had shipped to the station on her word, disregarding their contraband status. He hoped the sheer fear of him would hold his debtors at bay until he could return to pay up and he managed to intimidate the human station director if not the droid one for the time being. They knew he was good for it or remembered that he was in the past. Brede traded on that now and when the last crane disengaged from his ship, groaning and screeching back into the recesses of the walls where it belonged, he didn't wait for the receipt. The Scythe shot off the station at maximum power blowing his debt across the landing strip like dust.

****

"Narita!" Brede barked at her as she squealed and clutched his neck red nails digging into his flesh. She screamed with every blast from the attacking ship. "Let go of me! I cannot defend if you're piercing my throat." She let go and stood behind him, grabbing the seat to support balance. "Go sit in the jump seat and lock down."

"Which one is the jump seat?"

"Behind me. Get the fuck in it and shut the hell up."

"I can't get to it with all this bouncing and shaking!" she said, toppling on the back of the pilot seat again. "Can't you make them stop?"

"Do it Narita." Brede ignored her concentrating on making the attacking ship stop. If she fell on her ass it was her own fault. Two more ships fanned out heading directly for the Scythe, guns preparing to blaze. For one instant he visualized the memory of Elektra in the crow's nest gunnery. But she wasn't really there and he blinked the image away, charging up the volt guns and hoping the power surge wouldn't kick in too late. He received two direct hits on the starboard sending the ship flying and the fighters out of his field of vision. He righted it then skidded the Scythe into a half-circle to come alongside the two remaining ships, giving the mother ship direct hits to its hull with little result. The mother ship launched a deadly volley that vibrated the Scythe dangerously and ripped off two hover rotors. The explosion blinded him for a moment and the last fighter veered away from the Scythe in a wide sideways arc. Brede twisted the Scythe the same direction to cut off the attacker's path and let go with the volts full force. They weren't there. He stomped on the floor pedals trying to manually pump them up to firing levels as the mother ship navigated for another round of firefight.

"Shut *up* Narita!" he screamed over his shoulder again. She'd begun squealing again when the volley began and hadn't stopped. He pumped the volts over and over as more fighters exited the mother and maneuvered to his port and starboard to box him in for her. Brede counted the seconds until the volt guns revved up and realized there was nowhere to go. The mother blasted and two more rotors disintegrated as they wrenched off the Scythe.

"We're going down…" Narita's voice was loud and warning next to him and he ventured a glimpse at her terrified face pale around her red lips. Without warning she reached out and pounded on the eject function. He had no time to respond and clung to the wiring as the ejection bays opened and sucked out half the dashboard. An air mask dropped to her and she pressed it to her nose.

"Hit the AutoSave!" he screamed in earnest.

"What?" her face looked stupid as she struggled to hear him over the roar of the rest of the rotors.

"AutoSave! Hit the AutoSave! Now!"

She inspected what was left of the dashboard, peering closely at it as if she needed glasses. Brede wanted to scream again but air began to suck out of his lungs and his body dangled half out of the cockpit. At last her expression changed to one of recognition and she pointed to a key with raised eyebrows.

"This?" her voice sounded muffled beneath the mask.

Brede nodded.

"Okay," she pressed the key and the AutoSave sequence engaged.

He managed to force his muscles enough to swing back into the pit as the auxiliary shields closed over him and secured lockdown status. His problems still weren't over. Three more fighters emerged from the belly of the mother armed with major firepower. Struggling to get back into what was left of his pilot seat, he spun the ship to face them and squeezed the triggers of both volt guns repeatedly, relief washing over him as he nailed all three with full power. They broke apart and the Scythe shot through the debris toward the mother ship, revving the volts again and again for maximum effect. He geared full speed and stopped just short of collision and fired the volts simultaneously. Unprepared for direct attack the mother's shields did not engage in time and his volleys hit the cockpit windshield, blowing it out completely and setting a series of explosions that wracked through the ship's frame like dominoes and incinerated the monstrous ship as it went. Brede glared at Narita clutching her lockdown bar with white knuckles.

"You almost killed me." He said quietly. 'Do you fucking realize that? I almost died."

"You didn't." the petulance returned to her voice. "You know I could have died too."

He couldn't trust himself to speak and ignored her concentrating on setting the course for Arc Cariian, the next nearest planet from Amphidia. He decided against setting down on his own planet again, bounties of all types placed on him by at least three Amphidian competitors and two known enemies desirous of both his head and the Vessel of Beket-Re.

Once he sequenced autopilot he relaxed as much as his flowing adrenalin allowed. Besides himself he had Narita to take care of now; all those enemies would take her head on a plate as well and he refused to imagine that—it was too close to possibility. He glanced back at her from the co-pilot seat where he moved after the fight. She really was rather helpless for all her dramatics and emotionalism; she had hold of him all right. He couldn't resist her sexually and wouldn't resist her in any other way. Brede didn't know why he wanted her and didn't question it either. He just did. At least she didn't wear a stupid grin all the time like Elektra Tate.

****

But she did insist on being treated as a visiting interplanetary sovereign monarch and referred to herself as such after demanding audience with the Arc Cariian government, no small feat with the Senate of the planet numbering 1,000. The Senate Supreme comprised five heads of state. Extremely civilized, Arc Cariian cared for its people and planet and welcomed any visitors from anywhere in the galaxy a policy that Narita almost brought to its knees.

"I am a royal emissary and I demand to be taken before the Senate!" she shouted at the Senate Concierge when advised she needed both a passport and identification before being announced before the Senate and allowed to present her demands of special treatment once they touched down on Cariian. She made such a disturbance that he interrupted the governmental meeting just to appease her. She followed him and shoved him aside rudely, announcing herself once more as a "royal emissary" and demanding a hearing by the Senate who sat stunned at her behavior.

"I am the royalty of New Cairo, planet Earth and I require attendance and accommodation immediately according to my importance!" Narita folded her arms across her chest and pouted her lips. After a protracted silence one of the members stood up and spoke to her.

"This is highly irregular Madam…"

"Narita Sabbad," she informed him.

"Madam Sabbad. We are usually well-informed of any visiting dignitaries or emissaries and prepared in advance. How is it possible you have arrived here with no advance announcement?"

"I am fleeing my home planet of Earth. I seek both refuge and sanctuary here. There was no time to set up protocol, let alone announce we would be stopping here. This was an unintended landing. If I had known I would be treated in such an uncouth way I would have refused to touch down here at all!"

The entire Senate Supreme hustled to acquiesce to her demands, shocked into it by her rude behavior and placed her into the penthouse of the hotel reserved for the highest, most important dignitaries. It surprised even Brede when the Concierge ushered him into their new penthouse apartment and introduced him to a battery of new attendants. Narita sat upon an enormous bed, simpering at him surrounded by a handful of what amounted to handmaidens and he wondered how she managed to create a retinue everywhere she went. He left her there every day as he sought out work and information on the possible whereabouts of the Vessel of Beket-Re assuming that his consort still wanted it.

She did not unbeknownst to him. In fact she'd long forgotten it and now attended to creating havoc anywhere she could. "I heard there's a banquet tonight for the Senate's guest dignitaries," she said to one of her women, designated as the maid of honor. "I was not invited. Please find out why and find out who I have to speak to for an invitation." The woman nodded and exited the penthouse without a word. Narita immediately contacted the Senate Concierge.

"Concierge," she said when his visage appeared in a corner of her mirror. "I'm trying to be patient here but I find this personal insult difficult to accept, especially when I've had to accept and deal with so many of these 'unintentional' affronts to my dignity. I am sure you do not want to have to face your supervisor with yet another one."

"Uh, no, no, Madam Sabbad," he stammered. "What is the difficulty now?"

"Don't take that tone with me," she snapped, faking upset. "I am not the cause of these slights of my dignity! I have not received my invitation to the banquet tonight and I demand to have it in my hand before I dress for the celebration. Can you manage to arrange that?"

"Uh, Madam Sabbad, I am not seeing your name on my list—"

"Oh!" Narita said. "That does it! I will take no more slurs against my dignity! I shall speak with the Senate myself!" she slammed a fat palm against the mirror and his image disappeared wearing a frightened and frustrated expression. She beckoned another woman to her side at the vanity. "I want you to bring me a list of the guests at the banquet tonight. I want it within an hour no later. Go." She waved a hand and the second woman vanished through the doorway. Narita sat, chin in hand, staring at her reflection in the mirror wondering how she might rope Brede into attending with her. He'd been out every day claiming to work and come back every night exhausted, both of which infuriated her. Not tonight she decided, inspecting her nails and lips. Tonight he'd join her or suffer for a long while and he'd better not give her a fight or he'd suffer even longer. She stood and looked at the clothing hanging between wispy, white material lengths that kept them fresh and clean and called for more servants to appear. "I need a new gown for tonight," she told them. "Please have the in-house tailor see me immediately for my measurements and please charge it to the Senate at large. Thank you," She waved them away and waited for her maid of honor to reappear. In twenty minutes the appointed one entered the suite and stood before her.

"Well?"

"Madam, the invitations have gone out and you were not among them," she told Narita. "I have ascertained that you should speak to the wife of the Senate Leader to ask a late invite. Should I do this for you?"

'Hm, no," Narita said. "I will speak to her myself. What is her name?'

"She is Arias Savarna, Madam. She deals directly with the Senate Concierge and presides over functions of this sort."

"Thank you, you may go." Narita sat back down before the mirrored communication block and scrolled through the pictures in the mirror's corner until she came to Arias' name.

"Hello?"

"Mrs. Savarna?"

"Yes, who is this please?" The woman, a full alien breed spoke with a pronounced accent. Narita smiled wider. Arias would be so much easier to confuse.

"I am Narita Sabbad, political refugee from Earth and royal emissary. I dislike troubling you with such a trivial matter, but I am wondering why I have not received an invitation to this evening's celebration? I know it's not your fault, I know how things fall between cracks and I'm sure that's what happened. Perhaps you could check this oversight for me yourself? It would be extremely embarrassing if I did not appear tonight. The oversight would be obvious to the other dignitaries. I know your Concierge is frantic so if you could spare a moment to have an invitation sent up it would help relieve some of the stress from him, I'm sure."

"Oh," Arias Savarna said. 'Oh, I am so sorry Madam…"

"Sabbad, Narita Sabbad."

"Oh, Madam Sabbad, I am so embarrassed now. I will have my personal assistant rush an invitation up to your suite immediately! The Concierge should not make mistakes such as this. I will have a word with him in the morning! Once again I apologize! Is there anything else I might do for you?"

"I will need a new gown. I hope you won't mind but I've asked the tailor to work up a new one for tonight. I will pay for it myself—"

"Oh no no Madam, the Senate will be happy to produce a new gown for you as restitution for your inconveniences. Will that do?"

"Yes, quite. I thank you so much Mrs.—"

"Arias, please call me Arias. I shall seek you out tonight and perhaps we can speak further. If there is anything else, let myself or my assistant know immediately! I shall see you this evening!"

"Thank you Arias. I look forward to it." Narita pressed a thumb against the square and it shrunk and disappeared. The machine of her plans began to whirr into life to scramble the life of the rude Senate Concierge she'd taken a dislike to immediately and she moved to the large bed and flung herself down to sleep before the tailor showed up in an hour.

****

She argued with the Senate Concierge until she pulled out one of three invitations that came up to her room and insisted on being announced, unlike all the other guests at the party. Brede stood beside her clothed in whatever he allowed the tailor to put on him, another charge Narita had bullied someone into paying.

"I see no reason I should stand here Narita," he said standing below the giant monitors, their presence imaged on it almost defeating her argument with the Concierge. "I've got other things to do, including finding the Vessel."

"Don't be silly Alekzander," she smiled through fury. "As my consort, you must be shown at my side at any and all public events. It wasn't easy to wrangle this invite and I'm going to make the absolute best of it." She smiled into the monitor, showing small, pearly teeth and blood-red lips. For some reason he found them irritating and refused to look directly at the cameras, let alone their supersized images onscreen. She elbowed him slightly.

"Smile damn it and be polite if you can't be friendly. And for God's sake let me do the talking. You're so…antisocial."

"That would mean I'm psychotic."

"Precisely, now behave yourself Alekzander and I mean it or you'll be sleeping in the hallway for the rest of the month."

"Try it,' he gave her a dry smirk.

"Just fucking behave."

He snorted quietly and the Concierge waved them down the ramp into the central room. She turned back to him and drew her brows down in a frown. He scrolled through the names, pressed hers and Brede's names and the words popped up on the monitor below their images announcing their attendance. Once down the ramp she threw Brede an approving glance and then ignored him as she sought certain people from the list of guests she'd obtained earlier.

Once she'd ensconced herself in the most important and impressive circle, she dismissed Brede to fetch drinks for them both and immediately turned to join in the gossip and spread a bit of her own. "Oh, I didn't know that," she jumped into the conversation without knowing what it was. "But then I barely got into this soirée'," She paused waiting for effect and questions. "My invitation apparently was lost inadvertently and the Senate Concierge claimed I wasn't on the list even though I'm in the best of the penthouse suites! Probably trying to save his…career if you know what I mean," She paused for effect again, watching their shocked expressions. People rarely spoke so openly at gatherings on Arc Cariian and its Senate parties. Narita continued, unperturbed. "I had to go through several channels just to find someone who could help and finally had to contact Arias herself. Of course she tried to defend her Concierge, but I wouldn't stand for it. Oh, here she comes now, the phony."

Arias approached the group and Narita rushed to greet her with an air kiss on both cheeks. "Arias, my new darling, the party is wonderful! You've done such a marvelous job, even with that forgetful concierge of yours!"

Arias looked confused for a moment and then returned the kiss with a smile of recognition.

"Ah, yes, Madam Sabbad, I hope the corrections satisfy you and I am happy you are enjoying the celebration! We will speak further when the fuss settles down! If you'll excuse me please everyone."

Narita waited until she was out of earshot and turned back to the small crowd. "Ugh! See how she fakes friendship? She ignores the fact that I am royalty on my planet and that I condescended to touch down here than another society planet. Really, I almost think she planned to snub me all along," She assumed a wounded and indignant expression, eyeing those around her who now assumed expressions of their own, mostly distrustful and slightly angry. Satisfied that she'd unsettled them all and planted the seeds of suspicion she swept away from them announcing she needed to find her consort, one Alekzander Brede and waved goodbye dramatically so their eyes followed her to his impressive form.

"I thought you wanted a drink," he said as she stopped beside him at the automatic bar.

"I need one now believe me," she said, dropping pretence. "It's not easy dealing with backwater planet fools." She took the drink from his hand and discreetly downed it in one gulp. Brede's eyebrows rose in question. She rarely spoke so honestly and it did not become her at all.

"What the hell have you been doing?"

"Nothing, just socializing," she said holding out a hand for another glass. "It's what royalty do Alekzander. You might want to take note of that."

"I don't like the look on your face."

"Get used to it. You're mine now handsome."

****

The Concierge had a name. It was Hetsutu Manso. He also had a limit to the abuse he would accept. First Arias reamed him for 'misplacing' Narita's non-existent invitation and then guests of the Senate began acting oddly toward him, exhibiting surliness and resentment. He knew who the cause of it was and thought about how he could rectify his ruined reputation, one that had taken five human lifetimes to build. From the day he laid eyes on Narita Sabbad, his life's work deteriorated rapidly through no fault of his own and he watched her profit from it in silent fury.

Then came the day the Senate Leader accompanied Arias to tell him his services were no longer necessary and would he mind training his replacement? They thanked him for his long years of service and said due to recent unpleasant reviews by the guests his pension and benefits would no longer be valid and for planetary security reasons he would be farmed out to one of the satellite moons of Arc Cariian to worry about his own retirement life. They hoped he understood, they said.

"Does this have to do with that…that bitch, Narita Sabbad?" he asked tasting acid in his throat.

"Not just Madam Sabbad, but many others. We had no idea you had been so remiss in your duties and attitudes toward them all." The Senate Leader said stiffly. "I am truly sorry to lose you but sorrier still to learn of your ill-considered treatment of our dear guests."

They turned their backs to him and walked down the center aisle of the Senate Supreme to the podium at the bottom center to call the meeting to order.

All the meetings were broadcast throughout the planet so that the citizenry could watch their government openly and on occasion join in the meetings from the two thousand communities; almost all of them watched and participated.

Hetsutu decided he would not stay for the humiliation in training his replacement, surely young and attractive much as he had been when he'd devoted his life to the service of Arc Cariian's society and government. He had nothing to lose by refusing; he had nothing at all now, except his knowledge of every facet of the Senate's operation from security to catering, and he almost laughed imagining the faces of the entire planet if he tossed a five foot dessert in the face of the Senate Leader; *almost* laughed. He decided to at least make the rounds and thank all the co-workers who'd stood by him, teaching him over the years, helping him avoid scandals and generally making the system work flawlessly. That is until Narita Sabbad showed up demanding special treatment and destroying his life.

Hetsutu stopped by the kitchens, numbering three and hugged the chefs, the staff and ran his hand over the blue light of the instant grills, remembering times when he'd worked overtime and handled food he had no time to eat. No tears filled his eyes, too deep were the feelings, and he said goodbye to each who let their own tears flow. He thanked the staff who managed the robotic housekeeping and finally thanked security who backed him up the rare times he needed it when violent races, like Amphidians, confronted him, keeping him and the rest of the Senate Supreme safe. Hetsutu hugged the head of security, patting him on the back.. He visited his own quarters, touching the treasures he'd been thanked with, memoirs of his service, his uniforms of Concierge; all the basics of his life.

****

Narita hated anything she deemed boring and the Senate meetings she decided she hated worst of all. So when a note came from Arias requesting her presence at the meeting she nearly spat on it, tossing it to the ground, ignored for the moment while she contemplated how to finagle another visit from the Senate tailor.

Brede opened the door just in time to see the parchment fall to the floor, watching it float downward like a leaf from one of the Amphidian trees. He stooped to pick it up then read it and held it out to his sworn consort. "You've dropped something."

"On purpose Alekzander," she said in a plaintive tone. "I never drop anything unintentionally."

"This is a formal request Narita. I don't think you should ignore it."

Narita heaved an exhausted sigh.

"It's probably that idiot alien bitch Arias waiting to either chew my ass off or humiliate me in front of the Senate. I'm not going."

This was yet another new side of her. Apparently she'd forgotten he was alien, half at least, and the prejudice surprised him and pissed him off as well. "Oh you're going alright." He said, walking to her. "I don't want you pissing off anybody here. These people have been very helpful to me, not to mention gracious, something you need to work on."

"Well, they haven't been gracious to me Alekzander! It's been a dreadful struggle for me here."

"It's a formal request and you're going. I'm going with you."

She immediately relaxed and smiled at him, appeased.

"Well, if you're willing to make an appearance, I am as well. Now I'll need new clothes—"

"Just get ready." He pushed aside the creeping feeling of suspicion and resentment leaving the room before he had to examine it.

****

The enemy had a plan. He watched the Senate of Arc Carillon gather for their session, no missing Senators, no missing pages scampering about, and all cameras activated to broadcast yet another of the legislature and intergalactic relations. They moved to their seats slowly filling up the three thousand seat room with the small hum of uncounted languages spoken in hushed voices that sounded over the nine-story room and its velvety walls. Protocol and respect, strictly observed in the enormous gallery, presided over the meeting more than even the Senate Leader himself and quiet attention was the order of the day, providing everything the enemy needed to destroy his enemies. He waited in a small side antechamber, watching the proceedings begin on the wall screen inside it, waiting for the perfect moment to appear to devastate them all.

The Senate Leader stood as the last participants sat down and called the Supreme Senate to order. The rustling of seats being filled faded and soft silence filled the room as the lengthy roll call was taken. He waited until the Senate Leader sat back down and walked out of the antechamber and down the right aisle, pulling out one of Alekzander's own weapons and spraying the room with bullet fire before heading to the bottom front of the room. Hetsutu cut down the Senate Leader, his aides and the other Senate officers along with Arias Savarna and then turning back toward the audience, screaming unintelligibly until he spat out Alekzander's and Narita's names claiming they incited his violence by their own. He pulled up the heavy gun again and aimed it at them still screaming.

Brede yanked Narita to the floor as the occupants of the room spread out, fighting each other to escape the gunfire and threw himself on top of her. People ran screaming past him, having never experienced violence of any type in their lives and chaos reigned. From the ceiling in the Senate room, guns disengaged and swung down, collectively sighting Hetsutu in their crosshairs and vaporizing him into a swirl of pink smoke that curled against the grey of the room. In that moment Brede yanked and dragged her up the aisle to the outside of the building and toward the Scythe parked not far away, waiting for just such an escape.

When Narita began to complain about her torn clothing and the insolence of the homicidal Concierge, he shoved her into the ship and down onto the couch he'd installed for her.

"I don't care how inconvenient this is for you.' He said. "He used my weapon and fingered me as the instigator of that scene. We're leaving now while we're still alive."

CHAPTER FIVE

"Why do we have to leave?" It came out whiny whether she intended or not. Brede grunted in response, checking out the Scythe one last time. He'd reconstructed it, redesigned it, and made it four times larger and ten times more luxurious to accommodate not just himself but Narita now as well. He'd kicked out the walls of the fuselage and reconstructed the frame to expand the ship to three-story height; one floor dedicated entirely to sleeping and created a lounge area as well as putting in escape pods for the first time. When he traveled alone the concept never occurred to him. Brede assumed he'd go down with his ship or save it, nothing in between. To handle the extra heft he added eight more hover rotors and spread out the wing frames to include two smaller volt revolvers above the originals. It passed its initial test flight and he could spare no more time to work out the kinks and bugs; he possessed only enough time to shoot it out into open space and en route to their next destination.

"I like it here," Narita continued.

"Well, if you could manage a bit less pretentious and troublesome, we might be able to settle somewhere." He kicked over the hover rotors, numbering twelve in all now and climbed into the cockpit. He locked the Scythe down and spun it slowly to face the open docking bay. The ship edged out until it cleared the bay and Brede accelerated up and off the planet Praeclaire Savat, the fifth civilized planet he'd set Narita down on and then taken her off at maximum speed. She couldn't keep her mouth shut and blabbed about their relationship and exactly who they were and exactly why that was important—to her—and the growing number of enemies tracking them across the galaxy.

Praeclaire Savat was as highly developed civilized planet as Arc Cariian, the only difference was the topography and location. It too had lovely shining buildings, shimmering in its moonlight and doing the same in the sunlight. Where Arc Cariian was bathed in buttery yellow light from its five suns, Praeclaire Savat lived in perpetual darkness far from its sun, a small one by galactic calculations. Its people pale, thin and tall, taller than Brede himself, practiced peace as their culture and Brede guessed it was due to their physical frailty. While it was a nice philosophy Brede counted it as impractical and anemic, just like its people and he wondered how anything requiring authority or punishment got handled. On Amphidia most of the disagreements or reparation, even out-and-out murder was left to the participating parties. Whoever lived considered it justice done.

The Praeclaire took Brede's arrival as a good sign and presented him anything he asked for with joy. Hanging so far out of the galactic community, they rarely received visitors and hungered for anything that might revive their struggling economic situation. Their only trade item was a form of obsidian: used mostly for jewelry and buildings though it could be used as fuel by lesser developed societies with more primitive power requirements for energy. Praeclaire's problem was that few people knew about it, hampering their trade agreements. So when a visitor arrived, they took extra pains to accommodate them in the hopes they might spread the word around. Brede would have been happy to do it, but once again Narita got in the way, this time insulting everyone she could and referring to them not so privately as "those white alien freaks" as she took rabid advantage of their desperate hospitality by commissioning them to create entire robes and clothing hung with the obsidian as jewels and fussed about unnecessarily to rush them for her convenience. She even demanded a black crown of it, informing them that it should outshine even the gorgeous buildings they lived inside. She considered them below her, thinking her humanness as the superior race. After three months even the gentle Praeclaire took umbrage at her behavior and crowded around them, herding them like a pair of cattle back to the Scythe and threatening to call in their nearest neighbors and allies to remove both permanently from the galaxy.

He looked back at her now, pouting lips frowning as she sat arms folded on the couch behind the cockpit, another new addition to the Scythe, built to accommodate her wish to watch him while he piloted the ship.

"You know," he said over his shoulder. "I'm running out of places to take you. You might think about being more discreet."

"You aren't my consort because I'm discreet Alekzander." She grinned at him.

He keyed the autopilot and walked back to where she sat and dropped down beside her.

"What is this sick need you have to impress everyone?"

"I'll show you."

****

He held up the little compact world again and opened it.

"Why would you want this Elektra? What is it good for?"

"I was only nine when I saw it. It was so beautiful I'd never seen colors like that so soft and pretty. I crawled under a table in the souk and took it. If anyone saw me they said nothing."

"I still don't understand. Why did you want it?"

"Sometimes...when things would get...hard in Garbage City...sometimes I would open it and look at it and imagine that I would have a house like that. I knew I never would but...you know...it made it a little less hard and easier not to cry. I could almost sleep through the whole night after I looked at it."

"What about this?" He dangled the locket. "What the hell is it?"

"It's called a HoloLocket. Everyone had one at the turn of the last century. I wasn't lying, I didn't steal it." She paused. "Did you open it?"

Brede stared at her. After a moment he flicked the lock and the locket popped and opened, two hologram images turned toward each other, away and back toward one another again in time with tiny tinkling music notes. One was Brede, the other Elektra. He stared at her again and watched her expression change to shame.

"It's—it's just something that teenage girls do, Alekzander. You know how teenage girls are, they do stupid things." She swallowed. Still he said nothing. "You know how teenagers get, all hormonal—especially if their families don't have the money for regulator implants. They do stupid things because they get emotional and fantasize. It's like the compact house, that's all. When I moved in to the City of the Dead, I tripped over it. It was embedded in the dirt floor. I cleaned it up and kept it." When he remained silent Elektra spoke again. "At night, when it was dark, I would take it out and look at it and listen to the music. It was like having a friend there, in the tombs. Then the dark didn't seem so…lonely I guess. It—it was just something to keep the dark away, that's all. Just to keep the dark away," She lowered her eyes and gazed at the floor. Then she looked back up at him. "It doesn't mean anything anymore Alekzander. You can throw it away. It doesn't mean anything to me."

"And yet you kept it for the last four years. It must mean something to you."

"No, not anymore," She pressed her lips together as if the words required a massive effort. "I'm an adult. I don't need it."

Brede tossed it against the wall though not hard enough to break it. Elektra sucked in an unwanted breath and made a short lunge for it before realizing what she'd done and caught herself. He laughed.

"I thought it meant nothing to you."

"Well, well it doesn't! But you know, its habit and—and it's one of the two things I own. Besides, I could probably get something for it in the souk—the chain itself would probably bring in some money…" She stopped and looked at him.

He hated himself for it but he still enjoyed watching her suffer. At times emotional torture surpassed physical by a thousand percent.

Why he remembered the scene in his dreams Brede didn't know. He rarely ever dreamed just submerged into blackness, a trait from his Amphidian mother's genetics passed down to him. Elektra invaded that black sleep more and more now and the dreams grew more frequent and more unsettling—yet somehow not unpleasant. He wanted—*needed*—them to stop. Elektra was gone forever and so the memories of her should be as well. The only person he should be dreaming of was Narita Sabbad.

****

Two of the bounty hunters killed each other before Brede came into shooting range. The third, Attilio Melivilu, laughed as he ripped his ship through their debris knowing that murder in competition was a risk inherent in the job, especially with a little help from him. He did what he did so well: playing them against each other but not against him and not realizing it. He planted a seed in each of their minds and cultivated them carefully into violent fruition.

"I hope you are aware of what our mutual *associate* is up to," He said to Keelan Jaide. Jaide eyed him suspiciously.

"I have heard nothing. What are you talking about?"

"You know…" Melivilu paused with an innocent expression. "Oh…maybe you don't. Damn it I should have kept it to myself. It is nothing, never mind." He turned away from the other hunter.

"If this is something that I should know, please tell me." Jaide still regarded him with distrust.

"I don't want to cause dissention here," Melivilu said and then hesitated. "I assumed you know since he's done it before."

"Done what? There are a million things he has done—all bad. Which is it?"

"Well, you know…the worst thing…"

Jaide's eyes blazed with fury.

"Oh no. He will not try that again with me! Once was enough to burn me into learning his tricks and terrors. He will not get away with it."

"But I think he has a new twist on it. Something about disintegrating anyone who tried to stop him this time, I believe. He wants Brede and he wants extra bounty on him and I daresay he might just get the higher price with what he's planning." Melivilu gave him a droll, gossipy expression.

"Damn him. Dylis McGuinne will not cheat me a last time. I will die before I let him. I swear it." Jaide turned to leave but Melivilu grasped his sleeve.

"Wait Keelan," he said. "You might want to check with someone who knows his plan better than I do; someone who has dealt with him before."

"Why?" Jaide snorted. "I know him and his trickery. I said I will not allow it." He turned away and then turned back to Melivilu. "Thank you for this Attilio."

Melivilu grinned and followed him to do his own search for Dylis McGuinne and play the same game with him. He didn't have to look far; he found McGuinne at a local bar hung in the far end of the Aoko sub galaxy as a weigh station for tired and thirsty independent contractors such as bounty hunters and assassins. He leaned over the bar counter and asked for a Double Helix straight up. Still leaning on his elbows he glanced at McGuinne with a sarcastic smile.

"What the fuck brings you here Melivilu? Shouldn't you be out somewhere digging up the body of Alekzander Brede? That's usually how you work—as a scavenger—picking up the leftovers from professionals like me." McGuinne asked voice hard.

"Normally, yes I would. But I've been privy to certain information that..." he stopped when the bartender slid the amber glowing glass at him. He sipped deliberately taking his time in tasting the liquor. He sighed after the second sip and raised the glass toward the bartender as praise.

"What information?" McGuinne snapped at last. He was not a patient man. "Do not try playing games with me Attilio. I'm used to your games."

"My games yes. But it's not my games you have to worry

about. It's our mutual…competitor. He has some new technique or plan to abduct Brede and ask for a higher price than both of ours combined when he presents him before we get close."

"Hah! What possible technique can Keelan have? He's a complete tech idiot."

"That might be true but he has some way or…some*one* who can direct him straight at wherever Alekzander Brede is hiding. Jaide plans to scoop him up from under our noses."

"Hah." McGuinne knocked back his drink in one gulp. "I've yet to see Jaide scoop us on anything let alone a huge bounty like Brede." He slammed his glass down so hard it cracked. "Hah." He repeated and brushed hard against Melivilu as he stomped past and out the door to the docking bays.

Melivilu downed his own drink fairly beside himself. He'd planted the seed in the exact way in each of his enemies to make them destroy one another over fabricated plans that did not exist.

It could prove so much the easier for him and the surety of his reward now that he alone would chase after the elusive Alekzander Brede and whatever the hell it was he carried with him that interested his employers so intensely. He tracked the Scythe as it traced its way along the galaxy his great-grandfather called The Milky Way waiting, biding his time and learning to predict where Brede would set down next. The job now intrigued him from the chase to the reward to the object d'art that captured the attention of the most influential of human people and the price he could command made it a true joy to destroy the prey. It promised to be a profitable ride.

****

Brede lay beside Narita, staring at the muted chromatic lighting, thinking not of his just ended lovemaking with her but of another earlier round with Elektra. Why he should remember it at all he didn't know. It should have been just one of many encounters with women; entered into and exited from and barely memorable yet it was burned into his brain, his body and his vision and he couldn't shake it. He explained it away as association with Elektra's annoying personality and behavior and the fact that every time he turned around she did something to piss him off worse. The fact that she'd confessed to stowing away only to sleep with him pissed him off most—or second. That she'd sold him out pissed him off to no end. So why did the idea of an Elektra Tate-less future wake him again and again and unsettle him so damned much? Why the hell did he want it back?

"What are you thinking about?" Narita broke into his thoughts.

"Huh?"

"Well, you're twisting and turning and sighing. What the hell is wrong with you?"

"Just…thinking about someone."

"Who?"

"Just…someone from the past, no one."

"'No one' doesn't make someone sigh like that," Narita said. "Who the hell is it?" she sat up. "Is it a woman?"

For an instant Brede lost control of his stone-faced composure.

"So it is. Might I remind you that you participated in a little ceremony that bound you to me as consort?"
Narita gave him a cruel smile.

"So that binds me to you forever?"

"For all practical purposes yes, now who the fucking hell is she?"

"Someone I knew on the streets in Cairo, that's all. You wouldn't know her."

"That *thief*?" Narita let out a surprised laugh. "A nobody! A nothing! *That's* who you're pining over? If I'd known that I'd have left her in the under prison until she rotted. Alekzander, you've gone soft on me—in more ways than one lately. I should have just put her to death but I didn't know she'd keep interfering with us."

Brede narrowed his eyes and gazed at her. She looked different somehow. Fat and ugly and cruel; not the sensuous creature he saw her as an hour before.

"That nobody sacrificed herself to save your ass."

"She *deserved* it! You told me she was the one who got us into that mess! *She's* the one who made us fucking refugees. She *should* have died in our place!"

"When and why did you put her in the under prison?"

"When she came back after you ejected her from the job I asked you to do for me."

"How could you possibly know that?"

"Alekzander don't be naïve! Royalty have spies everywhere watching everyone. I knew who she was and why she wanted to join you out there. You'd sent her to deliver a gift to me once and it was written all over her. She was only a girl then but I knew when she grew a couple of years older she'd be a threat to me and that I needed to teach her a permanent lesson in staying away from you—my intended consort."

"What did you do?"

"*Oh please*, how do you think she knew immediately when we sealed the deal so to speak? My people fed her that information! They'd been doing it since she brought the gift. When you kicked her off the Scythe, I had a howdah placed strategically where she'd have to pass and she fell right into the plan, not to mention the howdah. I had her dragged in front of me at the royal court and accused her of both stealing it and stealing my consort. It was quite funny really though I think my royal guard took the proceedings a little too literally."

"How?"

"Oh, you know how guards are Alekzander. You've seen how they get overly enthusiastic at *any* opportunity. I think one of them stomped on her hand. I tossed her into the under prison for seven days to teach her some respect for the royalty. She was entirely respectful when she came back up, I can tell you. Not one of my guards had to step on her again to make her obedient before the throne. She did it herself quite willingly."

"What happened after that?"

"I don't know. She knew to stay away from you. That was all I cared about." Narita ran a finger along his breastbone. "And now she's gone completely. I don't have to think about her again and neither do you." She smiled at him, a wolfish grin. "Though she did say something odd when I accused her of sleeping with you," Narita frowned, confused. "She said she'd already been punished for it. Stupid girl. You're lucky you're rid of her at last. I know she irritated you, though why you put up with it so long is mystifying to me. I'm surprised you didn't kill her years ago." She slid a hand into his pants. Brede grabbed her wrist, pulled it out and twisted it hard.

"Ow, you're hurting me, damn you!"

"Perhaps I should step on it for you."

"That wasn't my fault! I never told my guards to hurt her; she just wouldn't press her face to the floor and they got angry."

"So you let them crush her hand?"

"I didn't *let* them do anything! What the fuck is your problem Alekzander? It was five years ago. Why do you even care? You hated her."

That stopped him. He did hate Elektra, didn't he? She sold him out at the first chance she got… didn't she? He never figured she might have a reason. A crappy reason maybe but a reason nonetheless. In the end her betrayal betrayed her and it no longer mattered to anyone. Why it haunted his dreams more and more now Brede didn't know but *did* know that he shouldn't care. Elektra Tate was gone with her stupid grin and her pesky personality and her perpetual following him around. He looked at Narita lying beside him smug and superior and wondered if he hated Elektra because he hated her or because Narita hated her.

Did he find Narita so attractive simply because she was the peak of societal Earth—the highest social rank as royalty? Had Narita poisoned him with her obsession for social snobbery? Brede stood up and looked at his sworn consort.

"Get out."

"What? Are you fucking crazy?" She jumped from the bed and stood naked, fists on hips. "We're in the middle of fucking space you idiot! Where am I supposed to go?"

"I don't care. Just get out."

"What do you think you're going to do? Drop me off in the middle of nowhere in some lifeboat pod? I happen to be *your* royalty Brede if you don't remember. You're the consort. You do what I tell you not the other way around."

"Get out Narita."

"You can't do that you fucking alien bastard! You can't do that to *me*! I'm the fucking *queen*—"

Brede picked up his gun from the bedside shelf. He aimed it at her chest and pulled the trigger.

"Not anymore." He said quietly.

He didn't bother to send her body back to Cairo. It would cause an investigation and though he'd get out of it easily enough he didn't want the inconvenience. She was a bitch in life and was proving even more so in death so he bundled her body, the one he'd lusted after so long and so constantly, put her in the trash chute and shot her out into space as a fitting tribute to the last bit of monarchy in the New Middle East.

****

He thought he saw her weaving in and out of the midday crowds of the city, a glimpse of her light hair against the brunettes, a hint of her pale green jumpsuit among the Djellabas and turbans and though he pushed through the throngs clogging the streets, he never got close. He walked the blocks and neighborhoods she haunted without luck; knowing she could not be there, knowing it impossible, and yet the Amphidian extra sense told him that she was there just out of his reach. He could almost feel her heartbeat. At last he gave in to the ridiculous and asked those she once lived with and among the tomb houses if they knew where she was, if she was there at all, whether she was even still alive. The only responses he received were angry, hostile and suspicious yet not directed at him but at her.

"Elektra?" One of them said, spitting out illegal tobacco mixed with espresso, "thought she was better than us, hah! Thought she could live up town and ignore us, the bitch. She no longer welcome in this neighborhood, not around here anymore, not in the City of the Dead. If you find her spit on her for us."

After he ran through everyone who lived on the streets or alleys of Garbage City Brede walked back out of the criminal neighborhoods accepting the inevitable until someone caught up with him, falling into step behind him. A hand dropped on his shoulder and by instinct he stopped walking, spun and grasped the handle of his gun.

"Peace my friend," the man said quietly. "I have information that you are looking for. My name is Mahmud and I am the doctor to these proscribed citizens."

"And what information could a doctor have for me?"

"I know who you seek and I know her location."

"Why are you offering this to me? What price is to be paid?"

"No price other than helping a friend."

"I am no friend of yours."

"No but she is. I was unable to help her in the past but I believe I can now."

"You don't even know who I'm looking for," Brede said. He doubted the man's story and doubted it would be free either.

"I do. I can give you her address."

****

Brede knocked on the door and waited. After three more times he lost patience and pounded on it with full strength.

"Elektra let me in!"

He heard a slight noise from the other side and the door slid open. She backed away from him, pulling something behind her long skirts to hide it. She said nothing but blinked rapidly, truly terrified of him for the first time.

"Why didn't you contact me? I thought you were dead."

She said nothing but tugged whatever she hid further behind her. Brede, already impatient, frowned and reached behind her to pull out a small boy. He looked at the boy. The child was his own image. He looked at Elektra again.

"Why didn't you tell me?" He said without smiling.

"I—I didn't know until after you were gone."

"I didn't think you made it out of the pyramid. You should have contacted me." He glanced at the boy again.

"I know I should have told you but you were gone with Narita and I figured you wouldn't care." Her terrified expression turned desperate. "Alekzander, I know you have full rights but he's all I have. Please don't take him, please. I don't work the streets anymore, I—I have this place now. We live here and I actually do legit work. I wouldn't do anything to make him ashamed of me, ever." She swallowed hard. "He's all I have."

Brede stared at her a long moment and then knelt to look at the child.

"Do you like your mother?"

"I love my mommy."

"Is she a good mommy?"

"Yes."

"Would you be sad to leave her?'

"Yes! I don't want to leave her!'

"Even if you could have anything you wanted?"

"Alekzander," Elektra's voice warned.

"Be quiet Elektra."

"This isn't fair Alekzander—"

"I said be quiet."

She clamped a hand over her mouth and stood without moving.

"What if you could have adventures all the time?"

The boy looked at him, eyes glittering. He looked up at Elektra.

"Alekzander this is cruel. Stop it. He's a little boy. It's him you're being unfair with not me."

Brede glanced up at her.

"I just want to know. Would you leave your mommy behind for adventures?"

Again the boy looked at Elektra with Brede's eyes.

"Would you be sad Mommy?"

For the first time in all the years he'd known her Elektra could not speak. She swallowed a sob but said nothing. The boy looked at Brede again.

"Why can't my mommy come with me?"

The question jerked laughter out of him. He rose and looked at Elektra.

"Well, I don't know if he gets the negotiation gene from you or me."

"Alekzander please, please don't take him. I'll never ask you for anything. You don't have to support him, I told you I work now—real jobs—I don't make a lot but…he's all I have…" Her voice squeaked and tears wobbled at the rims of her eyes.

He looked at his son, put a finger under the boy's chin and lifted his face. He looked at Elektra without emotion.

"I'll be back." Brede spun and walked out the door.

"Stay!" he heard Elektra hiss and turned as the door slid shut behind her.

"Do I have to beg Alekzander? Is that what you want? I never had anything you know that but if you take him I'll have nothing at all. I won't have any reason to li—"

"Elektra you need to learn to shut up. I said I'll be back."

He didn't turn back around but walked away and didn't see the stricken look on her face.

****

He also didn't see her leave in the night with his son. When he returned to the small room it was as she left it, as if she just grabbed the boy and ran. He knew that was exactly what she'd done. The trick now was to find out how and where she'd gone. Brede had his own list of contacts; an extensive one. He bypassed her old haunts and went directly to the Travel Ministry.

"I need to find someone who left Cairo recently." He sat across from his highest contact, Bryn Aras the Supervising Director.

"How recently Brede?" he asked.

"Within the last two days. And I need that information now."

"Left legally or illegally?"

"Both. But most likely illegally."

"Description?"

"A woman and a boy—she's a proscribed petty outlaw."

"And the boy?"

Brede hesitated for a long moment, considering.

"My son."

Bryn stopped touching his air screens and stared at Brede.

"Your son," He snorted out a laugh. "Hard to believe Brede, last I heard you were consort to the Cairo royalty remnant. A proscribed citizen hardly seems like a choice you'd make."

"Do I get the fucking information or not?" Brede jumped up and leaned forward over the desk not smiling. He pulled his gun sticking it under Bryn's jaw.

"Okay, okay Alekzander! Don't shoot me." Bryn squeaked.

"Then don't make me."

"It's that important to you?"

"More than that," Brede said. "This is my son."

"Alright," Bryn said. "If they left via this travel axis I should be able to find them. I need their names or at least the woman's."

"Elektra Tate."

"Hm," Bryn frowned at his screens. "She has a record. Of course, it's through the royal court which makes it a bit messy and convoluted."

"Make it un-messy."

"That would take a long time and I'd have to contact the royalty—"

"There is no more royalty in Cairo."

Bryn stared at him again. He could believe that of Brede. "What—"

"*Just*—give me the information." Brede remained standing and still holding the gun.

"All right, Brede. Let me run the cameras and flight information."

It took less than ten seconds.

"She didn't leave legally, Alekzander."

Brede was already halfway through the door.

"Hey," Bryn said. "What are you going to do when you find her?"

Brede's expression told him.

****

"Shush, Zander go to sleep now."

"I'm not sleepy Mommy."

"Just try baby, okay? Mommy will hold you," She clutched him against her and rocked him slightly, brushing his hair from his face. He fell asleep within minutes and she dozed along with him.

"Time to pay."

Elektra's eyes opened and she stared at the captain. There was no excuse to get out of it, she'd agreed to the bargain. She squeezed her eyes for a moment wishing it away and then slowly rose without waking her son.

When she returned he woke and looked at her.

"Mommy what happened?"

"Nothing baby, Mommy went to the bathroom and…fell down that's all. Go back to sleep."

"I can't Mommy. I'm not sleepy anymore."

"Okay, we'll talk for a little while. You'll be sleepy after that. Zander, listen to me. If ever Mommy can't come to you and you feel afraid of anyone or anything, do you remember what I told you to do?"

"Yes. I remember."

"You do just like Mommy taught you, okay? You promise? You won't be afraid to do it?"

"No Mommy, I will not be afraid. I promise."

"Alright then baby. Want to try to sleep now?"

"No. How long will it be till we get to our new home?"

"Tomorrow afternoon I think. It will be soon I promise."

"What will it be like there?"

Elektra swallowed and thought.

"It won't be like Cairo. It won't be dry and hot. There will be trees, real ones green and fragrant—that means they smell nice. There will be lots of water, rivers and streams and you can drink from them right there and wash in them—" She stopped and glanced at the hallway where she'd just been.

"What else Mommy?"

She stared into Brede's eyes.

"Oh, well, let's see. There will be birds Zander! Remember I showed you on the holograph? Like your fuzzy bird? Except they fly free up in the sky and they are beautiful. There will be little animals too, rabbits and squirrels and maybe even deer. I'm not really sure what will be there but you'll like it Zander and I will too."

"Have you been there Mommy?"

"Yes, once a long time ago. Before you were born."

"Hmm…"

He let the sound fade out as his eyes closed and Elektra prayed that the trip would be over soon. She clutched him against her again and cried into his hair.

****

He tried every technological trick he and everyone else knew, from aerial facial recognition to DNA skip tracing to physically threatening the manager of the building she lived in without success and as a last resort he brought his request before the true legal system of Cairo.

"I request a warrant for Elektra Tate." He said to the panel of judges.

"For what reason?"

"Kidnapping."

"What level of citizen?"

"Proscribed petty outlaw," He said for the thousandth time.

"That is a serious charge against such a citizen, Mr. Brede. It carries a deep penalty. Are you sure you want to do this?"

"I want a warrant to arrest her. Whether I will press actual charges will depend upon her."

"You are requesting only an arrest warrant at this time? May we ask why?"

"She has my son. I want him."

The panel looked at each other. After a moment they nodded.

"Considering that fact and the fact that you have full citizen rights on most planets, Mr. Brede we will issue only the arrest warrant. If she is in Cairo she will be taken into custody. Warrant granted."

The panel pressed their hands on the signature station and called the next case into court.

Brede didn't bother to thank them or his legal counsel, who remained standing, silent and unnecessary. He walked out of the court and headed toward the new version of the Scythe, redesigned and rebuilt after his escape with Narita. It now measured three times larger with twice that in speed and firepower and features far more luxurious than he ever planned. He'd used it so much in the last three days he no longer bothered to hide it. Besides, Elektra would be the only one foolish enough to try to steal it. But she didn't, it still hovered there. She couldn't have piloted the ship anyway. He climbed into it and revved up the engine letting the hover rotors speed up. No, she'd stowed away and ridden at least halfway to his destined planet before announcing her presence by shooting up two hostile ships and giving him that stupid, lopsided grin. Pissed him off at the time but it pissed him more when she suddenly abandoned the job, the Scythe, and him. And to add insult to injury, she'd even given him up to enemies for a mechanical hand. It didn't matter that she'd gotten him out of it again by sacrificing herself, it wasn't kosher, was a rotten thing to do. She wouldn't get far he'd make damned sure of that; just like he'd make sure he got custody of their son.

****

He'd only allowed her to join him on one job before that, nothing special, a vehicle recovery job on his home planet and 16-year-old Elektra wandered off sightseeing forcing him to track her down after he'd been paid.

"Alekzander, this planet is amazing! There are trees, there's cool clean water to drink its beautiful!" She said when he finally zoned in on her and connected their com mics.

"Yeah right, get your fucking ass back on the Scythe and I'll pay you your damned money. I've wasted fucking hours scanning for you."

"Oh," she said. "Sorry, I—I just got carried away. You grew up here?"

"I grew up everywhere. Get back on the fucking ship."

She said nothing more even when he handed her the money, just stared out the windshield with a stupid wistful look on her face even as they broke away from orbit.

"You think you could live there Elektra?"

"I'd practically die to live there."

Yeah, well maybe you will if you don't learn to stop being a fucking pest.

"It's not what you think. It's an aggressive society. Weapons are used openly, people die, and I don't think I even remember seeing a

Sheriff or police force." He shot her a look. "You may be an obnoxious little thief but you wouldn't make a week there."

"But it's so pre—"

He kicked off from the seat and grabbed her by the hair. He jerked her head back and hissed into her face.

"I learned to kill when I was ten Elektra. At eleven I learned not to regret it. I haven't since."

"You are hurting me Alekzander."

"That's the least that will happen to you there. Get that idiotic expression off your face. Even I wouldn't let you go there alone, as annoying as you are."

But he knew Elektra well and intimately, especially after the last job when she stowed away and he knew she didn't believe him. Brede kicked the Scythe into gear and screamed out of orbit. Any thief worth their salt knew the trick of hiding in plain sight.

****

He had every right to kill her if he needed or wanted. Once more he pounded and kicked her door and when she did not respond he shot the keypad making the door slide open as far as its now bent frame allowed it. She stood waiting for him. Elektra pointed a gun at him, arms straight forward in shooting position.

"Why can't you leave us alone Alekzander?" she asked, voice shaky. "All I want is to raise my boy and make him feel safe and happy."

"He's my son too Elektra. I want him."

"I can't do that Alekzander."

"I want him."

"Please Alekzander I don't want to do this. Please just leave us alone,"

"I want my son."

"Don't make me do this *please.*"

"You think you can?"

"Alekzander *please.*"

"Do you think you can—what—wound me and run away again Elektra—?"

"Alekzander," she broke into his sentence. "I can't wound you and leave it at that. You once told me that you learned to kill at ten and then learned not to regret it the next year. But I never told you, I've been a crack shot since I was three. I won't miss." She openly cried now but never lowered the weapon.

Brede looked at the floor and snorted out a small sarcastic laugh. He shook his head.

"So none of those shots were lucky?"

He didn't give her a chance to answer but moved forward and twisted back her real hand, the right one until she dropped the weapon with a cry.

Brede laughed.

"Did you really think you could take *me* down Elektra?"

"Stop hurting my Mommy!"

Brede looked down at himself in shock. The blast went through his back and exited through his chest, tearing a large hole. He staggered back a little and looked at the boy and then at Elektra who backed away from him just in time to miss being hit herself. Her face, spattered with his blood, paled beneath it.

"You taught him to shoot his father?" He asked astonished.

"No! No I didn't Alekzander! I taught him to shoot in self-defense if I couldn't be there to protect him, that's all! I never thought he might—" She turned to the child. "Give me the gun Zander," She held out a palm.

"But he was hurting you Mommy. He always hurts you. He always makes you cry."

"I know honey and you were very brave to try to help me but you made a mistake."

"But—"

"I know baby. Give me the gun and you go back upstairs. Mommy will come up after a while."

"But—"

"*Zander! Do what your mother says!*"

Both of them stared at Brede. Whether it was the tone, a deep growl, or that the boy somehow recognized the voice of his father, he ran up the stairs, two at a time, the gun on the floor where he laid it.

'Do you see now Elektra? He needs a disciplinarian, not a coddler." He grimaced at her from the floor and wall that he now slumped against. "Now, you're going to fix me up."

"I don't know how."

"Doesn't matter, you're going to do exactly as I tell you. And don't think you can kill me through this. You won't."

"Alekzander, I didn't want to hurt you I told you that. I never thought he'd think to use it on you—"

"Yeah, that's great. Now shut the fuck up and listen to me. Do you have a cauterizing tool?"

"Yes but that's only for—"

"Go and get it."

She started to respond but then thought better. She stood up and ransacked the shelves on her walls seeking the little torch. She tossed whatever she found over her shoulder and behind her and when she found it Elektra spun around and held it out to him. He grunted and slid almost flat on the floor.

"I'm not going to use it you are."

"But Alekzander—"

"Listen to me." He grasped the collar of his shirt and ripped it in half, exposing the deep wound. "You are going to power up that thing. Then you are going to reach into this hole, grab the edges of my torn rear aorta and then squeeze them together. When they touch you are going to run that tool along the edges and cauterize them shut—seal them. Do you understand Elektra?"

She nodded once again unable to speak. He could see the white around her irises. She was afraid again, a good thing for once. He grunted.

"Do it now."

"But—"

"Do it now."

She reached inside him with shaking hands and he watched her breath unevenly as she followed his instructions. Amazingly he did not scream.

"Is it done?"

"Ye—yes."

"Alright, I'll live. Now do the same thing with the frontal aorta and until the skin is the last thing you solder together, got it?"

She pressed her lips to squelch another sob and nodded.

"Do it." He inhaled with pain and then looked at her. "Now."

To Elektra's credit she managed to do it competently and with little unnecessary pain to him.

'Leave me," he said. "Go check on the boy."

She nodded again and entered the lift after wiping his dark indigo blood from her hands on her skirt. He watched her thinking the small apartment primitive and probably all she could afford though it was relatively safe and hidden from most of Amphidia and somehow she'd managed to keep them both alive in the planet's violent existence. At last she'd done something right. By the time she returned Brede stood at the half-open door, its power source constantly buzzing in frustration unable to open or close completely. Already his body was healing; his alien half took care of that. Zander's shot nicked the rear heart but tore through the frontal one. Luckily the rear cardiac system was the crucial one. He looked at her.

"He's sleeping as if nothing happened.' She shrugged, surprised. "I've never seen him do that before. He gets upset so easily."

"I told you he needs discipline Elektra."

"He's only a little boy—" She stopped and shook her head. "I'm tired Alekzander. I don't want to fight now. I'm just so tired…"

"I'm going. But know that I will be back, Elektra." He turned toward the door.

"Alekzander."

He turned only his head looking over his shoulder but not at her.

"Look, I know you still hurt and well, as always this is my fault, but if you want, you know, you can sleep here on the sofa tonight," she waved a hand at what looked more like a bed than a couch. "You know…if you want. I mean, if you think it will help with…the pain and everything."

He turned fully around.

"You won't let my son *kill* me this time?"

"Don't be funny. I'm trying to be nice—I just want a—a truce for tonight, okay?"

She turned toward the kitchen space, letting him make his own decision. She bent to pick up some toy of Zander's and her hair fell half way out of the clip she'd swept it up with. Ignoring it she tossed the toy over the Permaglass partition, their son's obvious play corner and he stood behind her, brushing a stray strand from her neck. Elektra stopped moving and he watched a shiver run down her back. Brede ran a finger along her shoulder.

"You know, the last time we actually spoke civilly to one another, you confessed that you only stowed on the Scythe was to 'get close enough to have an outside chance with me," he said quietly.

"That was a long time ago Alekzander."

"Not that long."

"You didn't want me you wanted Narita. I was just a convenient substitute."

"Not this time. You'd have more than an outside chance."

"Look what happened last time Alekzander. He's sleeping upstairs."

He kissed her neck and she shivered again but still did not move.

"If—if I do this, will you leave us alone?"

He twisted her head around to face him.

"This is not about custody."

He twisted her face farther and kissed her. She responded greedily, surprising him and they tumbled down on the couch. Brede's eyes were closed when the secreting began. As he licked her body, anywhere his tongue touched her the sweet, granular gel called Sugar by humans and Amphidians alike, spread over her making her moan and arch toward him. In Amphidians it was a sign of great emotion; an automatic response uncontrolled and unbidden and once begun unable to stop until their bodies pulled apart in satiation. Sugar served other purposes as well; to enhance the human pleasure and to prime her body for pregnancy. It happened once before when she'd stowed away on the Scythe. After they were through Brede laid on his back thinking. At the time he didn't realize it was happening or didn't want to realize it. It never occurred with Narita, not once, even during the most intense sex. The Sugar caused Elektra to conceive Zander but Brede put it down to his general fury at her, especially when she'd hitched a ride with the express intention of sleeping with him. The anger was the reason it happened at all. He'd never been that angry with Narita until he killed her and then it was cold anger, no real emotion at all. The Sugar was also responsible that the sex with Elektra burned into his brain and body never wiped away or forgotten.

This time it wasn't for quick intense release and when they finally finished with each other, Elektra lay in deep sleep with her back to him, hair askew and soaked with sweat. He watched her, moving her hair from her eyes and then put an arm around her, against her breasts, and his leg over a thigh enjoying the feel of her flesh. Her hair, grown out and long, was no longer cut short and childish and her face less thin and angular; living off the streets made her healthier. Her body was not long and thin and boyish now, but softly rounded no doubt from giving birth to their son.

"Mommy?" Zander stood at the open lift door, eyes wide with fear. "Mommy!" He rushed toward them and stuck his face into Elektra's. When he was sure she was breathing he stared hard at Brede. "Did you hurt my mommy again?"

Brede shook his head in the negative and held a finger against his lips. "She's sleeping," he mouthed at the boy. Zander promptly climbed on the 'bed' and sat at their feet.

"Who are you and why do you make my mommy cry?" The boy asked in a mix of curiosity and hostility.

"I am your father Zander."

"But why do you make her cry if you're my father?"

Brede thought for a moment.

"Because I am a man…and something else," he said finally. "As you will be a man."

"When I am a man I won't make my mommy cry."

"You will Zander."

"I won't ever! I'm not like you! *I'm* not mean."

"You are like me regardless you like it or not. And one day you will find that you have another side, like me, that is different from a man. A side that likes to hurt just because he can do it." Brede stared into the boy's eyes, identical to his own, until recognition dawned in them and the child looked away.

"But you still need to learn to be a man Zander."

A small tapping sounded on the frame of the twisted, half-open door and Zander leapt off the bed and ran to it. Two children, Amphidian, asked the boy if he could play with them. Zander spun and ran back to Elektra's face.

"Mommy, can I go outside and play?" He worked a finger between her eyelids. "Mommy is it alright?"

Elektra grunted, pulled his finger out of her eye and then opened them both. She sat up a little.

"No Zander. I've told you before that it's not sa—"

"Let him play Elektra."

"No! It isn't safe. He's only four—"

"And he needs to learn how to deal with things—with people."

"But—"

"No. He needs to learn to be a man. There isn't any better place to learn it. Let him go." He looked at his son. "Go on Zander."

The child spun and ran outside, laughing and talking non-stop in Amphidian with his newly allowed friends.

"Besides, I don't believe that we are quite through here," Brede grasped a handful of her pale hair. She struggled against his hold.

"Are you trying to condition me that every time I let you countermand me I get some sexual thrill from it?" Elektra snapped.

"Hm, hadn't thought of that but it's damned a good idea." He snickered and pulled her face toward him again. "And where the hell did you learn the word 'countermand'?"

"Shut—"

"Up." He finished for her.

****

"Alekzander, I can't do this. I can't be the other woman." Elektra shifted on the bed and lay on her back. She stared at the ceiling and Brede readjusted his arm to continue pressing it against her breasts.

"You won't."

"Yes. Look I've tried to be—mature about everything but...I tried to get you out of the pyramid when they activated the tracking device in my palm. It started blinking off and on red and I knew they were trying to find you again. I couldn't let that happen. I tried to cut it out of me, to dislodge it but I couldn't. That was when I got back into the pyramid and told you to leave with Narita. I told you I'm a crack shot. When they came in after you, I had an old ball detonator full of processed napalm. I tossed it to them and out of reflex one caught it but as he did I shot the ball in the direct center. The firestorm rolled over them and exploded detonating away from me. It did throw me out of the pyramid and how I landed without losing Zander I don't know. I didn't even know I was pregnant, that's probably why."

"I saw the firestorm from the ozone," Brede told her. "I figured nothing was left of the building or half the city."

"Why did you come back to look for me if you thought I was dead?"

"I had a…revelation of sorts."

She gave him a curious frown.

"I heard something that changed my plans."

"What about Narita? Does she know you're here with me—or looking for me?"

"Narita doesn't matter anymore."

"Don't lie to me Alekzander."

"I'm not lying."

"I have a right to know if she's going to come after me with murder in mind," Elektra said.

"It's not something you have to worry about anymore."

Elektra sat up completely.

"Where is she?"

"I took care of it."

"Took care of what?" Elektra stared at him eyes wide.

"Took care of it—of her."

Her eyes widened.

"You killed her?"

"Yes."

"Why?"

"Because she needed it, that's why."

"Alekzander, you were her sworn consort! Why would you possibly do that?"

"I told you. I learned something that changed my mind."

Elektra looked away.

"Will you kill me too if I don't give you what you want?"

"I doubt it."

"But you might. I know you Alekzander. If you want something badly enough, killing someone to get it isn't beyond you."

Brede laughed.

"I could have killed you at any time Elektra. I haven't so far."

"Only because you don't want Zander to see you do it," she looked away again.

"He'd get over it."

Her head whipped back around.

"You're hateful. I don't know why—"

"He's more like me than you know Elektra. He has more sides than one—and one that you don't and *shouldn't* know about."

"I'd never let him grow up like you—"

"You have no choice in the matter. And neither does he," Brede sat up and grabbed her shoulders. He twisted her to face him. "I want him. He needs me more than he needs you."

"No he doesn't—"

"Elektra," it was a statement. "This isn't open for discussion."

"I—"

"*Don't*—" He licked his lips. "Make things harder than they need to be, Elektra. Especially for yourself."

She glared at him.

"You really will kill me won't you, you bastard!"

Brede said nothing. There was nothing he could say. He merely stared back at her.

"Oh! I don't know how I could ever think that you were someone or some*thing* I wanted! I hate you! You hold all the fucking cards here Alekzander and you think that makes everything you do all right. If you take him Alekzander I swear that I will hunt you down until my last breath. I will destroy you."

"No you won't."

"Oh!" Elektra slapped him. He caught her arm and held it.

"Don't ever raise your hand to me again woman."

She grasped his hand with her mechanical left one and tried furiously to twist herself out of his grip. Although surprised by the power of her left arm, Brede simply held her until she exhausted herself.

"I mean it Elektra. Don't ever do that again."

She made one last weak attempt to wrest her arm out of his hand.

"You are not my master Alekzander. No matter who I am I still have rights."

"I care nothing for rights Elektra—yours or anyone else's. Not even Narita's," He smiled at the memory of her body floating aimlessly in space. "The only rights I care about are mine. And I have the right to my son."

Elektra began to weep, hands covering her face.

"I can't fight you Alekzander," she told him between sobs. "I have nothing—no right to him whatsoever. Why do you have to take him? Why are you being so cruel?"

"Because I can."

She wept harder for a long moment and then wiped the tear streaks from her face.

"If you take him, I'll never see him again."

Brede paused. Her response crept up his neck like a dark prophecy and he secretly shrugged it off.

"He'll get over that too."

If she wanted to strike him again she managed to control the urge. He watched her face tighten and her jaw set. His Elektra Tate was gone; the little girl pestering him for attention, taking all the cruelty for just a moment of his time had disappeared for the time being; perhaps for all time and Brede wondered for a moment if she could ever come back. He also found himself wondering why he wondered at all.

****

"You take that back!" Elektra jumped up and faced her accuser by sticking her face into the other girl's. "Alekzander Brede is my friend!"

"Yeah, your perverted friend," the girl said and the others murmured assent.

"He is not! He's my friend. He pays me to work for him."

"What kind of perverted work does he have you do?"

"Ooh, you liar," Elektra's face screwed up in fury. "He—he pays me to find information out for him and—and sometimes I take stuff to people for him!"

"If he pays you, how come you still steal food?" Another girl asked.

"Well…" Elektra breathed hard for a moment. "…well because he owes me money right now. But he'll pay me. He always does,"

"Yeah, I'll bet he does. He probably pays you by stuffing your—"

Elektra lost it. Her fist shot out and connected with the first girl's eye. The girl staggered a moment and then her own fist shot out and smashed into Elektra's nose sending blood running down to her lips. They jumped at each other and scuffled furiously dropping into the filth and dust of the main street of Garbage City as the other girls in the group screamed to encourage the fight to dangerous levels.

"Go! Go! Go! Fight! Hit her Saara! Hit her!"

"Hey you girls! Hey, stop that now!" one of the men who lived in the city ran to them and surveyed the scene for a moment. He pulled Saara up from Elektra and stood her before him. "What are you doing daughter? Fighting?" He looked horrified. Women didn't engage in physical fighting ever—it was prohibited and akin to sinning.

"She hit me first Daddy!" Saara pointed at Elektra, still on the ground.

"She was lying about me! She was saying lies about my friend!" Elektra stood up, rubbing the back of her hand just above her lips where the blood still flowed.

"Your man friend," he gave her an angry look. "It is not right for a man and a child to be 'friends.' It is sinful. Go on you little bitch. Get out of Garbage City and don't come back. I mean it. You will be punished if you do, I swear that. Go on," he waved at the edge of the city and Elektra backed away slowly until he took steps toward her. Finally, she turned and ran out of the city walls and didn't stop until ten blocks away. She knew that Saara's father meant business and she wandered the darkening city blocks, panic building in a steady wave. She pressed it down with the thought that Alekzander was one of the few people who hadn't used and abused her and she'd defended him, her only friend.

Alekzander! She realized the Scythe was hidden in the area and ran to get into its hangar before anyone dangerous saw her on the street alone. When she found it, she managed to lift the door a few inches and *slide under it calling his name. No one answered and Elektra walked under the wings of the ship and curled into fetal position in a corner where she slept deeply knowing she was safe for the moment.*

She slept even when he returned and began to rev up the engine of the Scythe, seeing her seconds before the rotor blades began to spin. Alekzander killed the engines and the ship ground into a hard halt at the immediate power drop. He crawled out of the cockpit and walked to the back of the hangar.

"Elektra?" *he asked in an astonished voice.* "Jesus Christ I almost shredded you! What the fuck are you doing here?"

She woke up at the sound of his voice and stood up twisting knuckles into her non-bruised eye.

"Oh...uh, I was walking and saw someone auspicious passing by. I thought I'd sleep here to protect the Scythe."

"Suspicious. Not auspicious." *He gave her a disbelieving gaze.* "Stop lying for once. What the hell are you doing here and—" *he leaned down and looked at her dark purple and yellow face.* "What the hell happened? Did someone hit you?"

"Oh, uh..." *she repeated and again wiped her hand under her nose where blood dried in black streaks,* "well someone was lying about me and y—lying and I got mad and..." *she stopped not wanting to expose too much information.*

"You got into a fist fight?" *He actually laughed and she watched a tiny wisp of approval cross his face. Then he sobered.* "But that still doesn't answer why you're sleeping here."

"I—" *she gazed up at him debating whether to tell him the truth. She decided he was her friend and would let her stay there.* "I—got kicked out of Garbage City. They don't allow girls to fight there ever. I can't ever go back, I'll get punished bad," *She thrust out her lip again and shrugged dramatically.* "I don't care. I didn't want to be friends with them anyway. They're stupid and they lie. So I was walking and I saw—" *she inhaled.* "I saw the Scythe parked in here and I knew you would say it was okay."

"I didn't," *he said.*

"Well, you weren't here and—"

"You know it was a stupid thing to do. If I hadn't seen you, you'd be splattered across the walls right now Elektra. Don't do it again."

She swallowed hard. He wasn't going to let her stay. It was unthinkable. He was her friend, the only one who protected her whether he knew it or not. From the moment she saw him she knew instinctively that he was someone who could safeguard her just by their association. More than that he was her friend and she didn't have many of them. In fact she didn't have any at all.

"Okay Alekzander." A burning began in her chest and rose up to her face. She refused the urge to beg. It could only lower his opinion of her and he might banish her from their relationship altogether.

"Find somewhere else to sleep," he said, turning to inspect the now slightly damaged rotors on the ship. "I don't want you here again."

"I don't have any place to—" She lost her temper and cut the sentence too late.

He turned back around, frowning in thought, and then breathed out through his nose.

"Alright you can sleep in the Scythe tonight. But you'd better find someplace tomorrow."

Elektra breathed out herself.

"Thank you Alekzander! I'll find someplace else I promise!"

"Get in." He lowered the rarely used ramp and she walked up it and stopped at the door. She'd never been inside the Scythe; never been that close to his life and it looked like Xanadu to her. She entered slowly and tried not to run her hand over the seats, the controls but couldn't resist and touched everything she could until he climbed inside after her.

"The sleep compartment is over here," he grasped her shoulders and turned her away from the control console. "It's small but you shouldn't have any problem." He guided her to it and let her climb up. "There's a bathroom here," he pointed to a door. "And the temperature adjusts itself. I'll be back in the morning." He turned and walked back toward the cockpit.

"Thank you Alekzander," Elektra called after him in a small voice.

"Right," he didn't look back and the ship bounced a little when he jumped out of it. She heard the doors lock behind him and snuggled herself into the mattress and blankets that carried his scent. She inhaled it and smiled with security. He really was her friend just like she'd told the other girls of Garbage City. Elektra shook her head. She didn't want to think about them, the filthy city or that she had to leave in the morning and scratch desperately to find a place to live that was fairly safe. Alekzander wouldn't let her spend another night.

She sat awake and waiting for him in the morning. She'd washed with the tiny amount of water in the ship and smelled cleaner than she had in a long while and sat in the pilot seat with a smile on her face.

When Alekzander finally climbed back aboard, he gave her an angry look, his mood dark and impatient.

"I thought I told you to leave this morning," He plopped down in the co-pilot seat holding some type of food wrapped in hard plastic, half-open.

"You did. But I wanted to say thank you again for letting me sleep here. Alekzander," Elektra tried not to eye the food in his hand or that he stuffed into his mouth.

"Okay you're welcome. Now get the hell out."

She hesitated.

"What?" he snapped. When she could not tear her eyes away from his hand he shook his head. "No, you're not getting any. I let you sleep here last night, that's more than anybody in Garbage City would do. Do you know how lucky you are? Nobody sleeps in the Scythe besides me, nobody. Now get the hell out and go steal your damned breakfast like you always do."

"Okay," she said and blinked hard. She stood up and waited as he pressed the key for the exit ramp to drop. When it did she walked out off the ship and out of the hangar, looking about the street for someplace she might go. There wasn't any.

CHAPTER SIX

When they hauled her up from the cells Elektra looked both terrified and broken. Brede stood behind the glowing gently humming tabletop, Zander next to him, helpful to impressing their likeness upon the panel of judges.

"Please don't let him see me like this, Alekzander," she said in a quiet voice. Her arms cuffed behind her at the elbows and her own legal counsel shoved her against their table. "Please?"

Instead of responding he shifted his gaze to the judges and then down at Zander. Like he'd told her before, the boy would get over it and would probably forget her in two years. It wasn't an accident he neglected to tell her about the kidnapping warrant. The decision to press actual charges still hung in the balance and hung upon her behavior in the proceedings. For the first time in a long time, perhaps ever, Brede hoped he could show her a little compassion and mercy instead of enjoying her pain. It was akin to an addiction, enjoying cruelty and killing; murder as a victory of sorts and pain of any kind as the maximum high. Brede knew he couldn't remove it from his make-up any more than he could change his eyes or his height or his skin color; it was a part of him and he rarely tried to control it, in fact he never had.

"Call to order, justice circuit court New Cairo is now in session." The female judge in the center of the panel of nine said. She inspected the monitor embedded in the tabletop and then looked up at Brede and Elektra.

"Elektra Tate, you are held under a requested warrant for kidnapping. Do you understand?"

"Ye-yes," Elektra's eyes rounded as they blinked

"You understand that the penalty accompanying this charge and warrant is particularly deep and possibly prolonged?"

"Yes."

"Then we will not waste time reading the warrant and charges. Before we get the interrogation underway I will ask you how you plead."

Elektra looked at her legal counsel who ignored her and remained silent. She looked back at the judge and inhaled a shaking breath.

"Not guilty?"

"Recorded response as not guilty," the woman said. "Elektra Tate you are charged with kidnapping the son of Alekzander Brede—"

"I wasn't kidnapping him! I—I was afraid I'd never see him again. He's my son too—"

"Silence Miss Tate. Outbursts like that will not help your case. Now as I was saying, kidnapping the son of Alekzander Brede a fully righted citizen in most of the galaxy; as a proscribed citizen here in New Cairo, you do not have the right, in fact any right, to this child in any way. Now that that is out of the way, we will begin examination of you and your actions. Do you understand that Miss Tate?"

Elektra nodded.

"So noted as understood," the woman looked at the monitor on the wall where the proceedings appeared on its screen. "Now, Miss Tate, we will start at the beginning as I have discerned it. Did you advise Mr. Brede when you learned you were pregnant?"

"No," Elektra shook her head. "I didn't even—"

"One answer at a time Miss Tate! Now, did you advise Mr. Brede when you learned you were pregnant?"

"No."

"Why not?"

"He was gone when I found out."

"Gone? Gone where?"

"He—he left New Cairo with—as the sworn consort of Narita Sabbad, of the royal court. I did not know until after he was gone."

"And you did not try to contact him?"

"No." Elektra licked her lips.

"Why?"

"I did not think he would want to know. I thought he would not care."

"Did he indicate that to you?"

"No. There was never a chance to talk about it."

"So you let him labor under the impression you were not only *not* pregnant but that you were not even alive?"

"Well, not exactly."

"What does that mean, not exactly?" another of the judges, a man, asked.

"I never told him I was pregnant because I did not know until he was gone. And then I was so busy after Zander, our son, was born, I just didn't think Alekzander would want to know. I never kept it from him intentionally, I swear! He was the consort of the royal court, I was afraid to let him know…"

"So, because you were afraid of repercussions to yourself you refused to tell him."

"Well, if—if something happened to me, who would raise Zander? I was afraid for my son too."

"Yet you have no rights to the child. You knew you were in the wrong?"

"I—I didn't think about it. I never thought Alekzander would come back to find me. He thought I was dead. Why would he come back?"

"Yet he did. And when he did find you, you tried to hide your son from him, did you not?"

"I—I was afraid. I didn't want him to take Zander from me—"

"And when Mr. Brede informed you he wanted his son, you knowingly left with that child and hid yourself and the boy from Mr. Brede, isn't that correct?"

Elektra nodded.

"Yes, sort of, but I wasn't kidnapping him, really I wasn't. I just panicked. I didn't think about what I was doing I just—"

"You have admitted that you absconded with a child not rightfully yours and hid him from his rightful parent, Alekzander Brede. What is your final defense?" the woman looked at her again.

Elektra huffed out fast, shallow breaths.

"I just want to see my son, to raise him and make him happy. I just wanted to be able to see him, that's all—"

"That does not excuse your behavior, Miss Tate. You are still guilty of kidnapping whatever your reasons."

Elektra looked at Brede.

"Please Alekzander please don't take him, *please*. Tell them. Tell them that I panicked, that I was afraid. *Please* Alekzander!"

He gazed at her without emotion.

"Please Alekzander," she gave him one last desperate look before the security officers headed toward her. "Please?"

Still he said nothing.

"Miss Tate, cease disruption of the order of this court! One more outburst and you will not be given any further consideration for your own defense. Now, we will try to proceed to the next segment of this case. Mr. Brede, you have heard Miss Tate's defense and now is your opportunity to decide whether you will officially press kidnapping charges and sentence can be pronounced." The judges looked at Brede.

"Considering that she was concerned for my son and that she *is* the mother of my son, I suggest that she serve only a short time if I press charges officially," he said, glancing at Elektra and then at the panel of judges.

"What is your interpretation of a "short time" Mr. Brede?" another judge, female asked him.

"Perhaps a year in prison, perhaps six months if she exhibits good behavior."

"You are aware that Miss Tate is a proscribed petty thief Mr. Brede?"

"I am fully aware of that. Miss Tate and I have a long history of acquaintance. She's made some mistakes but she is not of a dangerous or malevolent nature."

"So you're suggesting a six month sentence?"

"Actually, thinking about it now, perhaps even three months would suffice."

"And you still intend to press charges?"

"With reservations, yes."

"Expressing reservations will affect her sentencing Mr. Brede. Are you aware of that?"

"Yes."

"Then why press charges at all?" the male judge asked.

"I want her to understand that she has no rights to my son." He finally glanced at Elektra who stood bleary eyed and stunned. "Regardless that she did give birth to him. But I don't want her killed in the process."

Brede looked at Elektra fully. It was as close to compassionate as he could get. She didn't look at him; didn't look at anyone or anything but the floor. She hung her head, finally defeated. It didn't matter. He'd made the decision to take his son, to make sure that she was at least punished for selling him out whether she knew it or not and the part of him that was not human refused to let him back down on those decisions. That part recoiled from human emotions as if *they* were alien to *it*.

"Then I will pronounce sentence upon Elektra Tate: three months in the under prison to begin immediately and to terminate at the end of that time. Court adjourned for lunch." The judges placed their hands on the signature terminals and exited the room into their quarters.

Elektra gulped a huge breath and looked at him.

"Could I—could I see him sometime? Just maybe once a year Alekzander—maybe on his birthday—he wouldn't even have to know I'm there. I just want to see him…grow up. Just that Alekzander—I won't ask for anything else. I'll just come to see him on his birthday, that's all Alekzander. Please?"

"Where is my mommy going?" Zander asked him as they pulled Elektra out of the courtroom though she put up no struggle.

"She's—going somewhere for a while Alekzander." He grasped the child's hand and led him out of the courtroom and down and out of the building.

"When will I see her again?"

"Not for a long while, but you'll have other things to think about," Brede said. "Do you remember I promised you adventures?"

Once again the boy's eyes gleamed and he smiled up at his father.

"Yes. I remember."

And you'll remember those longer than you'll remember your mother…or even her name.

****

The scraping of the steel doors echoed around her head and Elektra jumped to standing as they slid back into the walls. Three men entered, dark with dark hair and eyes, and they stared at her. She'd stopped counting the days since there was no light to tell her the passing of time so she did not know how long she'd been there.

"We have come to retrieve something," the tallest one said to her, his grin lighting up his face with white teeth.

Another one caught her arms and slammed her against the wall without speaking. The man holding her grabbed her head with his hand and pressed the side of her face against the wall so she could not see what happened behind her. She heard more scraping sounds, sounds like digging, sliding and grinding and she could not imagine what could be in her cell that was of value.

"Do not be alarmed. We are not here to harm you," he said. "...unless you do not give us what we want. Then you'll be raped a dozen times over." She shook with fear; no one could hear her if she called out and if they did, no one would come to help. Elektra tried not to whimper. She heard more scraping and the sound of something heavy being dropped repeatedly as they hissed in urgent whispers.

"Where is it?"

"It is here, keep looking."

"I cannot find it."

"It is here damn it! Find it!"

"Does she know? She was here before."

"I doubt it. Only they knew and it was a punishment."

"Ask her."

"She doesn't know."

"Ask her anyway."

The man with the grin walked to Elektra and the one holding her. He let her go and spun her around to face them both.

"Do you know where it is?"

"I don't even know *what* it is."

"Let me put it another way Miss Tate. When you enjoyed your time here before, did you have any visitors? Did you find anything unusual?"

"I was chained to the wall for seven days. Nobody came except to chuck in food from time to time. If there was something here other than me, I never saw it. Like I said, I don't even know what you're looking for." She looked at him trying to keep her voice from wobbling.

"Did you know Alekzander Brede was looking for it—for something?"

"I knew he was on some type of job for Narita Sabbad. What it was I didn't ask."

"He didn't tell you? We heard you joined him on that particular…job. I'd think you would know exactly what he was doing."

"I didn't stay long enough to ask. I…left early."

"I find it difficult to believe you had no idea what he was seeking Miss Tate." The man stopped grinning at last.

"I didn't go with him to help," Elektra said. "I was there for an entirely different reason. And I told you, I left early."

"Ah, a lover's spat perhaps." He grinned again.

"Something like that," her lips twisted down and for a moment she was too angry for fear.

"I hope so for your sake. If you are lying to us, when we are finished with you we will kill you and you will welcome it as a mercy after what we've done. Now, where is it?"

"You can't get something out of me that I don't know. As for lying, I've been punished for telling the truth lately. I can't see how a lie can hurt me at this point. But I'm not lying."

He turned back to the man at the wall speaking in another language and Elektra hit the ground with a hard thump. The one who held her kicked her ribs and she heard and felt the crack of them as they fractured. He picked her up again punching her so hard her head hit the wall each time. She didn't have time to scream or fight back. He flung her to floor again and knelt over her chest holding an ancient knife with serrated edges on both sides. He drew a thin cut from her jaw down to her breast and held the tip of it there laughing through an evil grin. She did cry then, tears running down the sides of her eyes toward her temples and ears, tickling her as they rolled. Death had never come so close to her and she took shallow breaths to avoid angering him further. They scraped their fingers and various tools both primitive and advanced along the wall feeling for anything out-of-place or loose or uneven. Whenever they thought they'd located something they ripped or blasted the stone wall with small explosives leaving piles of rubble where they fell.

"It is not here. Perhaps Brede already found it."

"It is here! Look again."

"I am telling you it is not here. None of the instruments can find it. If they cannot find it, how can I?"

"Then he has found it. Or someone else has. We must track down all those seeking it and remove them by process of elimination."

"What about her?" the knife edged closer to her nipple. "I can remove her easily."

Elektra knew exactly what they meant. She squeezed her eyes shut to stop the whimper escaping her. The other two men turned and stood over her as well.

"I—I didn't lie." She said, voice shaking hard. "I didn't lie. I don't even know what you're looking for."

The man who'd remain silent spoke at last.

"I think we should do what we like and kill her anyway. Who's going to care if she dies? She's nothing but a street whore. Her own man doesn't want her—half-man…half-bastard." He laughed at his own joke.

"And then we'll kill her." The one kneeling over her cackled as if he found that the most exciting part. "I'm going to cut you up at the end…"

Even the man who abducted her as a child didn't frighten her as much as the three who stood over her. He at least hadn't threatened her with death. She began to struggle and one of them wrapped a hand around her throat and squeezed cutting off her breathing. Terror clutched at her and in desperation she grasped the hand that choked her. She felt small snaps as the bones cracked and tendons ripped and he screamed jumping back away from her. Without thought she grasped the wrist of the one with the knife and twisted it completely around. It stuck that way and he made a fist with his other hand. She grabbed that too and wrapped her hand around it, the bones and ligaments crushing and she pushed him backward as he sat up grunting in pain. He fell backward unable to catch himself and she clamped the same hand around his crotch.

"I'm sorry! I'm sorry! Let go! Please let go!" he cried, eyes wild voice half an octave higher. Elektra hesitated barely winded from the exertion. "Please," he begged quietly. "Please let me go."

"No." she said shaking her head. "If you would do that to me, you'll do it to another woman…or child. Can't let that happen."

His screams didn't stop even when they dragged him hemorrhaging out of the cell and up out into the street.

She stood silent as they grouped back together and headed toward the door. It shrieked shut again and Elektra was left to her own devices. She looked down at the clot of blood and flesh on the floor and held up her left hand, staring at it in shocked wonder. "I'll have to remember you," she told it and walked to the doors that only opened from the outside. She leaned against the human-sized lock and thought about the reason that the entire horrifying scene took place at all. Alekzander had been searching for something when she'd tagged along—something important enough for two fighters to ambush the Scythe. Narita hired him to search for it whatever it was.

He wouldn't play lap dog for anyone but her.

Elektra's lips pursed with bitterness. So whatever he was searching for he was doing it for her. What could Narita want that was so precious? The woman possessed everything—including Alekzander—what could make her promise him money…or making him her consort? Alekzander couldn't want it himself he was too sensible…too convinced of his own power, his own control…definitely not the type to want something frivolous as Narita would. It was something that a free hand reconstruction—damned expensive—was given gladly to trade for him. Elektra thought about the doctor and Alekzander in the glass walled room being tortured. She hated him at the moment he insulted her but she relented and contacted the priest-warriors of Hatshepsut. Something niggled at the back of her head and it wasn't the lumps from being slammed against the wall. She walked away and sat down on the only dry spot in the cell, knees up arms resting atop them. Why would Alekzander visit a tomb? He cared nothing for history, his or anyone else's so whatever he searched for was old…very very old. And he was searching for it in the resting place of the dead…not unlike the City of the Dead.

Apparently Brede's reputation carried all the way down to the under prison. It no longer mattered to her what he or anyone else considered her or if no one cared about her, her only thoughts were of Zander and possibly never seeing him again. Slowly, so slowly she was barely conscious of it, Elektra Tate began to devise a way to see her son, if only one last time.

CHAPTER SEVEN

"Alekzander Brede?"
Brede walked around the Scythe, docked back on Aedificer Industrial Port Station, where he'd taken several jobs of re-designing ships for other pilots to pay his debts, holding a grind blade he'd used to clean the rotors. "Who's asking?"

The small balding man gazed up at him without trepidation.

"I am Arthur Asad Directing Supervisor of the New Cairo Intergovernmental Finance Department. We oversee the financial transactions between the governments of the royal courts and the New Cairo courts."

"What do you want with me? I'm in the process of paying any debts I might have accrued—"

"No no Mr. Brede! This is not about any debts. In fact, it's the opposite. You are the sworn consort of Narita Sabbad?"

"I am."

"Well, the last known record we have of her is that she is deceased, is that correct?"

Yes but—"

"And we also have listed that she died as a result of a violent outburst on Arc Cariian, correct?"

Brede said nothing in response.

"Well Mr. Brede since you are the sworn consort and only living relative per se of Narita Sabbad, you are entitled to her entire financial inheritance. Congratulations."

Brede cocked his head slightly in disbelief.

"Narita had money?"

"Yes Mr. Brede and quite a lot of it too. Not to mention the accumulated wealth in jewels, artifacts, and various other invaluable items. They are now at your disposal to do with as you choose."

"And I have to do..."

"Nothing but put your hand on the sigstation Mr. Brede. Once you do that, Queen Narita Sabbad's fortune is yours. Again, congratulations." The little Directing Supervisor smiled earnestly and held out the small machine. After a long moment Brede placed his hand on it. The little man smiled again.

"And there you are! The official transaction is complete and you have access to the account as of now," He turned away and then turned back to face Brede. "Oh, and the taxes have already been taken out. You do not need to worry about them again. Good day Mr. Brede."

He watched Asad walk away and get into a small chauffeured craft that lifted off the Port immediately. Then he looked down at the blade and shook his head with a laugh.

"That bitch." Still shaking his head, he walked to the front of the Scythe and tossed the blade into a tool box in the corner of the bay. "Zander! Come. We launch in half an hour."

****

Elektra was long gone by the time Alekzander and their son arrived to collect their new booty. She'd been released from the under prison with the plan she devised underway. Once again she stood before the captain whose ship carried herself and Zander to Amphidia to ask for passage and sanctuary.

"Miss Tate…Elektra if I may…although your method of payment on the last trip was very enjoyable, payment for a permanent seat on this ship warrants something a little more…valuable. No offense intended." Quentin Richart gave her a greasy smile.

"I can shoot." Elektra didn't smile back.

"You? The mother of a small child?" Richart snorted in disbelief.

"I wasn't always the mother of a little boy."

"I still find it difficult to—"

The lights above his head shattered before he saw what happened. Elektra held up the gun in her hand, elbow resting on the other arm. She'd confiscated the gun in her childhood. It was old but still effective.

"Need another example?"

"No!" Richart laughed out loud. "That is enough proof and enough payment—as long as you don't shoot me!" He walked to her and put an arm around her shoulder. "I hope you won't mind sharing the captain's quarters with me."

She let him lead her there eyeing the ship trying to memorize the details of it as they passed through. Once in his quarters Richart told her to unpack and left her to supervise passengers and property loading the unnamed ship that transported anything and anyone for a price. She watched his back as he walked back up the corridor; he was tall but thin with black hair and eyes and pale white skin and she tried not to cringe as he disappeared through the loading bay. There could be no stopping now, no turning back, no hesitation over things needed to get to Zander, no matter what. When he returned she asked him what people paid him to spirit them away from whatever danger they faced.

"I prefer the term 'trafficker' my dear. Pirate makes me sound so…cliché. I'll take whatever highest price I can get out of them, depending on their level of desperation." He sat down across from her. "I accepted your payment didn't I?" He flashed the repulsive smile again.

"I had nothing else." She looked away from him, trying to picture Zander and what he might be doing.

"You had enough for me."

"Where will you take the...passengers?"

"Anyplace they want to go. I have no qualms and no preferences." He leaned toward her. "The loading is complete now. My first mate can handle the launch. I think it is time for us to bed down for the night."

Elektra closed her eyes and the picture of Zander vanished. It did not matter. Whatever it took her to get to her little boy.

****

"Do you remember what I told you about adventures?" Brede looked down at his son sitting in the co-pilot seat.

"Yes. That I would have them all the time...will I?" The six-year-old gazed up at him; a miniature of himself.

"Yes. In fact, they're going to start today, now. Take over." He stood up and walked out of the cock pit.

"But I can't—I don't know how!" Zander said. He spun the seat frantically seeking Brede. No one responded and the boy turned back to the dashboard. "I'm scared!" he squeaked out to no avail. The Scythe began to list and he stared at the dashboard frowning before he ventured touching a few controls. He tried desperately to remember what Brede taught him about piloting but his mind blanked and his throat tightened with fear. The terrifying tilt of the ship forced a sob out of him and he shook down to his bones.

"Father!" he yelled, looking over his shoulder. "Father, help me! I'm afraid!" No one answered and he called again with the same results. Zander's stomach clenched and tears filled his eyes. Suddenly he knew there was no choice but to decipher the mechanics and he forced himself to read the key sequences before the Scythe could tilt once again. He closed his eyes praying that he'd figured them out and his fingers flew. The Scythe listed again and hung for a torturous moment before at last righting itself as he sat inhaling with relief though he still shook with shock. His memory returned and he reset the course his father programmed before testing him. Brede entered the cockpit again and sat down. He inspected the dashboard and then looked at his trembling son.

"Did I hear you say you were afraid?"

"Yes Father I did. I was scared." His voice still held a sob and his big eyes reminded Brede of Elektra.

"No!" Brede barked at him, sticking a finger in Zander's face. "No. Fear is not our way. Fear is weakness and weakness is death. Do you understand?"

Zander stared at him, frightened for a long moment. Then his face changed.

"Yes Father. I do. Weakness is death."

"Do not forget that. Ever," Brede eyed the child longer and then gave him a small grin. "Besides, that's what adventure is Zander. It's fear of the unknown, of danger, of success that makes the adventure worth the time and effort. And do not forget that we control our own adventures and destiny and do not follow or depend upon anyone for any reason." Brede added serious again. He turned back to the control panel and ignored his son's face growing dark and pensive in thought.

"Yes Father."

****

Elektra hid her pack beneath Richart's bed, a spot that looked as if he'd never cleaned it. She shoved it until it touched the wall and stuffed a few grimy cloths over and around it and then stood up and rubbed a fist into the lower arc of her back. A wave of nausea washed over her and she struggled not to vomit by pressing a fist against her mouth. In the next moment it disappeared and she decided to find breakfast wherever and whatever it might be.

All of the male crew stared at her as she entered the mess hall and she stared back at them ignoring their comments easily. Experience on the streets, in Garbage City and the City of the Dead that taught her the need to stare down an opponent kicked in at long last. She sat down in a space between them unnerving all.

"Hello. My name is Elektra Tate, what are yours?" She gave them a smile that could not reach her eyes.

"You a passenger?" one of them said, mouth half-full of food. Some of it fell out as he spoke.

"Yes a permanent one. I'll be here a while." She smiled again barely hiding the sarcasm.

"Permanent? What the hell does that mean?" Another asked, smirking at the others.

Elektra took a bite.

"Courtesy of Captain Richart," she said and picked up a cup. "Huh, not espresso, I'll have to get used to this." She looked at them all again. "I've drunk espresso since I was a child. When I couldn't get contraband gin."

That stopped the attitude in its tracks. One by one they identified themselves and their jobs on the ship.

"Aroone, First Mate." He reached a long arm across the table and held out a hand to Elektra. She smiled and held it a moment longer than needed. He nodded at the man seated beside him. "Dagfel cook." Dagfel grinned and inclined toward her a little. "These two, Hassell and Dafi, watches."

They grinned at her too though less lascivious. Elektra grinned back, this time not her lopsided smile the one she used to keep for Brede, but enough.

****

""So, do you have another plan of action?"

Melivilu stared at his employer, hesitant to irritate him. The bounty on Brede was high; higher now that the others eliminated themselves.

"I have not had time enough—"

"You have another plan now. It is to wait. I will not rush my chance."

"As you wish."

"I do wish. The others were bumbling fools. They would have destroyed this mission by their infighting alone. Brede is not only competent he is treacherous as well. We will never get another opportunity. Nothing must go wrong. Is this understood?"

"Understood."

"Good. Now find out what he is doing and where."

****

She stood close to him, watching him cook, hands behind her back just close enough to unsettle him.

"What is that?" she asked as he whisked something that looked like eggs and poured it over the griddle in one giant puddle. He looked at her and laughed.

"Don't you recognize pancakes when you see them?"

"I never learned to cook."

"What? Where the hell did you grow up—the outer Delta?"

"Garbage City and the City of the Dead in New Cairo," She said. "I mostly stole what I ate, I didn't cook it."

Dagfel Dafi stared at her as if she was an insect and then turned back to his pancakes.

"Would you teach me?"

"For a price."

Elektra gave him her most charming smile.

****

Once again Brede found himself seeking Elektra in New Cairo but not for any reason she might hope for; his search came from simple curiosity since he was in the city anyway and perhaps just to rub her nose in the fact that he now could have anything he wanted along with permanent custody of Zander. He refused to acknowledge the thought that he might give her some money if for no other reason than to enable her to buy new clothes and an amount of real food and shelter. No, the reason was to punish her a bit more with their son's fading memory of her before they abandoned her life forever.

Once again he haunted her neighborhoods and got the same response from those who shared their existence with her.

"Ack! She's no true Cairene," one of the men spat again at her name. "Whatever hell she's in now, she deserves it. Her and that bastard brat of hers—"

Without warning Brede grasped the man's throat and lifted him from the ground.

"That bastard brat is my son. Now where is she?"

The man's breath rattled out of him.

"Don't know."

"How long gone?" Brede squeezed tighter.

"Don't know."

"Useless." Brede flung the man down ignoring the crunch of bone that sounded when the body hit the ground. "Come,' he told Zander who stood watching the scene with an uncertain frown. They walked back out of the cemetery town and out to the main streets of the city. Zander skipped a step or two to keep up with his father, an unconscious imitation of Elektra's habit when she was younger. Brede jerked his head trying to shake her out of it. She did not belong to him; did not belong to anyone. Never had and never would try as she might. "Move your ass Zander," he stepped up his pace seeing the object he wanted. "There's something I want to show you."

They stopped outside the abandoned pyramid, slightly pink toned in the scalding breeze and Brede watched the boy's face change to astonishment. Elektra's did the same when she first saw Amphidia. He blinked away the image with anger. Damn, why did he see her so much in their son? They looked nothing alike and yet the boy reminded him of her constantly and without intention.

"Come with me Zander." He took the child's hand and led him into the empty pyramid with its now worn out accoutrements that still held traces of luxury. When he'd abandoned it with Narita they left nearly everything behind, merely glad to be alive. At least Brede was. Narita never stopped bitching right up until the time he blasted the hole through her chest to stop it. Zander ran a hand along the still sumptuous materials of the curtains and chairs and he stepped up on the small dais for a moment to turn about and survey the scene.

"What is this place Father?"

"I used to live here…at times anyway. What do you think of it?"

"This place is amazing Father! You lived here?"

"I told you I lived everywhere Elektra—" He stopped, swallowed hard and breathed out slowly. "I lived here for a while yes."

"It's beautiful. Was it beautiful when you lived here?"

"More beautiful Zander, everything was clean and new then. But that was a long time ago."

"Can I go upstairs?"

"You can go anywhere you like. It's yours now—if you want it."

"I want it." The boy turned toward the stairs cut into the wall and then turned back to Brede with a serious look. "And everything inside it." He didn't realize he sounded so much like his father. Brede did. At last the vestiges of Elektra Tate were gone and they could move on with their lives without her. He gazed about one more time, remembering Narita and her retinue and their relationship and then shrugged. She was out of their lives now too—his especially—and moving forward was the only option and the best one. He followed the boy upstairs.

****

"Ah, you cook so much better outside the kitchen galley," Dagfel said and ran a hand over Elektra's hair. She said nothing and in another minute he dropped into sleep and snored loudly. She crawled out of his bed and tugged on her clothes. She'd kept her jumpsuit but dressed in long skirts and tunic shirts reminiscent of Earth's feudal times. Most men appreciated it and she found it comfortable and easily used for their pleasure and her plans. Elektra glanced at him one more time and opened the door's airlock with slow movements so slow that its hiss could barely be heard. She stepped out into the corridor and then shut the door again in the same way.

"You know it's customary that the crew shares provisions," Hassel said behind her making her jump and gasp. "I don't think Dagfel would mine sharing you with me."

Elektra frowned for a moment weighing her options.

"On condition that you do not tell Richart."

****

He stood in the doorway of Narita's bedroom, people and things inhabiting his memory as ghosts, wisps of conversations floating in the air. Brede walked to the bed he and Narita shared and stared at it. He looked up at the shattered ceiling and windowsill, the scene of both violence and lust and then shook his head. The memories that lived there did so without great emotion and nothing remained to show the passionate activities that once took place in the room. He turned and looked at the windowsill, its turquoise tiles like broken teeth in an open mouth. He walked toward it, looking down at the street below, empty in the late afternoon sunlight. He shuddered a little at the vacant lane, a strange emotion creeping up between his shoulders. He ignored it; everything happened a lifetime ago. It was dead now and natural that it evoked sentiment over the past.

"Father, was I conceived here? Was I born here?"

Brede turned back to the bed's dais where his precocious son stood looking at him.

"No Zander, you were neither. That happened…somewhere else."

"Did my mother live here? Did she live here with you?"

"No. Your mother never lived here with or without me. In fact she's only been here twice. Once was to take a gift and message to—" Brede stopped. "Your mother lived somewhere else." He squelched the desire to look out the window again, to see if Elektra stood below wrestling her breakfast from some unsuspecting tourist.

"Is it true?"

"Is what true?" Brede remained at the window, distracted.

"Is it true what that man said that I am a bastard child?" Zander met his gaze evenly chin thrust out like Elektra.

"Listen to me Alekzander," Brede turned and walked to him. He pointed a finger at his child. "You are my son—my only son and my acknowledged son. That makes you legitimate."

"But my mother, why did that man hate her?"

"Humans hate each other for various reasons most of them idiotic. In any case it doesn't matter, that's all in the past now. You don't even remember her do you?"

"I—just sort of sleepy images," Zander said. "She had light hair I remember that."

"You're looking for me alright Alekzander. In fact it's the first time. I'd remember that."

He gazed at his son standing on the dais, identical to himself in every way. Zander wore his hair in box braids like his father, pulled back in a band. He stood taller now, twice the size of a six-year-old boy; closer to one of thirteen years, again like Brede. Only at times did he resemble Elektra and only in her movements, expressions, phrases. More than once Brede found himself thankful that his son did not sport Elektra's stupid lopsided grin.

"I imagine you'll eventually want to change things here, make this room your own," Brede suggested, wanting the entire scene and subject changed.

"Oh, I don't know. I kind of like it."

"Well, we'll see. While this is yours, you must stay with me until I've settled everything. It will be here when you decide to come back. Are you hungry? The souk is still open."

"The souk," Zander focused back on him. "What is that Father?"

"It's a marketplace. Come, we'll find you something you can eat." Brede held out a hand to escort his son back downstairs and out of the pyramid. He looked back one last time, planning to make sure the ghosts who lived there would evaporate when he returned.

****

"She is not with him. After her incarceration they have since parted ways."

"Where is she now? She will find him, she cannot help herself. Are you sure they have a son together?"

"I have seen him with my own eyes. There is no mistaking him he is identical to the father."

"And who has him?"

"Brede."

"So then she has double reason to find him double the determination. Find her and you will find Brede eventually."

"Indeed. The woman is obsessed with him."

"You have never had a son have you? There is little a parent would not do to protect their child. Find her."

"It may take longer than a week. It may take longer than a year. Are you willing to be that patient?"

"I would wait until the end of time if need be."

"As Ice Heretics do. I will then be on my way."

A son! It was more than he could have hoped for! The planets were lining up as if according to his plan, as if they knew what he wanted and desired to acquiesce. More than half his plan was complete now; the only things left were the machinations of the situation he needed. A son! He laughed again with sheer excitement, something he'd not done in years. And something he would do for the rest of his life.

****

"Whore!" Richart screamed into her face and then flung her against the far wall. Elektra grunted as she slammed into it and then dropped to the floor. She scrambled to her feet, one arm cradling her pregnant stomach.

"You will harm your child," she managed to gasp out.

"My child? *My* child?" He walked toward her. 'Do not put this bastard on me bitch. It could be anyone of us or all of us. This—*this* is why sailors never let a woman on a ship. It is not bad luck, it is betrayal." He spat at her, missing her face but hitting her throat as she crawled away from him. His shouts brought the other men to their room. They stopped and stood watching his rage spew, uncertain whether to fear it or encourage it. Richart walked toward her again and placed a kick at the base of Elektra's spine sending her flat on the floor with a cry of pain. He straddled her and jerked her on her back to face him.

"Since you love to fuck us all, perhaps you'd like to fuck us all at once." He didn't smile but looked at the men who nodded. "And then when we're all done, I'll kill you and your filthy child."

He kicked her again, crushing a rib and sending her sliding across the floor, an arm slamming against a leg of the bed. She cried out again and looked up to face him. "And if you give me any trouble I'll kill you now."

She looked up at him, breathing hard.

"...when we are finished with you we will kill you and you will welcome it as a mercy after what we've done."

She kept her face immobile when the memory struck her. Then she scrabbled to her feet pulling herself to stand. Elektra gave him a second to realize what was happening but not enough time to react before she squeezed his throat with her left hand. His neck crumpled like a tilted accordion and his vertebrae crunched with a squashing sound. The other men stood wild-eyed with fear. They backed up in unison.

"I'm guessing none of you want to meet the same fate," She let go and Richart's body dropped to the floor. She rubbed the back of her hand over her bleeding split lips.

They backed away farther.

"Get back to your stations—except you." She pointed at the First Mate. "You pilot this ship and don't bother to try anything stupid or you'll be lying beside him," Elektra nodded at Richart's body, twisted at an odd angle from his head. He nodded and scuttled toward the cockpit. Pulling Richart's gun out of his dead hand, Elektra waved it at the rest of the crew, dismissing them and walked toward the berth she'd shared with the now dead captain. She'd used them all shamelessly Richart was right about that, soaking up as much information as she could get out of them and playing them off one another to place her in a position of power. Though most of the time she merely tricked them with sex, stupid and cruel as they were and disgusting as well, many times she had to control the urge to vomit when doing what they preferred. She learned everything about everything except the one thing she needed most: piloting the ship. Elektra carefully cultivated Richart, the only one intelligent enough to be wary of her and she'd done practically anything he wanted to gain his trust. It took over a year to gain it and he'd begun to show her little tips and tricks when she wasn't servicing him in the cockpit. Only two snags hitched her plan and they both proved critical. She miscalculated the time it took to learn to pilot the ship and her unexpected pregnancy. She didn't however underestimate their ruthlessness—it was the reason Richart chose them—they represented the lowest of the low and considered very little beneath them, not even killing a pregnant woman and one who might carry their child. So she waited, lying in the filthy bed she shared with the dead captain. They came just as expected, killing the corridor lights and twisting the airlock silently. They clambered inside the doorway and stood trying to distinguish the bed in the blackness. It lit up with a blaze of fire that spat out in an arc, killing them almost instantly. She rose with difficulty as quickly as she could, knowing the First Mate would realize something happened within minutes. It took less than that. Apparently he planned the failed attack on her and stood waiting at the end of the corridor his own gun cocked and pointed at her.

"Don't think you can do to me what you did to Richart," he told her smiling. "I am no fool who is easily blinded by a female."

"Apparently not," Elektra said.

"And don't bother trying to impress or kill me with your marksmanship. I've shot guns longer than you've been alive. By this time, I never miss."

"Neither do I."

"Hah. You would never put your child in danger. Please don't try these feminine theatrics with me, Elektra Tate." His smile turned grim and he pointed his weapon at her. "I know you. I know who you are and where you come from; Richart was stupid not find it out for himself. I could kill you and no one would care. You know that and so do I. So," he relaxed a little. "...the question is what do I do with you?"

"You could just shut up and kill me."

"You're very funny staring down death. You have much more courage than I expected."

"How do you think I slept with all of you? *That* was courage." She shifted her weight and placed a hand on the wall. "Please," she said between shallow breaths. "...please just let me go back to the berths. I won't bother you again and you can drop me off anyplace you want. Please, I just feel so…sick."

"I can do better than that," he said the grin returning to pleased. "I can put you out of your misery altogether—"

"As I can yours," Faster than he could see Elektra reached out and wrenched the airlock wheel until it ripped off with a loud screech. She flung it at him, striking his forehead directly and embedding the sharp jagged edge into his frontal lobes. He dropped with a look of disbelief on his face and did not move again. "You should have just shot me." She advised as she stepped over him. The ship listing radically stopped any further commenting and she realized he did not key in autopilot. For the first time she regretted killing the crew and knew she had to reach the cockpit as soon as possible to prevent the rest of the passengers including herself and the baby joining the flight crew in death.

Elektra ran with clumsy steps and bumps into walls or seats until she reached the cockpit and sat down with difficulty. She looked at the dashboard and tried to remember what little she'd seen Brede do on the Scythe. She cursed herself for her blind adoration of him and reached out to touch a keypad. She couldn't. A gigantic spasm twisted her and she bit off a scream. It lasted a long moment and she inhaled rapid breaths until it stopped. Shaking her head to clear it, she leaned forward to inspect the board more closely and again contorted out of shape. When it happened a third time she knew the baby was coming and before its time due to Richart's brutality. Before a fourth contraction the ship began to shudder in terrifying thuds that grew powerful enough to fling her from the co-pilot seat to the cockpit floor. Groaning in pain, Elektra stretched as far as she could fingers clawing their way up the console, grasping anything that might work as autopilot. As the last of the contractions curled her body, she pounded her fist on the dashboard again until she hit something that stopped the shudders momentarily. The last thing she remembered before falling into drowsy exhaustion was the face of her second son and his tiny mewling cries.

CHAPTER EIGHT

"Pull *up* Zander! God damn it, pull *up*!" Brede screamed at his son and dropped into the co-pilot seat. He tried to wrest the control of the Scythe from the boy to no avail. The ship dived after two attacking fighters, riding their asses, all three headed into the ozone layer of Amphidia at suicidal speed. *"What the fuck are you doing?"*

"I locked it on manual," Zander told him, never taking his eyes from the fighters. His voice remained calm, infuriating Brede who glared at him. His son's face resembled stone, tight with determination, eyes narrowing as he shot the Scythe after the nearest ship. He did not use the volt guns but cocked the cannons and squeezed the trigger. The shots hit their mark and the little wing fighter burst apart like a shattered comet.

"Now for you," he said to the remaining ship, rolling the Scythe end over end, cannons blasting the entire time. That ship burst apart too; its engine parts falling into the planet's atmosphere like fireworks. 'Hah!" Zander shifted the gears at the last possible moment and pulled them up with barely five thousand meters to spare. He righted the ship and adjusted for gravity guiding it smoothly into horizontal flight. At last he unlocked the manual and allowed autopilot to engage. He looked up at Brede and gave him an Elektra smirk.

"I'll kill you if you try that again boy."

Zander assumed an innocent expression.

"But Father you told me weakness is death. I was exhibiting strength."

"Don't fuck with me Zander. Get rid of that fucking attitude or I'll kill you just for that. I might kill you for endangering the Scythe. Get the hell out of this pit." Brede refused to look at him again, the scene strangely familiar. He ignored it, concentrating on taking the ship to its hangar bay at their new home, still under construction.

Brede was no fool when it came to money. He might have been born with all rights in all classes and highly educated but he was not born with riches. It showed when he took work recovering stolen ships, designing new ones for other pilots or when he killed as a mercenary. The lessons he learned reinforced themselves when he indebted himself trying to appease Narita Sabbad's insatiable lust for luxury at any cost mostly his. So when he inherited her unbelievable fortune, he lost no time in building what he considered the most important thing: a new home in the form of a pyramid.

The difference between the old one and the new one was not only the sheer size of his, but also its amount of security; basically it served as a fortress. Brede docked the Scythe on the platform atop a stem that sunk below the pyramid and once locked in he went in search of his son. Zander sat watching the firefight he'd just engaged in on monitors in the underground floor that served as a recreation room. The room while austere gave off a velvety silence, enhancing the quiet sense of understated wealth. White walls and floor contrasted with brown, black and blue décor, mostly masculine.

The wall of screens unfolded from the floor, walls and ceiling and Zander sat dead center in front of it as it showed the firefight from every angle from his point of view. Zander's face did not look like an excited nine-year-old but rather a shrewd warrior sizing up an opponent. Brede sat down adjacent to him.

"Do you mind telling me what the *fuck* you think you were doing?"

Zander's face never changed even when he looked at his father.

"I was eliminating the enemy Father."

"No you were endangering us unnecessarily. There was no need to follow them and nearly kill us both. What were you thinking?"

"I told you Father. I was showing power." The boy sighed as if Brede was stupid. "You told me that to show weakness is death. They showed weakness and they died. You were right."

Brede stared at him. Was the boy being sarcastic? He suspected it but could not put a finger on his son's exact mood. He sat up and sighed as well.

"I didn't say for us to die in the process Zander. Next time I give you an order, you'd better fucking obey me. Otherwise I'll show you what weakness is. Get yourself to your rooms. I'll speak to you later." He stood to walk to his own wing of the pyramid.

"Father,"

"What?" He turned back to his son.

"I saw their insignia. I've seen them before. They were tracking us on the last two trips to Cairo… and back."

****

They had a taboo against harming orphans. Those whose families counted hundreds of years in Garbage City eventually developed their own set of rules and laws and superstitions and Elektra Tate was one of them. She'd been abandoned literally on the street at the entrance of Garbage City and wandered back and forth unable to understand what happened. When they found her, confused and questioning anyone if they might be her "mommy" many of them backed away and a handful ran to the city's leaders to ask what to do with her. Her fine blonde hair and blue eyes nearly terrified them as if she'd sprouted from alien or human seed pod on her own than from parents who dropped her off for unknown reasons. The people in Garbage City were dark-haired, dark-eyed and dark-skinned and more than a few believed she was cursed and able to curse them as well. Regardless why she'd been abandoned or what the city leaders said to pacify them and allay their fears, the people mostly stayed away from her. Due to the taboo however, they occasionally tossed food to her or placed it where she could find it easily and as they worked separating trash from treasure on top of the mountains of filth, also tossed clothing at her that she dressed herself with after a year or two. Other than that they felt no obligation to help her but left her to grow up alone as a type of pariah dog. Only the other children took notice of her as children did; mostly to ridicule her. When they allowed her to join them they made sure to keep her at the edges of their groups, at times ignoring her when she tried to take part in their conversations.

"How would you know?" they asked her when she ventured an opinion. "You're not one of us. You don't know anything and the only reason we keep you around here is because you will curse us too,"

"I am not cursed! My family… my family got lost. You'll see! They'll come back and they'll take me away with them! And I don't even know how to curse you so there!"

But as the years passed everyone realized no one was lost, no one was looking for her and no one was coming back. To maintain her own sanity she carefully crafted a series of lies that she could almost convince herself into believing and by the time she encountered Alekzander Brede she owned an entire history built from scratch.

Sometimes she would leave the city and wander near the desert dunes to sit and cry alone and at night she laid in terror of being assaulted or abducted or attacked by the demons the other residents of Garbage City would speak of in hushed terms that they cared not if she heard. When she approached teen age, she adopted an attitude of false bravado to mask her emotions and lied shamelessly when anyone got too close to the truth. Only Alekzander Brede could break her façade into pieces and he was the only one that took the time to do it.

****

New Cairo's heart sometimes beat faster at night, its trillion eyes lit and blinked while warning signals beat out a tattooed rhythm to help night flyers navigate tricky perceptions of depth between the towers. Those more active at night, the ones who could afford the power bills, came out and came alive in the throbbing pulse of the city while the poor ones struggled against the stifling heat in both day and night. Innumerable craft dotted the black skies, making the real stars indistinguishable and faint. The lights from the crafts blinked out their own SOS cadence mostly out of synch with the others and only the pilots and air traffic coordinators knew where they went, when and why. They flew between the buildings, diving in any direction when needed to maneuver the air space in the city diving straight down or tipping on their sides to squeeze in between them. It kept the city alive in the midst of an otherwise useless desert ruined by an encroaching rise in sea levels and abandoned for three centuries by its own race of people until Midinium arrived as the new savior of the Earth. Earth's government, when the economic catastrophe occurred, experienced such gratitude that they did what they did best throughout human history: they pandered shamelessly to any and all beings that could financially benefit them even to the detriment of their own race of citizens. And Amphidians topped that list. Closest in physiology of humans and easily could cross-breed, the Earth government granted them rights of priority over most of the poorest citizens of its planet. The Alliance also carefully hid their terror of the violent, war-like tendencies of Amphidians, praising them as superior, even when bred with humans. To neutralize the Amphidian threat and keep their fingers into every galactic pie, Earth formed The Star Alliance, a hastily created inter-galactic entity to oversee relations between itself and other planets and races interested in stellar trade. The Star Alliance quickly grew into the major governing body creating legislation between races and trading laws as well as interstellar race relations. Most of the races and planet governments concerned themselves with their own existence and planetary functions, except those the Star

Alliance deemed not yet evolved enough to participate in the actions of the Alliance. It worked out well for Earth.

****

When the sudden grinding vibrated the ship, Elektra placed the baby in the net sling on the co-pilot seat and then pulled the lock bar down over him. As the decibels grew she sat down in the pilot seat and stared through the windshield wondering if the noise was an alarm or if the ship struck something. The space ahead was clear and no sign of an alarm presented itself so she sat a long moment staring at the console. LEDs blinked in steady rhythms, gauges flickered and the autopilot beeped happily to itself. Nothing indicated a problem anywhere in the ship and Elektra thought for a moment. She clicked the monitors on the ship into life and watched the twenty small camera screens placed throughout. Corridors looked strangely silent, mess hall and kitchen stood empty and nothing moved in the sleeping berths except a small ribbon of material or thread blown about by the air conditioning vent. She shivered. The ship reminded her of a lock-down mental facility without the need for lock down. She'd seen the inside of one once on a floating monitor screen that hung between the monolithic buildings in downtown New Cairo. No one walked the halls or spoke into com links and the effect was eerie calm. She switched views and looked at the engine room. The strangeness was less there; most of the time it stood empty and only occupied when inspected or repaired. Nothing looked out of place there either. Power drums and rotors hummed in steady even pulses, readouts showed perfect power levels. Perplexed she sat back in the seat and frowned at the screens until the grinding turned into breaking sounds. She flipped the outside cams on and scanned the outside of the ship. Cameras on the underside showed enormous rings one outside the other unlocking grate by grate, reminding Elektra of a jar lid unscrewing. She blinked, watching the screen another second before she leaped from the seat and ran from the cockpit toward the area. Once in the corridor she slammed a hand against the doorjamb and its control panel, opening all the corridor doors and kicking on the monitors in each one. She glanced up once to see the sector of the ship separating and then continued full speed toward it.

"No…no…*no!*" she screamed as she ran. "No…stop…*stop!*" The grinding sounds deepened and slowed and Elektra hesitated. "Slower and deeper, what does that mean? What does it mean?" She shook her head. "No…no please not that. Oh God…" She ran again and stopped at a decompression hatch and stared at the walls beyond it. She hit every key on the control panel to no avail; the machinery was locked into operation from the cockpit. Elektra glanced up at the monitor of the inside of the walls. Pale terrified faces stared back at her and she closed her eyes to shut out the horror of it. She fell to her knees in front of the hatch door pressing her fingertips and forehead against it, drops from her eyes covering the floor with tears.

"You son of a bitch Richart," she said through sobs. "You ground them up after they paid you. You never dropped any of them anywhere. You killed them…you murdered them…for nothing. You already had their money…you bastard …"

She finally stopped vomiting as the rings separated completely and what was a group of living beings now turned to ground meat ejected into black space forever. Refusing to look Elektra stood up as the rings began their re-lock sequencing, the grinding sound gone replaced with metallic twisting and screeching. Pressing her palms against the wall she managed to stand and walked stiffly back toward the cockpit where her baby son sat locked in the co-pilot seat.

****

"Ack!" The old man coughed, cleared his sinuses and spat. "Why have you engaged subcontractors to find Brede? Why is it so difficult to apprehend him, his son and his woman?"

"I cannot be everywhere. I am regretting it now believe me. I have lost two more fighters."

"I heard that Brede sent them screaming back with their tails between their legs and then destroyed them as they did. I *am* everywhere." He waived away Melivilu's protests. "I suggest you do the same with or without assistance. I grow tired of your excuses. I want him now."

"Yes," Melivilu refrained from bowing to his employer, a sign of weakness. "I will do so."

"See that it is not an empty promise again. Patience is one thing; incompetence quite another." Once more the old man waved him away and he made his way out of the old blackened building that served the old man as a grim residence.

****

He walked slowly through the burnt-out hull of buildings, dragging his body with a pain that never ended, physically, emotionally or spiritually. He often carried the weight of all three throughout the rooms that marked the horror that ended his true life and threw him into a surreal one of hatred and plotting revenge against the man who caused it. He'd been a man once himself, a whole one with family and future and a career on a fast track in politics in Thebes Two. There were connivances of course expected and he never shied from confronting those who played games of greed or power or simply incompetence. But he'd never known the fear that rode along with those who played the most dangerous of games—murder—until Alekzander Brede entered his life. From that second his life swirled in a horrifying, helpless downward spiral never to emerge up into the light of day, though he knew it not at the time. Ashes of the one he loved most now scattered as dust in the unswept corners of both his mind and his residence and flurried as he dragged himself past them. Sorrow, more than pain bent him and icy fury kept him alive through the deadness that was his life now and forever. He felt the old injuries, old pain less than he did the emotional; at least what was left of it. But the worst pain of all was not physical but cerebral: the knowledge of his ruined life and love twisted in his brain robbing him of sanity and curling him into a snail-shell of a body which he carried on his back at the snail's pace; no longer in a hurry: there was no one to hurry to, no one awaiting him now or ever. Only the insane demand for revenge kept him from cutting off his own breathing apparatus and letting himself die in pain as he lived. No, he would not allow himself to die until justice was torn from the most horrific scenes of his life. Brede would pay there could be no doubt of that; Brede would suffer long and painfully, in just the same way that he had suffered. Oh, yes, now he could finally, *finally* make Alekzander Brede pay.

****

Zander no longer asked about his mother and if he still wondered about her he gave no outward sign, no indication or interest in learning of her in the least. Brede satisfied himself that he'd been right; that his son would forget Elektra after a few years and now he watched Zander grow into an Amphidian in his own right with little regard for others as long as they were weaker than him. Brede carefully refused to recognize that his son was more Amphidian than he was or that his own human side was concerned about it. Zander needed to be tough; tough enough to kill if he had to. Already he'd proven himself by blowing apart two fighter craft that trailed them. At times it appeared that Zander enjoyed killing a bit too much for Brede, whose opinion didn't matter any longer; only the fact that his son behaved as he needed to behave to survive on Amphidia.

For his part Brede kept from thinking about Elektra by keeping busy focusing on completion of the fortress home. He designed and redesigned various wings and suites for no one; he owned few friends and those he did were unlikely to drop in for extended visits. After his infatuation with Narita, he rarely even spoke to women, Amphidian or otherwise and laughed at himself for getting old, at least by human standards.

The pyramid fortress home sat in a small valley between two mountains covered with the dark green forest three kilometers from a river that supplied fresh water and the occasional fish-like creatures that were inedible but beautiful. He'd bought it outright with Narita's money choosing it specifically for its location, geographically protected by the mountains to its sides and rear. He built it large, ridiculously so, and armed it with huge arsenals of weapons and ammunition as if expecting war to descend upon them.

He owned many enemies, some earned and some acquired by default, but enough to keep him paranoid and tightly supervising construction suspicious of any weak spot in the edifice and demanding testing and retesting the security. He knew he could destroy any of them, yet the same extra sense that told him Elektra was alive when he knew she could not be, now tugged at the edges of his mind trying to name barely remembered threats. And so he concentrated his efforts toward making the technological fortress impregnable.

****

Colin Factor tossed his tiny communicator on the onyx table beside him. Melivilu was incommunicado again, probably to cover the fact that he'd lost two more fighting mercenaries in a fire fight with either Brede or someone near him. Melivilu didn't want to talk about his growing failures or address the whispers that he played more than one employer at a time. Colin might do better himself, if only his body would work with him instead of gorging itself on Egyptian delicacies. He'd been a rival of Brede's back on Amphidia though on a minor scale when they were younger and Colin watched Brede win every occasion. Not always fat and doughy, Colin at one time thought himself a real contender for Brede's crown, even believing he threatened his reign in athletic fighting.

They stood waiting to be picked off in order in the early

spring of perennial green Amphidia, the season so faint that only Amphidians noticed and that by scents on the air. The Elimination Games officially opened and Colin, Brede and Treffayne Brede's best friend, aged ten faced each another, Brede without emotion, Colin filled with it. He needed to participate not just to claim superiority but for his very survival. Those who lived on Amphidia did so through sheer survival skills and strength. Colin desired the win as well. He worked for it, unlike Brede. He'd practiced without stopping at times, working himself to near death in preparation to compete and finish first. Winning embodied his persona, his life, his existence and without it, he stood as nothing.

When the rare warm sunlight warmed the chilly air the half the city crowded the arena and the other half crowded the city monitors to watch the games and lay bets on the favorite, Alekzander Brede. Silence dropped and the names chosen and as expected the three called to the starting line to wait for the signal. The contest consisted of running, shooting and wrestling a water devil to the ground, killing it if needed. Colin's bones shook as if the morning air vibrated through his flesh all the way to the marrow; he forced his mind to still using most of his nervous energy to do so—a mistake. By the time the signal sounded he experienced a small trill of exhaustion though he followed Brede as second and maintained it almost all the way. No one could touch Brede; he was tallest, fastest, strongest, and most put it down to the right DNA combination between his Amphidian mother and human father not that it really even mattered. Winning, surviving at all costs, that mattered on Amphidia. That thought caught up with Colin's mind and he missed a stride shaking it from his head. He lost his footing and the crowd sucked in one collective gasp, exhaling when he regained and sped past Treffayne to Brede's shoulder again. He matched Brede shot for shot as hit targets along the trail and managed to grapple a river devil and twist it backward against his chest and forcing its head beneath the water. Long hours and days of practice kicked in and he easily overcame the creature, snapping its neck as he slammed it under the water one final time. As they both went down he heard the crowds scream his name again and again before the currents filled his ears. He'd somehow overcome Brede and now held the lead—little could stop him now.

Something was wrong. Another river devil rose before him in the depths of the clear rapids, grasping him this time and forcing him backward and down deeper and deeper. He struggled against his breath being wrung from him when he realized it was no devil at all; at least not one from the river. Colin struggled harder and with a massive effort lifted himself and his attacker above the water, Treffayne's hands still around his throat. He managed to drag them both to the bank where Brede stood watching them, his own gun cocked and ready. The second Colin unlocked Treffayne's crushing fingers from this throat, Brede shot. Treffayne staggered back from Colin, hands suddenly crushing his own neck trying to stop the hemorrhaging flood of indigo blood. He looked at Brede horrified.

"I was...protecting your victory...Alekzander..." he said through a mouthful of bubbling red.

Brede cocked the gun again.

"You cheated." He told his best friend and pulled the trigger again.

In that instant it all changed. The victory that was legitimately his was scooped out from under him and bestowed by the hysterical crowds upon Alekzander Brede and Colin was left screaming himself; screaming that it wasn't fair, it wasn't supposed to happen that way, that the win was his and not Brede's regardless what happened. Those who took any notice of him at all told him with stern expressions that he should exhibit good sportsmanship. It was only the first thing Alekzander Brede took from him, initiating a lifelong series of thefts that might have made Colin Factor a happy man.

If Alekzander Brede stole his youthful victory with ease, it counted as nothing when he took the one thing in life Colin wanted more than his own sanity. She was beautiful. Long black hair and eyes and lips sweet and round and red and her laughter made Colin weak. He'd been content as a friend, planning on being more in the future and wanting to enjoy every second of everything he was to her. So he refused to rush things regardless what his heart urged.

That made what Brede did even more agonizing and atrocious. The day ended at the closing of the souk in New Cairo and they ended their haggling for prices as the sun began to descend below the pink-tan horizon. Brede passed by and foolishly Colin hailed him toward them.

"Alekzander!" He said, beckoning. "What are you doing here?"

Brede walked slowly toward them, people brushing past him appeared half sized in comparison.

'Working,' he shrugged. "Nothing you'd be interested in. What are you doing here?" he glanced at the young woman at Colin's side.

"We're shopping!" She squealed, grasped Colin's arm and blasted her smile at Brede.

"Um," He shrugged again and turned back to Colin. "Actually I just bought a place to dock the Scythe. Expensive but worth it."

"Why don't you join us for dinner…?" The woman let the sentence hang.

"Brede," he said. "Alekzander Brede. Colin and I go back a long way."

"Then we insist you join us Mr. Brede don't we Colin?" She grinned this time showing white teeth and a shiver of excitement. A cramp of foreboding clutched Colin's throat but he managed to smile.

"Yes, of course Brede. Join us."

He remembered many things about that fateful meeting but the one he recalled most clearly was answering Brede's negligent question afterward.

"Her name is Narita Sabbad."

****

Colin consoled himself by making a killing in the Midinium market and leveraged that into a position as something akin to a modern-day sheik that he secretly suspected Brede found humorous. Colin saw it in the excessively respectful behavior Brede exhibited with the smallest of smirks and he hated Brede for it. He hefted his large mass up from his favorite chair—the one that still had puffy cushions—and moved laboriously to the windows across the room. He gazed out Thebes Two that blinked its glittering night eyes at him, knowing himself a figurehead, his powerful position merely a façade, bought by the highest bidder. He'd bid damned high too flattening his competition. Few could match his sheer amount of cash and gave up early securing the position for him. He'd had to make the choice between respect and riches and he chose the latter. But he'd still lost out on the one thing he desired most and could not buy.

Now he stared at his pseudo-kingdom, lit up against the dusty sunset and busy preparing for the real activity that came with the velvet blackness of night. It contrasted with his memories of business and scaling the heights of fake social climbs. Colin shook his head, watching the ghosts of his past flicker on the city streets below. Then he smiled. After so long, after all the things Alekzander Brede had taken from him, he could finally take something from Brede.

CHAPTER NINE

Elektra tucked her breast back into her jumpsuit after nursing the baby and carried him toward the sleeping berths where she'd made a makeshift cradle. She ignored the monitors as she went; there was no one to watch anyway. She wrapped the baby in blankets she cleaned over and over to rid them of any undesirable substances or germs, rocking him with her hand and humming a song from somewhere in her long distant happy infancy. She closed her eyes and tried to erase the memory of Richart's final horror inflicted upon innocents who trusted him with their very lives. Exhausted by it all, she kept her eyes closed, drowsing off, waking only when her chin touched her chest or the baby made some small sound.

****

"Listen to me bounty hunter," the old man wheezed at him. "There is a change to the plan."

"Another one?" Melivilu couldn't stop the frustration in his response. "You've changed plans on me at least three times. What the hell do you want now?"

"You are aware I can replace you immediately, in fact, completely if need be?"

Melivilu hesitated, biting his tongue. He wanted to tell

the old man to drop dead; that he grew tired of pandering to his senility and that the old man should get himself to an Alzheimer's Rehab Center. But he needed the money and didn't want his already shaky reputation diving even deeper down. Taking this now high paying job caused his status to rise unexpectedly and if he finished this one successfully he could name his own price in the near future. Not to mention the satisfaction and downright glory of killing Alekzander Brede that would be his to claim. So he refrained from telling the old man to go to hell and nodded as if intimidated.

"It is good for you to remember that. Finding Brede and bringing him here to me is now insufficient—I want to find Brede where he lives."

I have a better idea. What do you think of a public execution?" Melivilu said.

"Don't be an idiot Melivilu. That might please you but does not aid my plan. You still don't understand do you?" The old man hacked out a breath again and waved away the bounty hunter's movement toward him. "Eh, never mind. Your job is to do what I tell you and that is to find him in his home, wherever it is now, and report back to me. I will take it from that point."

"I hope that will not affect my pay."

"You will get your money don't worry about that. Worry about doing your job. Find Brede. There is little time to waste now. Get out of my sight."

Melivilu nodded and turned his back on the old man. He walked toward the outdoor launch pad, an ancient edifice at best, and climbed into his own craft. He'd never personally met Brede; never cared to until paid to do so and that was now. He'd find Brede alright and he couldn't help it if Brede got killed while resisting apprehension could he? The old man was an idiot. He'd get his pay and get the praise and admiration for murdering Brede as well, and if the old man met with an accident, well, he was old and sick and it was to be expected eventually. Melivilu maneuvered his small ship out of the heavy gravity with difficulty. He shook his head.

The faster Brede and the old man died, the easier his life would be.

****

"I am telling you Father, I saw that insignia!" Zander walked beside his father and looked up at him with frustration.

"And I am telling you there is no such insignia. It's not possible son." Brede glanced down at the boy but kept walking. Zander insisted that he'd seen the insignia on the two small fighter craft since he'd destroyed them. He could see how his son could make the mistake. Zander was young and inexperienced and had never seen any other insignia— and he highly doubted that Elektra had the wherewithal to teach their child, if she could identify any at all. Besides, it was too close to another that he knew and he didn't want to think about that. "I don't want to hear about those insignia Zander. I am telling you there aren't any like what you're describing. We have other things to take care of and one is finishing this place. The security has to be impeccable."

"After it's done can I go to New Cairo and work on the pyramid?" Zander looked up at him again.

"You can go and get an idea of what you might want done with it. But you can't work on it legitimately for a few years."

"Can I go all by myself?"

Brede sighed for the millionth time. Sometimes he found it difficult to remember his son was still a child. He wondered if Zander got that from Elektra and then forced himself to stop thinking. They stopped outside Zander's suite of rooms and stood in the doorway side by side gazing in. Like his father Zander did not tend toward ostentatiousness; he preferred things functional and while the building appeared white and innocuous on the outside inside it was high tech as everything was on Amphidia, and made of Midinium iron and Earth granite composite. The two substances reinforced each other to the point that the fortress could only be sieged from within and neither father nor son was about to let that happen.

"Are you satisfied with this?" Brede asked.

"For now yes," Zander said.

Again Brede looked at his son. The boy swung back and forth between child and adult which concerned him. He didn't want Zander to swing toward child in an emergency though he showed no trace of it when he calmly took down two enemies. Still, Brede didn't like it and once again Elektra's annoying, immature personality was to blame.

"Come," he told his son and they walked throughout the building double checking against one another for any flaws or weak spots. Finding none, they ended the inspection in what served as a great hall; something worthy of kings in the Earth's dark ages down to the throne chair set in the center of it. He never stopped to question where he'd gotten the taste for that; he just did. He justified it to himself thinking he needed it due to own his sheer size and didn't need an excuse to do what he wanted. Narita's money was his now and he could and would do just what he pleased with it and if he wanted a damned throne, he'd have one.

He sat down on it now and Zander stood before him waiting.

"I've hired a small staff to live here." Brede announced.

"To do what?" The boy frowned tone resentful.

"Well, to maintain this place for one thing. It's a home too Zander, and unless you want to become an Amphidian chef we need one. We need the other staff as well. Leave that to me. I just wanted to let you know so you don't panic and kill one of them." He finally smiled at his son who didn't.

"I'm not stupid Father."

"I know that."

"Sometimes you forget."

"Zander, stupid is something you will never be...unless you let emotion get in the way. Allowing that is almost always stupid. Remember that."

"I will Father. I remember everything you've taught me."

"Very good."

Zander shrugged.

"Now I am going to take some target practice." His face lit up with excitement and his brows rose in question.

Brede nodded and the child spun toward a side door and vanished through it. He watched the back of his son disappear and decided he liked the fact that Zander was beyond a marksman; he qualified as an out-and-out sniper. He just couldn't decide if whether it was a good or bad thing. Brede closed his eyes against the memory of Elektra telling him she'd been a crack shot too, and the memory of four-year-old Zander blowing a hole through his body to protect her made him shiver. All in the past now, he convinced himself, all in the past and gone forever. He gazed around the severe walls and wondered if he should add more security to the guest suites for visitors, unlikely as that appeared.

CHAPTER TEN

The scope of those who now counted as enemies of Alekzander Brede expanded. A new player entered the hunt wearing the insignia Zander swore he'd seen on the wing fighters. No longer was the chase given by people with personal agendas but now a full-on militia, half human and half anything else that could be bought for the right price. They advanced toward Amphidia determined not to lose any more wing fighters and to overtake Brede s place of refuge.

****

"Ah I see the little Prince is in a mood today," one of the female human servants said with a sneer after Zander demanded his lunch early. "That one will be worse than a terror when he ages a little more." She busied herself cooking the Misor that Amphidians subsisted upon with distaste. "Ugh! I don't know how they can eat this."

"He's always in a mood and it's always both bad and sly. He terrifies my children by telling them he killed two fighters when he was six. One day his father will regret having that son. He's supposedly half human but I've never seen it in him. He's colder than the father."

Her counterpart, the man who served as Brede's major domo, snapped. Zander had taken a dislike to all the servants, thinking them stupid and weak because of their humanity.

They let their emotions drive them and that made them weak and vulnerable and easy targets for him.

"Huh!" the woman continued. "He roughs up my boy and then threatens him to keep him quiet but I know. I know," she shook her head in anger. "One of these days—"

"Is there a problem here?" Zander stood in the doorway staring her down. "If there is, perhaps this is not the place for you to work. I can talk to my father about replacing you and securing you another source of employment."

She couldn't stare him down. Few could. She scuttled toward the cupboards and pulled down dishes to ladle the Misor.

"Oh no, no," she said. "I've just been thinking about my son's bad behavior that's all. He's enough to drive me to drink," she added a small nervous laugh.

"Perhaps he needs some discipline. I could help you there too." He continued to stare.

"Eh no, no. I can take care of it myself. Thank you just the same."

Zander took the plate without looking at it.

"Just so you know that I can help you if you need it." He smiled without emotion and left the room.

The old woman turned and looked at the man. His face paled when Zander entered and it remained so even after the boy left. They gazed at each other another moment and then turned back to their jobs.

Neither of them nor any of the other staff felt comfortable enough to approach Brede himself about his son. None wanted to brave him, the one with the real power to eliminate their jobs and possibly them. So they waited.

****

Colin could smell it even in the recycled, sterilized air of his own war frigate. Victory carried a particular scent and now he could literally sense it coming. His "frigate" was a dressed down version of a pleasure ship with little to no firepower that merely ferried him about when he chose to embark on short journeys. Another faint fragrance, something remembered but buried deeply, wafted in and out of his sinuses, and he closed his eyes trying to place it.

"Sir, we are in orbit over Amphidia. What are your orders?" One of his soldiers stood in stiff salute and Colin opened his eyes. He'd insisted the crew address him as Sir though he had no idea of anything military, but then neither did Brede.

"You may ask the Captain. I defer to him."

"Sir." The soldier kicked a tiny salute, spun on a heel and left the room. Colin did not see the man roll his eyes as he turned.

Colin walked to the three-story high viewing window and stared at the planet, hands folded behind his back. How many years passed before the two of them, himself and Brede, stood together on their own planet? What expression would cross Brede's face when they did again? Shock? Fear? Confusion? He imagined Brede's face when his army touched down and besieged his fortress, Colin fronting the lines. Brede could fight one on one or in a firefight but he'd never confronted a battalion. He could do nothing but surrender. At that point Colin could call victory and as a trophy he would take the one thing Brede prized most and do nothing about it. He grinned at his mini-armada of wing fighters breaking away from formation and heading down into the icy atmosphere of Amphidia. Not only did victory have a scent; it had a taste as well. Colin licked his lips.

****

"Say you were wrong!" Zander stood over his friend, foot on a shoulder, gun barrel aimed at the boy's head. He whimpered and Zander repeated the order. "Say it!"

"I—I was only—"

"Say it."

"I—"

"Say it!" He cocked the gun and pressed it against his friend's forehead. "Say that you were wrong—say that you

cheated." He paused. "Say it or I will kill you."

"But—"

"Alright—"

"Wait!" the boy squealed. "I—I was wrong. I cheated."

"Say it like you mean it." Zander pressed the barrel harder.

"*I cheated!* I cheated okay?"

He waited another moment and then raised the gun's barrel. The boy broke into angry tears as Zander walked away from him. "I was only trying to help you Zander," he sat up and called out.

Zander stopped but didn't turn back.

"I don't need help. From anyone."

He resumed walking away, ignoring the boy with the red, wet face and fists that dug into his eyes. Then he stopped again.

"You're the one who will need help if I see you on this property again." He said still facing forward. "Do you understand?" Zander didn't wait for a response but walked to his suite in the fortress home.

Behind him, the boy managed to stand up still shaky but dusted his clothes off with one hand. He shot Zander's back a hateful glance then ran out of the enormous gate toward his own home and where he could find new friends. Zander banished him from their friendship entirely.

The staff that watched the scene take place were not alone. Brede waited until dinner before confronting his son with his actions.

"I thought Rezah was your friend," he said as they sat at dinner.

"Yes, he was. Why do you ask?"

"Well, you behaved as if he was your enemy instead Zander."

"I guess," Zander shifted in his seat and shoved a spoon into his mouth. "You know how I feel about people who are weak Father. You taught me that yourself you know."

Brede said nothing for a moment.

"What did he do?"

"He cheated in a game we were playing."

"He cheated you?"

"No, he cheated *for* me. Which is the same thing really," the boy looked up toward the ceiling at nothing, thinking. "I guess he thought I wouldn't win—which is stupid I always do—and so he cheated on my opponent so that I couldn't lose."

Brede waited another beat.

"You know Zander I was in the same situation once."

"What did you do?"

"I killed the cheater."

"Then I will too when it happens again."

"Zander...I'm older and see things a little differently now—"

"Are you saying you were wrong Father?"

"No what I'm saying is—"

"Because if you are saying you were wrong that would be weakness wouldn't it?" He held his fork pointed down at an angle and gave his father a pointed stare.

"And what would you do if I said yes? Kill me? You've already tried it once."

"I did?" Zander's eyes widened with surprise.

"Yes. When you were very young you shot me."

Zander blinked and Brede couldn't decide whether it was from glee or shock.

"Why did I do that?"

"You—you were protecting someone. You thought I was—hurting her."

"Who was she?"

"That's not the point Zander. The point here is that mistakes are made; that you can make a wrong choice."

"Then that would be my weakness and I would deserve to be destroyed."

"It's not always that simple. You made a mistake when you shot me—should I have killed you?" Brede stared back at his son.

"I—" Zander began and then clamped his mouth shut. "Well, yes. That is what our race believes. It is our way isn't it?"

"But you made a mistake. It wasn't weakness it was an error of judgment. You didn't have all the information and chose incorrectly."

Zander pursed his lips in thought. He looked up directly into Brede's eyes.

"It was my mother."

They locked stares and said nothing for a few moments.

"Do you remember?" Brede asked at last.

Zander gazed down.

"I—no I remember nothing." He said in a flat tone and his face shut down. Brede let the conversation die. The last thing he wanted to talk about with his rapidly twisting son was the mother he'd striven so diligently to erase.

****

The young man who tailed Brede in New Cairo now followed a new agenda. He discarded the Djellaba and now wore the clothes common to Earth as he approached his fellow humans on Amphidia. They spoke in hushed, fearful voices, glancing around them always.

"I tell you it must be done for all of us not just for me," he leaned down a little toward them. "It is a simple thing. You do what I ask when I ask and then it is over. I shall take all the blame. That I promise you."

"Why should you involve yourself?" one of them asked. "What are our concerns to you?"

"You are not the only ones. There is a long list of those wronged. Now is the perfect moment to regroup and retaliate. You are a small but important cog in the wheels that are grinding. The enemy will be ground up in that turning. If we do not stand and fight for our rights what is left of them will disappear. This is more than revenge my friends."

They hesitated a moment longer. He leaned in again and gave them an earnest expression.

"This is for all humanity."

That clinched it. They nodded silently and then received their instructions.

CHAPTER ELEVEN

    He dragged his now emaciated body across the floor he'd paced so many times, a long indentation was created in it. Despite the huge weight of the tech apparatus that kept his scarred lungs functioning he walked the length of it once more, giggling to himself over his coming vengeance upon Alekzander Brede. His machinations were coming to fruition after eons and he could hardly contain his elation. He'd have done it all for free; money meant nothing to him now. There was no one to inherit it, to use it in support of humanity. The dungeon, once a magnificent home, remained dark and dank from non-use and no maintenance. It suited his life perfectly now. The bright open windows patched with plaster and cement and Midinium no longer gave light; no breezes brought refreshing air. When his son was taken away so was his life; he no longer had purpose but for one thing: to do the same to Alekzander Brede and do it in the same horrendously painful way.

    He paced more and more as the plans came into view, rubbing his blackened, gnarled hands against each other. They functioned but he could not feel them; the nerve endings burned away causing his fingers to curl and twist, making everything he did a massive effort even the simplest things like opening a door. Still, he kept no servants. He had no need for them.. He didn't believe in hell, it would not compare with the living hell he suffered for decades with no relief. No, hell was on Earth not the other way around.

****

Melivilu sat in his pilot seat, his ship hovering in orbit over Amphidia cameras magnifying the planet below and giving the effect of standing on the ground. He snickered to himself, watching the final phases of the fortress home executed, knowing Brede had no idea what was coming and could do nothing when it did.

"Idiot," he whispered in his own language. "Too stupid to know you cannot take any of it with you."

He also kept an eye on the staff, noting its habits, comings and goings, work hours and where any chink in the security might occur; his job was stealth and he did it well. So well, in fact, none of his employers knew about the others and none of them could have guessed he had his own plans for Alekzander Brede. He plugged his liquid life support line into a frozen canister of alcohol and relaxed ready to watch the show.

****

"Is everything ready?" Brede asked his major domo.

"Yes Sir. All is complete, all plans are in place." The man smiled at him.

"Fine, I will present my son with his gift."

Brede left him to make one last tour of the grounds. The building of the house and property took three years longer than expected, giving his known and unknown enemies ample time to organize and deploy their resources against him. Some advanced upon Amphidia with small squadrons of individual fighters while others came with virtual armadas at their disposal. Even if Alekzander Brede knew about his coming destruction, he could do nothing about it. For some the anticipation of a surprised Alekzander Brede facing certain doom whet their appetites; others merely wanted him gone in the most efficient way possible. But not all wanted him dead.

Brede finished his last round of checks and double checks and returned to the side of his servant. "Satisfied," he said. "Make sure my son is in the main room at sunset. He has few friends. Make sure those he does have are present as well."

You have few friends too Brede.

"Yes Sir."

When the one cold sun of Amphidia began its descent under the horizon the major domo ushered Zander's handful of friends into the main room and seated them around the table leaving the Captain's chair and Zander's seat to the left of it carefully empty. The table brought in for the occasion weighed nearly a thousand kilos and required two hauling droids to lift, carry and set it into place. At the end of the evening it would be removed in the same manner.

Far too much trouble for one short dinner.

The major domo hid his disdain for Brede's developing flamboyancy, something Brede hadn't possessed when he hired him. It didn't matter. He excused himself to find Zander and seat him before the sundown was complete.

He found the boy cleaning his weapons as if he was a soldier, scouring every minute segment of them, face intent on his actions.

"Excuse me Zander but your father requests you join him for dinner."

Zander looked up, still frowning.

"It's hardly dinner time. Are you sure he wants me now?"

"Yes please. He's asked me to escort you to the main room."

Zander let out a frustrated sigh and set the weapon down on his bed. He'd taken it from the wall where he hung most of his weapons for easy access as well as décor. "Alright," he said. "Let's see what he wants." He slid from the sepia colored spread and followed down the dark wide halls to the doorway of the main room.

Which one is the real adult here—Brede or his son?

He motioned for Zander to wait ignoring the boy's slight squawk of impatience. He peered around the corner and caught Brede's attention and then turned back to Zander. "Now you may enter." The young man frowned deeper as he walked into the room and looked at his friends and then at Brede.

"What is this Father?"

"Please sit down and you'll see."

Zander complied and all sat in silence. At last Zander spoke.

"Is this some punishment for something I've done?"

Brede barked out a laugh.

"Why would I bring your friends to watch me punish you?"

"I don't know. Sometimes I find you…unpredictable."

"I just thought you might like to socialize and have your friends here when I give you your gift. Nothing unpredictable about that," Brede gave him a sardonic smile.

"Gift?" Zander's frown remained but suspicion now joined it.

"I'm not going to kill you Zander though if you keep this up I might."

"Alright," The boy glanced at his friends with a tiny, fleeting expression of childlike excitement. "I am hungry."

Without urging the major domo signaled the serving of dinner dishes while keeping an extremely close eye upon them.

****

He rode in his own ship ferried by a mercenary pilot. He watched them from his luxury seat above and behind the paid pilot who spoke little but obeyed completely. As the ships neared Amphidia he tugged on the special talon gloves with difficulty. He'd commissioned them made for this occasion specifically and they proved deadly in the most satisfactory way. Once he got them on, he held them up turning them around and flexing them in front of his face a thrill of anticipation running through him like neutron circuitry, keeping the infantile grin on his face all the way into orbit of Alekzander Brede's home planet.

****

Colin also rode toward Amphidia this time piloting himself. He broke with his frigate sending it back out to orbit deciding he wanted to fly himself to his destination. Revenge caused nervousness in him; an energy that burned the fat off him and brought him nearly back to his original weight and health. He noticed the changes but obsession with burning Brede prevented him from seeing anything else clearly. Shed of the ridiculous attire, he wore more comfortable, utilitarian clothes; the better to surprise his old nemesis. The closer he got, the more energy ran through him and his personal skiff charted a direct course toward his childhood enemy.

This time he planned nothing. All his planning in the past only led to Brede taking everything from him; everything he'd planned for and worked for physically, mentally and most of all, emotionally. This time they would just square off, one on one, a fight to the death if needed. He checked the coordinates on the skiff, checking the estimated time of arrival to orbit and any unforeseen circumstances that might bar his appearance.

He'd pulled out his old weaponry, cleaned and primed it himself, and practiced in his newly built shooting range on the rooftop of his five hundred story structure where he lived, worked and chafed every day over the wrongs done him by Brede. The weapons were outdated but he'd mastered them young and though he'd never killed anyone with them it was a distinct possibility. He knew Brede was a marksman too and only a firefight could settle the score over who was the victor at last. Even if he died in the process, he'd never give up unless some miracle presented itself to stop him. Colin Factor, like most other Amphidians did not subscribe to the belief in a superior being, considering themselves the superior race and religion, if they had one. If Colin had believed, he might have prayed for final victory even in death; but he didn't believe; only in himself was his faith and only in Alekzander Brede was his rage.

He checked his skiff once more set it into autopilot and climbed into his luxury sleeping berth for the long trip to Amphidia. He dropped into immediate sleep; the training habit of the athlete, resting for his coming contest. Not once did his semi-kingdom of Thebes Two cross his mind or his dreams.

****

The table floated atop the two hauling droids out of the main room and back to the storage wing where it resided until needed and Brede, Zander and his friends waited for chairs to return by the same droids. The boy spoke with his friends and Brede left them momentarily. He moved to an antechamber and flicked on the half wall of monitors that scanned the property and the sky. A few new ships orbited but no visible insignia presented itself and he made note to recheck their positions later. He shut the monitors down and left the small antechamber to join Zander and present him with the gift he hoped his moody son would enjoy. It was two minutes too early.

****

The ships screamed out of orbit and down toward the surface of the planet where Brede held court. The signal given, they swarmed toward the fortress home and began shooting up the walled quad with thundering volt cannons. Brede shouted for his staff and was rewarded with no response. Zander sped past him heading toward the explosions.

"Turrets!" he screamed at his father.

Brede had no time to appreciate his son's acuity. He nodded as he ran toward another turret quad. He leapt over three steps at a time, hearing the turret Zander occupied screech and lock into place. By the time he reached the top of the turret where the cannons sat, Zander engaged the guns and returned fire with thundering booms of his own. The darkened night provided both advantage and disadvantage; the ships' gunfire was easier to see than during the day but their lights mingling with the lights of the city and the quad made it difficult to distinguish their exact location. Brede engaged his own guns and shot off rounds at lines of lights and brought down over a dozen within a minute. He thought it a good run until he realized Zander had downed twice as many and showed no sign of stopping as the fighters fell like a meteor shower. Brede heard his son's voice over a comlink lying on the floor. He picked it up and shoved it into his ear.

"Where's the mother ship? Where is she?" Zander sounded as if he spoke to himself.

"Zander?"

"If we can see her I can bring her down—"

"The turrets don't have that capacity—"

The only response that came was the sound and sight of Zander's turret shattering into chunks and blocks and Brede thought he saw his son's body fly through the air. He flew down the steps and grabbed one of Zander's friends standing shell-shocked. "Here!" He tossed the boy toward his turret and resumed running toward the piles of crumbling Midinium and cement that lay stacked and smoking on the ground. Since a child, fear never played a real role in Brede's life the terror he felt now was not for his own danger but for the danger of his son and the horror of losing him.

"Zander!" He screamed tossing the huge bricks over his shoulder as if they were feather pillows. "Zander, god damn it where are you? *Zander!"*

He ripped apart the rest of the damaged material to no result. Brede paused a moment and then saw something wet and indigo. He attacked those bricks too but found only what could have been his son's blood. That thought spiked his terror even higher—what if that was all that was left of his boy? Scrambling faster through the rubble exposed more of the substance, thicker and gooey and suddenly he wasn't sure he wanted to continue. He did, pulling the darkened blocks apart until Zander's face appeared, still and pale. Brede pulled the bricks like a madman until he uncovered the top half of his son's body, a deep hole where his hearts should have been. He shook the boy to no avail; Zander lay limp and did not breathe. Brede sat back on his heels and surveyed the scene with the fighters still blasting the perimeter of the quad though no one was shooting back.

All this for nothing. All the security on this planet and I still lost him. I still lost him.

He paused a moment longer and then for the first time in his life Alekzander Brede hung his head and cried.

CHAPTER TWELVE

Brede carried Zander back into the compound main room, laid his body on the table and then sat in his chair. He stared at nothing, too shaken to even try to understand. The impossible happened. In one instant everything his life was about ended and there was no recourse, no rectifying it even if he tried. Anger, fear, despair couldn't enter the place he sat in now. That place was ice-cold hell, still and silent and brittle. Worst of all it was empty.

"I never had anything you know that but if you take him I'll have nothing at all. I won't have any reason to li—"

He heard Elektra's voice and opened his eyes and when he saw no one he closed them again. He'd fought a dirty fight to take Zander from her, never bothering to see her end of it. And now he sat in her place. He had reasons for it; reasons he once believed valid but now realized meant nothing. He refused her pleading to see their son on his birthdays—today—even from somewhere he couldn't see her. Might things have gone differently? He fought to regain his personality, the one just shattered, to find himself again and restore his Amphidian side—the one that never wavered—but it hovered out of his reach like a shimmering mirage.

****

Colin cut the main rotors on his small craft and followed another small ship apparently headed for the same place. He cut the outside beams and left nothing on but the running lights along the edge of his skiff. He didn't recognize the craft, there was no insignia and it was obviously custom-built but who would be landing on Brede's now thrashed property Colin couldn't imagine. If it was a friend of Brede he'd destroy him; if it was foe, he'd join him. Either way he was going to see Brede suffer.

The ship chose a spot at the far end of the quad that sustained less damage and the side doors lifted and spread like the wings of the falcon God, Horus. The thing that emerged from that ship could only be classified as half-man. So many tubes ran in and out of him that he looked mechanical right to the two artificial lungs perched on his shoulder blades that dragged air in and out, pumping with a rhythmic metallic ping. He hobbled to a door, moving like a hunchback due to the weight of the lungs and the pack that powered them, and rapped on the door twice with a deformed hand. Colin guessed he was foe.

****

Elektra shivered but not from cold space. A thrill ran through her and she could not identify what it meant. Both excitement and a brooding fear grew inside her like twin babies and she shivered again.

Arrian sat jubilant with a small pile of flour atop his head. He smiled broadly at her when she entered as if he waited to show her his crown. Already he showed signs of growing into a large man with a large body frame and ability to lift things he should not. His hair, like Elektra's was blonde and his skin was fair like hers as well. His eyes were Brede's though; dark blue glittering without pupils. Unlike Zander, dark and serious, he possessed an early sense of humor and generosity of spirit.

Elektra put her hands on her hips and gazed about the galley kitchen.

"I hope the food tastes better than it looks," she said "Here," she guided Arrian to a seat opposite her. She handed him a small piece of pita bread. "Taste it." She gave him a small smile. "Um…better than Earth!" Elektra tore off a piece of pita and shoved it into her mouth. She looked at Arrian. "You are magic little man!"

He burbled out what sounded like 'fank you' and she told him he was welcome. Elektra forced herself to eat to at least try to calm herself before they dropped into orbit over Amphidia. Her time on board the ship provided the steadiest eating regimen in all her life and she knew it. When she finished she left and walked to her own quarters deep in thought. Pulling out her clothes she wondered what to wear to see Zander after so long. Her old jumpsuit fit now due to her health but he'd never seen her in it. She wore the long skirt and tunic when she gave birth in Cairo and took him to the planet they now approached. Pain came with the memory; they dragged her to the under prison as Alekzander and their son walked away. Elektra clapped a hand over her mouth and made a small sound. She hated the memory. The horror of it caused the worst pain she ever knew and she could not imagine anything worse. What did she wear? Over the years she tried to bury it under the hope that she would soon see Zander. Closing her eyes she pictured the court room and the hideously dark and dank prison cells and her last glimpse of her boy: she wore the jumpsuit.

"No." she told herself aloud. "He'll see his Mommy. His Mommy wore a skirt. He'll remember me when he sees that—I know he will—won't you Zander?"

The trip toward Amphidia took nearly a year. Richart had skirted around the outer edge of the galaxy to kill and dump his passenger load. Arrian could now speak and walk and they made good, if slow, progress toward seeing Zander again. Elektra wondered how Alekzander would react to seeing her again. Would he be angry—angry enough to do something to prevent her from seeing their son? Would he be happy to see her? He generally treated her as if she carried some awful disease or as if he could barely tolerate her presence. After so many years and so much cruelty she knew she should hate him and for the most part thought that she did. Yet somewhere deep down inside her she still wanted him to like her or at least show her some approval. She shook her head without realizing it.

No, damn it. He's a bastard. He took your son away and put you in prison for wanting Zander back. He's been hateful and cruel to you since you met and nothing will ever change that. He'll never feel anything but hatred for you. You're not a little girl anymore Elektra so stop pretending you even had a chance. You never even qualified as his friend. You're an adult now. You've given birth to two children. They're important now, not Alekzander Brede. Not anymore.

****

Another player entered the game though none knew of it at the time. The new enemy carried the doctors who'd created Elektra's mechanical hand and their new techniques to apprehend and debilitate Alekzander Brede. This enemy trailed far behind the others so far it could not be discovered tracking them and waiting for its own descent upon the prey and his son, waiting…waiting…

****

"Well, well, well, Alekzander Brede." The voice cackled like an old hen. "Had I been a more vengeful man, I'd be rather disappointed to not have brought this about by my hand. But now that I see it, I am content to die a happy man instead. I suppose I should thank you for that. I thought to never smile or laugh again, even in revenge. I never thought I'd ever experience joy again. And yet this turn of events pleases me." Accompanying the voice was the sound of metal dragging in and out a crooked rhythm with gasping breaths.

Brede opened his eyes and stared at the speaker. "Nicolai, you did not do this. I did." His voice sounded dull even to his own ears.

"Oh, now, don't take my victory away from me Alekzander. Don't crush an old man's dream."

"I said you did not do this."

"Oh but I did. You can't imagine the machinations I've had to work to get to this point."

"Nicolai—"

"In any case think what you want about my participation. I've done what I dreamed of—I have lived to see you wishing you'd killed me for free. Though we are still not even on this account I am satisfied. I can die happy now. And best of all you can do it for me!"

"Maybe I should have killed you when we last met. Perhaps none of this would have happened." Brede gazed at his old enemy without seeing.

"Take heart Brede. You can kill me now. Go ahead. It won't bring you satisfaction however. That is my biggest joy of all." He walked with difficulty toward Zander's body and poked it with a metal claw. He looked back up at Brede expression daring.

Brede stared at him emotionless but sat up at the touch of the old man's hand against Zander's body.

"Touch my son again and you will die old man."

Nicolai Qitarah hobbled close to Brede and leaned toward him giggling a little.

"If you don't kill me now Brede, I will kill you."

"And take away my trophy old man?"

Both looked at the new speaker. Melivilu stood behind Nicolai Qitarah with his weapon against the back of the old man's head. The weapon was ridiculously overpowered for close range. If Brede could have laughed he would have.

"I think not." Melivilu continued. "I've been waiting for a big kill like this for decades. Brede's head on the wall of my ship is a trophy all right." He glanced down at Zander's body. "And his son's beside it. Hah!"

Brede stood up and advanced toward the bounty hunter. He said nothing but his blank expression froze them both. He reached out and grasped Melivilu's throat and picked him up, feet dangling. The bounty hunter struggled frantically to no avail; nothing he could do would release him and he saw his own death in Brede's eyes. That frightened him and he struggled even harder.

"Let me kill the old man only," he rasped. "I will rid you of him and then you will be rid of me."

Brede raised him higher.

"I swear you will never see me after that," he tried.

"I will never see you again now." Fury made Brede's face distant as if he was barely aware of his actions. He twisted Melivilu's head completely around and then tore it from his neck. Then he tossed them into the nearest corner and turned to face Nicolai Qitarah.

"I could kill you too Qitarah. Yet why? Now I know what a living death is. Since you insist that you masterminded this, you can suffer along with me until we both die."

"Are you afraid Brede? Are you afraid to be alone?"

"Fear of being alone is the last thing on my mind." Brede turned back to sit on his chair. "I won't waste another second on you." He gazed down at Zander's body.

"I will."

Colin Factor now stood side by side with Qitarah weapon and eyes locked on him. Brede shook his head. No wonder it happened. The entire security system was a sham. He shook his head again. Even if he killed every servant, Zander could not come back.

"Colin, how and why the fuck did you get in here?"

"I'll tell you once I prevent your revenge upon this man."

Colin's eyes never left Qitarah. "You've taken everything from me and now I'm taking something from you at long last Brede."

"That would be Nicolai Qitarah? That dish is already cold."

"What?"

"You'd be taking satisfaction from him not me Colin. I do not care whether he lives or dies now."

"Don't fuck with me Brede. This isn't Thebes Two. This isn't about money or power or politics. It's about you fucking up everything I ever wanted."

"I've barely been in your life Colin. What exactly do you think I've fucked up for you?"

"Everything you son of a bitch and now I'm going to take everything from you."

"Look around Colin. I have nothing of any worth left. Take whatever you fucking want. I don't care."

Colin stared down at Zander.

"You have a son?" He looked back up at Brede, astonished.

"*Had* a son Colin. *Had*. Past tense."

"And who is his mother?"

"It doesn't matter who his mother is or was."

"Was? She is dead then? I heard rumors…" he stared into space for a moment. His eyes focused again, red rimmed and he turned back to Brede. "So you've destroyed everything. Everything that could have made my life happy or worthwhile you've taken."

"Colin—"

"No you fucker. You're not getting off that easily. I can easily forget this thing—" he waved his weapon in Qitarah's direction. "And kill you. But you're not going to die until I call you out on everything you did to me."

"Colin—"

"No! I've got time and you have whatever time I give you. You're going to hear it before you die whether you like it or not Alekzander." He walked away from Qitarah and moved toward Brede. "If you have a weapon Brede, I suggest you use it now."

Brede said nothing.

"Alright if this is the way you want it. Sit down Alekzander."

Brede turned slowly like an aged man and sat back down.

"What have I done Colin?" A heavy sigh escaped him.

"Let's go in chronological order. I think it started with the race. Do you remember that race Alekzander or have you conveniently forgotten through your arrogance?" He paused for a moment but spoke again before Brede could respond. "I do. It's something I will never forget. It's the first of a lifetime of things you took from me."

"You're going to try to kill me over a childhood race?"

"Not just a race The Elimination. I worked for those games for over a year Alekzander. Physically, mentally preparing for that day, I gave up every day of the year to practice for the games. That victory should have been mine. I would have had everything—education, opportunity, the one person I loved. But no you had to intervene and steal it from me with your supposed prowess and pandering to the crowd. You made sure their response overwhelmed the judges' didn't you?"

"You were being strangled Colin." Brede's voice was flat.

"I would have saved myself! I would have overcome him! I didn't need you!" Colin screamed at him and then he collected himself. It took a few moments before he could breathe evenly. "You had to intervene didn't you? You had to take it all away by being the savior. Even if it meant killing your best friend, you had to have that win didn't you?"

"I didn't—"

"Don't try to prevaricate with me Alekzander. We've known each other a long time, you've done a lot of things to me; half of them you never realized or cared about. I've been patient—more than patient—to give back a little of what you gave to me. Unfortunately, the thing most precious to you I could have taken has already been stolen," Colin glanced down at Zander's body. "That takes much of the sting out of it. But in the end I think what humans call "karma" has come home to you most appropriately. Too bad it couldn't come from me."

Brede cradled his brow with his fingers and hand. Crushing exhaustion and sorrow set into him. Elektra must have felt that as they pronounced her sentence back in New Cairo. Brede remembered her face when they did. In the next second Colin's voice erased her image.

"In any case, I took the brunt of those games. Treffayne cheated, no one felt sorry for him. But me? I didn't even get pity. What I got was the title of bad loser when I tried to contest you. Because you acted the hero I got nothing. Nothing! I'd have won Alekzander and you know that which is why you stepped in to 'rescue' me and destroyed all my hard work and sacrifice. And in the end it meant nothing to you."

"Colin I told you I didn't—"

"Please Alekzander. Those games meant about as much to you as Zander's mother. When you took her, you took everything that meant anything to me. She was my world Alekzander. You took her and didn't care—either about her or about me. And in the end you even killed her." Colin's voice cracked with emotion and Brede looked up at him again. Colin Factor had apparently gone over the edge and was breaking right in front of him. An irrational urge told him to stand up and comfort his accuser but he held off remembering how much Zander hated weakness in any form and he wanted to be faithful to his son in death if not in life so he said and did nothing. He did wonder how in hell Colin Factor knew Elektra Tate. Then he wondered even more how Colin knew Elektra was dead—he himself didn't know despite his huge web of intelligence. Brede forced himself to stop thinking. Zander was dead and he did not know if he wanted to hear that Elektra was dead as well.

"Colin how did you—"

"Get inside? I told you I'd come to that. This man-thing is not the only one with machinations. I worked a few myself—even a few of the same ones," he nodded toward the separated head and body of Melivilu. "But mainly it came down to bribery. I've always found that's the easiest not to mention the fastest way to get things done. You chose a pathetic group of servants that gleefully gave you away in an instant. When I realized Qitarah here was landing before me, I hung back and then docked right beside him. It would have been lucky for you that he was flying alone, had I not followed him. But apparently I wasn't early or lucky enough to see you lose your most precious possession." He grinned insanely at Brede. "But it's rather bittersweet isn't it? Neither of us can get back what we want most."

"I was going to ask how you knew she's dead. And how the hell you know she's Zander's mother."

Colin snorted.

"They found her body Alekzander. They identified her immediately."

"Found it where?"

"There was a ship..." Colin's face threatened to crack again.

"Where? Where was it headed?" Brede didn't hear the panic in his own voice.

"Nobody knows Alekzander. What the hell difference does it make?"

"Was it en route here?"

"Could have been but there's no telling really. Besides, you'd be the one to know that wouldn't you?" Colin now sounded sardonic.

A million thoughts flooded Brede's mind. He'd known Elektra nearly all her life; she never appeared to have any friends let alone any male friends but it wasn't impossible. He could have met her in New Cairo; it wasn't that far from Thebes Two and she did ride the light rails on occasion. But were they close enough for her to reveal her pregnancy with Zander? Brede stopped thinking and looked at Colin. Was he the one who transported her and Zander when she kidnapped their son and left Earth for Amphidia?

"Colin. If you had anything to do with Zander's mother—or her death—"

"Stupid!" Colin spat back. "Harm the one person I loved most in the universe? You're the one who's crazy Alekzander."

Qitarah surprised them both by laughing.

"Oh," he said once he'd gotten his breath back. "This is truly wonderful. Next you'll be at each other's throats. Your son's death Brede will have gone for nothing! Nothing at all! I'll have destroyed him for absolutely nothing!" He cackled again until something ripped the main lung artery out of his skull and body. It landed against the wall next to Melivilu's head and slid to the floor making a dark red splash as it went. Brede and Colin watched his face blank out in shock until he realized what was happening and then shock turned to horrific fear as another of his tubes jerked out of his sinuses by an unknown hand. That same hand flung the tube against the opposite wall and then ripped the main plastic artery into his brain out slowly and tortuously. The other hand cranked Qitarah's head around to face whoever was killing him. The sound of his head cracking off his neck repulsed even Brede. His body finally dropped to the floor blood and snot covering not only his head and face but the top half of his shirt as well.

"Elektra," Brede whispered for the first time in his life.

She ignored him, pushing past Colin and dropping to her knees beside Zander. A deep moan of agony escaped her and she cradled his head to her chest. She rocked him for a few moments and then glared up at Brede.

"What did you do to him?"

"Elektra—"

"What did you do to him?" Her voiced rose higher.

"It—"

"What did you do to him?" she stood up and screamed it at him.

"Elektra—"

"What did you do to him? You killed him—you killed my son! You killed my son! You killed my baby! You killed my baby!" She beat her fists against him hysterical and Brede struggled to get

hold of her. She wriggled her left hand loose and struck him in the center of his chest with a deep thump sound. He staggered back a little and coughed out a breath. He inhaled and grabbed her again. "I'll kill you! I. Will. Kill. You." she repeated in a low voice.

"Elektra," He managed to hold her tightly. "*Elektra!*" He shook her hard. "Don't you think I'd have died a thousand times to get him back? Don't you think I'd have already done that?" She fought until she had no strength. He let her go and she turned her back to him and gazed down at their son's body.

"I don't know," she breathed at last. "I don't know. All I know is that I should have died before I let you take him from me. I should have killed you when I had the chance." She dropped to Zander's side again and stroked his face, his hair sobbing.

"Who the hell is this?" Colin asked.

"She is Zander's mother." Brede looked at him as if he'd never seen Colin before.

"*She* is?" Colin voice sounded as perplexed as Brede's.

"Who the hell did you think was his mother?"

Colin let out a small astonished laugh.

"I thought—I—" He sobered. "Then what happened to…Narita?"

"I made a choice. It was not the right one."

"What are you saying Brede? Are you saying you deliberately killed her?"

Brede sighed.

"I'm saying, for what it's worth, I'm sorry. You never said a word to me about her Colin. Things might have gone differently."

"*How could you have not known?*" Colin screamed himself. "*She was my life!*" He collected himself yet again. "You took her from me. She's not the only one who should have killed you." He nodded at Elektra.

"I didn't choose Narita Colin, she chose me."

"You arrogant son of a whore! There's no way she'd—"

"She wasn't in love with me Colin. Narita didn't love anyone but herself."

"You fucker—I'll kill you right no—"

"It's true." Elektra looked up at Colin bleary-eyed. "It's how I got this," she held up her mechanical left hand. "She had her guards crush my hand and arm. I had to trade Alekzander for this—" she paused and gazed around blank. "Doctors…doctors can do it Alekzander. They can save him. Aren't there any damned doctors on this planet? Aren't there? We can take him to them—" her voice rose again and Brede recognized hysteria returning.

"Elektra they can't—"

"Yes. They can! They gave me this hand! They can do anything! Come on help me Alekzander. You can pick him up and carry him! Help me," she grunted, trying to move the body.

"Elektra they can't raise the dead."

"But—"

"They cannot reanimate him. He's gone." He said the last in a gentle tone. He knelt beside her. "If they could he'd already be there."

"No," she moaned leaning down again. "I don't believe it. I won't. There has to be some way—I know there is—I just can't think of it right now. But I will. I'll think of it…I will."

Brede put his arm around her and looked up at Colin. He shook his head to say that she'd gone mad and sighed again. He'd at last destroyed Elektra.

For some reason Colin tilted his gun barrel toward the ceiling.

"I feel for her," he said nodding at Elektra again. "…and for you Brede. If it was my son with Narita, I'd be as mad as she is now. And that she's the mother of your son and not my Narita is a relief no matter how ridiculous. And, knowing Narita I can see how she'd choose you over me. You win again."

Brede looked up.

"No. It isn't how you think Colin. I wasn't even a person to her. You know how vain Narita was; how she had to impress everyone. I was just her biggest piece of jewelry. I wish I'd known how you felt. I'd have given her back to you with a smile."

"But you still killed her. Why?"

"She told me what she'd done to Elektra and thought it was funny. I didn't. I didn't think about it I just picked up my gun and—it wasn't my best moment."

"I don't get it."

"No, you wouldn't Colin. It was the same reason I killed Treffayne."

"It doesn't matter anymore Alekzander. Everyone loses here." Colin lowered his weapon toward the floor again and turned to leave. Then he turned back to Brede. "Why the hell *did* you kill Treffayne? He was your best friend. Why didn't you just let him kill me? You would have won either way."

"He *was* my best friend…but you were my brother."

****

"No, don't let me go. Don't let me go." Elektra pressed herself against him.

"I won't."

"If you hold me I won't think."

They lay in his bed after making love, each too wrapped in sorrow to speak. Neither wanted to think; to feel anything other than immediate release and neither one knew what to say. They listened to each other's breathing and finally fell into black sleep.

Elektra woke with a small jerk. So distraught by Zander's death she'd completely forgotten the baby still in the ship, docked in the bay at the outer edge of Brede's property.

Arrian must be panicked about now. I've got to get to him.

She slid slowly out of bed and threw on her clothes, running barefoot across the grass quad out to the bay and into the waiting nameless ship. She found him in his bed sleeping and tiptoed past the berths and into the bedroom she had shared with Richart. The realization stopped her in her tracks. She'd brought it with her—there might be a chance for Zander—a distant chance but a chance nonetheless. The concept was ridiculous—the whispers insane—but she was nearly insane herself: insane enough to take that chance for her boy. It now had no other purpose for her. Elektra walked the hall slowly, thinking, wishing. If it could only be, only work once that was all she needed. Perhaps God did think her worth his time...or whatever gods existed. She opened the door and shuddered once before she knelt and swatted her hand back and forth seeking something she couldn't find.

Where is it? Where is it? God it has to be here—it has to be. He couldn't have found it could he? He wouldn't know what it was if he did. What if he destroyed it or ejected it out with the trafficked passengers?

A full two minutes passed before she realized she wasn't reaching far enough and she flattened her body to the floor stretching as far as she could. The pile of clothing was still there and relief washed over her when her hand struck something hard. Elektra grunted, fingers grasping at the object until she moved it an inch closer and clutched it tight, pulling it toward her. She finally managed to fully grasp it and drag it out to her where she rose and kneeled to look at it. She'd never been brave enough to actually open it and she restrained herself, standing up and holding it to her as she traced her way back to the sleeping berths and out of the ship. She was grateful that she possessed the sense to set the ship on auto before she'd left it to find Zander. The ship hovered in hibernation, blinking lights dimmed and a steady nearly silent hum from the power cells lulled Arrian to sleep and kept the systems running efficiently. Elektra ran without sound herself, barefoot over the thick dark grass of the quad and slid silently through the still open doors into the house.

****

"Elektra?" Brede walked the empty halls perplexed. He'd awakened the fourth time and found her gone. A slight panic rose in him that she might have done something stupid while in her hysterical mental state. If she was near she gave him no response and he walked toward the main hall where he'd set Zander's body on the huge table they'd sat at just hours before. He guessed she was there or soon would be—she wouldn't leave their son alone dead or alive and he knew she would spend every second with him that she could. The room was dark, only the light lines on the walls flickered with LED lights and he could barely distinguish his son lying in state.

"Elektra?" He whispered again.

"No, it's me Alekzander."

Colin sat in Brede's chair in the dark.

"*Shit!* Jesus Christ Colin you scared the hell out of me! What are you still doing here?"

"I thought I'd come back and you know…sit with him a while. He is my nephew."

"Thank you. I appreciate it more than you know. Has Elektra been here?"

"No one has been here since you left with her. Is she missing?"

"I'm not sure yet. I woke up and she was gone."

"You think she's okay?"

"I don't know. I'm worried she might be over the edge entirely and do something…idiotic."

"We'd better start looking for her." Colin stood and walked to him. He put a hand on Brede's shoulder. "We'll find her."

****

She waited until she was alone in the corridor before entering the main room.

"Mommy's here Zander. Mommy's here. Just hold on a bit longer baby, please." She walked to the table and stood by his body, stroking his hair and his face, still solemn as in life.

"I love you my baby. Mommy loves you and has come for you. I won't let you leave me again."

After a few more seconds she placed the object beside him and opened it. She restrained the reflex to jump back not knowing what to expect. Nothing happened. Carefully and slowly Elektra peeked into the box and reached into it picking up the object within it. She turned it around, inspecting it, a memory kicking up dust in her mind. She'd seen it before in other forms but couldn't place it. There was no inscription, no prayer of supplication, no instruction at all and she gazed at it and then at Zander.

"Whoever you are, whatever god you might be, please bring my son back. Please bring him back to life—give him back to me please," she whispered to the god belonging to the amulet. Then she placed it on his chest and laid her forehead on his shoulder.

"Elektra!"

She straightened and stared at Brede across the room. His voice was an order and she reacted by rote—stopping where she stood.

"What the fuck do you think you're doing?"

"I was just—"

"Just what?"

"Just trying to...see if I could—"

"Stop it you god damned witch. I will not have you desecrating his body with some fucking worthless voodoo." He walked to her and stuck a finger in her face. "Do you understand me? I won't have it."

"Don't you want him back Alekzander? Shouldn't we try everything possible to save him?" She clutched his arm and stared into his eyes. "Shouldn't we do that?"

"No. He is gone, Elektra. You have to come to terms with that." He grasped her arm and pulled her toward his chair. "And don't think of doing anything stupid. I'll put you on a mental planet so fast you won't be able to blink twice. In fact I'm halfway to doing that now." He stopped and turned around to look down on her. "No more, do you understand me?"

She stood before him, refusing to let her face crumple completely. The expression jerked up a memory of her wearing it as a thirteen-year-old. He blinked it away and sat down pulling her toward him.

"What is that thing?" He nodded at the box and then the ankh on their son.

"It's—it's what you've been searching for—the Vessel of Beket-Re."

"Why did you bring it here?"

"I wanted to see Zander so badly…I had this stupid idea that I might…bargain with you…sort of trade it for him—"

"You really thought I would trade my son for something so worthless? Or trade him at all?" He stopped and then said through a sardonic laugh. "I don't want that thing. I've never wanted it. Narita wanted it."

"Well…well I don't want it either."

"You know, I had half the fucking universe chasing me and Zander for it. I built this fort to protect us—to protect him." Brede paused. "How long have you had it?"

"Since the City of the Dead."

"Why the fuck didn't you give it to me back then?"

"At first I didn't know what it was. It was in the wall of my room behind a brick. I kept it just like I'd kept the other things—" she stopped and bit a lip. "Anyway I only found out what it was after you put me in the damned under prison. Some men came looking for it; they nearly broke the cell apart searching. I—maimed one of them and when they finally left, I put the two together."

"Why didn't you contact me then? Our son might still be alive. I'd have tossed it to them as they skimmed over us." He gave her a bitter expression.

Elektra's face paled.

"I didn't know. I'd have killed to give it to them. I didn't know anyone still wanted it. Oh my God, it's my fault! It's my fault. Oh, my God, Zander please forgive me—I didn't know."

Brede relented for the moment. He gazed at her.

"How the hell did you get here?"

"I—commandeered a ship and brought it here."

"You—commandeered—a ship."

"Well, I had to…bargain for passage on it first. But I really did commandeer it in the end. I just wanted to see him so much I didn't care what I had to do—or what I did."

"What the fuck were you doing with that thing over the body of my—our—son?"

"I'd heard stories that it…I don't know…had powers or gave powers, something like that. I never really thought about it or believed it. But when I got here and found that he was…I guess I couldn't face it. I couldn't let him go without trying everything possible. I know it's crazy but I was so desperate to have him back that I would have tried anything. And I did. I don't know if it was right or wrong all I know is that I wanted my son back—I didn't care how."

Brede sighed and gazed down at the floor. He closed his mind to the fact that he wanted the same thing. It was wishful thinking and that was a weakness and if there was one thing his son hated it was weakness. It didn't matter that he now regretted teaching that to the boy; it mattered that he showed strength and moved forward. He looked at Elektra again.

"The funeral ceremony and procession is tomorrow."

"No! Just one more day please Alekzander? Can't you wait one more day?"

"To do what Elektra? Watch him decompose? I will bury my son with dignity and then it is over."

He watched her flinch and experienced a familiar feeling of satisfaction. He hated himself for it now; if he'd been a little kinder to her perhaps none of it would have occurred, things might have ended happily for all three of them. They might have had a life together. He focused on her again and this time watched her struggle with acceptance. Their son was gone—dead—and it would take strength; all the strength they possessed to move through it whether they did it together or alone. Elektra finally dissolved into tears, dropping to her knees and covering her face with her hands. Brede hesitated a moment then reached down and pulled her up. He rose to his feet as well and wrapped his arms around her and rocked her slightly hoping for once in all the time he'd known her that they would move through it together.

"Elektra," Brede said. "I know this is too late in coming, far too late but…once you asked me to stay and…well, I guess I'm asking you to do the same now. For more than one night though. You can stay for as long as you need to—or want to."

Neither one looked at the body of their son still and quiet or the tendrils of smoke that rose and curled about him, roiling over and around and through him like wisps of incense sent directly from the goddess Beket-Re herself.

Elektra's head rested against his chest, facing the table eyes closed against reality. Brede waited but received no reply. He moved back and held her away from him to see her face. She was no longer looking at him. Her eyes were round and her mouth hung slightly open and she pulled even further away from him, taking a step toward the light show emitting from her son's body.

"Alekzander—" she shook her head slightly in disbelief.

Brede followed her gaze and watched in silence. Elektra took a full step toward the table and then stopped, cupping a hand over her mouth. The smoke and lights froze for a long moment before Zander sucked in an enormous breath inhaling them both down into his body. Both Brede and Elektra froze with them waiting breathless as well as their son's life hung in a petrifying balance, waiting for him to either live or die. Zander stilled and Brede's heart solidified in his chest. The smoke and lights burst from the boy's body and curled one last time about his head before slowly evaporating, making a small fog around him. He sat up as if groggy and turned his head to look at Elektra.

"*Mother?*"

CHAPTER THIRTEEN

"He's a mongrel Elektra. I won't acknowledge him." Alekzander Brede sat in his chair chin resting on his hand.

"He is your son Alekzander."

"Mine and who else?"

"Yours and mine Alekzander. He's as much your son as Zander is." Elektra clenched her hands into fists and gave him a frustrated frown.

"No he is not. One thing you do not know about breeding with an Amphidian is that not only does 'Sugar' prep you for pregnancy it also allows other men's sperm to enter the egg as well. As I said, he's a mongrel."

That stopped her. Elektra blinked and stared at him with her crystal blue eyes. After a moment she inhaled.

"He is *your* son *first* Alekzander. It doesn't matter who else's DNA came after. You are the one who initiated the pregnancy."

Brede hid a smile from her. After all the time passed he still enjoyed upsetting her. Not as much or as cruelly as in their past; he'd learned deep and shattering lessons when he thought he'd lost their first son and her as well but he still secretly enjoyed it.

"I won't do it Elektra. Zander is my first and only son and he is my only acknowledged son. I will not have some mongrel you've conceived contest his inheritance—"

"He would never do that!" she interrupted. "Arrian is not that way. He is generous and loving and he worships Zander. That would never be an issue Alekzander and you know that."

"No I do not Elektra. I have a brother who thought I was hell-bent on destroying his life when I never gave a damn. His adult life revolved around wreaking vengeance upon me. When I murdered my best friend to save him he thought I was trying to upstage him and he didn't even *know* we were brothers. Even if I wanted to acknowledge this boy I couldn't. I won't—*can't* jeopardize Zander again in any way. Do I have to remind you that we almost lost him forever?"

Again she stopped, looking away and then closing her eyes.

"No. Of course not, it—it was the most—horrific time in my life. But we didn't lose him Alekzander. We don't have to raise them apart like you and Colin. They'll know they are brothers and we can teach them they need and love each other. They won't have a past like you have—"

"No"" he stood and thundered at her. "I will not acknowledge this child in any way Elektra. You can't even prove he is mine anyway. My DNA runs in you too since you conceived Zander."

"Look at him!" Elektra shouted herself. Her blonde hair, short again fell into her eyes. "His eyes are identical to yours—"

"And his hair is identical to yours. It still doesn't mean anything and it still doesn't make him legitimate."

"Oh!' she clenched her fists again and spun away from him. He waited until she reached the doorway and watched her flounce through it to smile. Whether it was due to enjoying frustrating her or sentimental sadness he didn't know or care; he just missed the skinny, scamming tomboy she'd once been and now would never be again. The older she grew the more feminine she grew and the more in control of her emotions and herself. He liked her hair short; he'd seen it that way since she was a child and it reminded him of that time when she'd do anything just to be noticed by him. Brede sighed. Did he miss her youth or just her hero-worship of him? Or was it both? Did it matter? Their problems, not so simple now, threatened to overwhelm them: when they thought they'd lost Zander but it also brought them together in another way, one they'd never experienced before. Their relationship tilted because of it; tipped them toward each other, him more so, causing emotion to erupt in him, playing out his human side, leaving him unable to control it.

Oddly enough it had the opposite effect on Elektra. Experience made her calmer and more thoughtful and careful; she no longer threw emotional caution to the wind and prayed it dropped her in front of him. Brede wondered briefly what might have happened had he valued her earlier and shook his head. He didn't and time did not flow backwards.

He meant what he'd said though. He couldn't and wouldn't jeopardize anything that might benefit Zander no matter how small the threat or who the contender might be—another son or not. Elektra should have kept her legs together. But she didn't; sleeping with not one but several men to get to Zander didn't wash as an excuse and he'd be damned before he acknowledged some bastard—mongrel bastard—as solely his own. He cluttered up the shattered fortress he'd built to protect Zander and interfered with their life.

Their life.

Brede shook his head half-laughing at himself. The older he got—in human years—the sillier he got. The second she came violently back he began to think and refer to the three as a unit; as a *family.*

You stupid old bastard Brede; you're jealous that she—

He killed the thought before he finished it. God *damn* her! After all that time she could still annoy him and piss him off as if they'd never left Earth, as if she'd never grown up. He should have killed her when—no that was something he could never do. He admitted it now hating himself and his weakness. Since Zander's death and miraculous return to life, his Amphidian side betrayed and then abandoned him and he despised the fact that now he could barely restrain any of his emotions. They flooded him and overwhelmed him and at times he knew what it meant to drown. Especially over Elektra—he laughed again—she'd finally pushed and shoved her way entirely into his life and he knew she would never willingly leave it, grown up or not. The worst part of it was that now he wouldn't allow her to leave it if she tried.

Knock it off Brede. She's made a fool of you—you've made a fool of yourself. You're stuck with her now—you've always been stuck with her and you know it. You've always known it haven't you idiot? What would she do if you proposed a union?

He shook off the shiver that ran down his spine. In the last few years he'd learned fear; what it felt like, what it could do and how it could destroy a life. It could destroy even a personality; crack it shake it apart and leave the pieces along the trajectory of existence. The thought of officially uniting with Elektra terrified him now who had known fear only once in his life. What would he do if he lost her permanently, how would he live? She was a part of him now as he was her; as much as his hair or eyes or mind and life without her inconceivable. As long as they weren't officially together in his mind it seemed safer somehow, easier to ignore anything negative but once it was official those images grew into frightening possibilities. He thought he'd lose his mind when Zander died and knew he'd do the same if it happened to Elektra.

Enough. It was time to behave like a man again—Amphidian and human. There were more important things to take care of than arguing with Elektra about her bizarre duo of children. One of those things was accompanying Zander back to Earth to renovate the Menkare property in New Cairo he'd promised the boy.

****

"You know my father won't acknowledge you don't you?" Zander said looking over his shoulder at Arrian who followed at his feet. "In fact, he calls you a mongrel."

"I an not a mongul! I an a little boy! My mama says I am his son." Arrian, four years old now, folded his arms across his chest as they walked.

"Do you even know what that is?" Zander asked.

"No. But I an not one."

"Yes you are. A mongrel is someone, usually a dog, who…has a…bad mix of genes from his mother and father. Or in your case *fathers*," Zander gave him a superior smirk.

"Fathers?" Arrian tasted the word, confused. "How many fathers do I have?"

"I don't know. You'll have to ask Mother, she'll know." Zander paused a moment. "But my father still won't acknowledge you and that means we're not officially brothers." He watched Arrian's face crumple.

"Not brovers? I want you to be my brover! I want to be for your brover too!"

Zander picked up the pace again, faster than before.

"Well, sometimes we don't get what we want. When that happens you have to be a man Arrian."

The boy stared at his back, swallowing tears frantically.

"I want to be a man! An I want to be a brover!" he grasped Zander's sleeve. Zander shook it off with irritation.

"Stop it! Men don't cry. Men don't act like babies. You're a baby. That's probably why Father doesn't want you."

Arrian didn't care about being a baby. He shrieked into tears spinning and running down the hallway as fast as he could manage. Zander glanced back once watching him go and then changed his own course to find his father, a satisfied expression covering his face.

****

Arrian sat on the steps of the only gun turret left standing, knees up arms on them, weeping deeply when

Elektra found him. She knelt beside him.

"My darling baby what's the matter? Why are you crying? Did you hurt yourself?"

He raised his face, red and tear-streaked and looked at her.

"My father does not want me.' He said between hiccoughs. 'He doesn't want me because I an a baby! Because I have many fathers."

Elektra's eyes widened and she crushed him to her.

"No no Sweetheart. You misunderstood that's all. Of course he wants you. And you are not a baby you are a brave little man. A very brave little man and I love you so very much." She kissed his hair and then his face and held him tighter rocking them both. 'You'll see Arrian your father loves you. He just doesn't know it yet, that's all. You'll see."

You'll see if I have to kick his god damned ass all the way back to Earth. He can treat me like shit but I won't have him doing it to you. I won't. You'll see.

****

"You wanted me Father?" Zander stood in the doorway of the bay hangar, staring at Brede.

"Yes. We're going to the Menkare today. In two hours as a matter of fact. Get packed and get ready for launch."

"Certainly Father,' Zander adjusted his formal collar. "How long will we be gone?"

"I don't know."

"Then I'll just pack…utilitarian." He gave Brede a small genuine smile. "I'll see you in an hour Father."

Brede watched him leave; watched him move in his formal manner in his formal clothing. After he'd miraculously come back to life, Zander had taken to wearing vintage clothing that could only have fit on Earth circa 1890. Vests covered long sleeved shirts with high pointed collars and dress pants with dress shoes completed the look. At some point Zander commissioned one of the house staff to replicate the anachronistic clothing from photographs he located somewhere in Earth's history. Why he chose the style Brede had no idea. He couldn't look more out of place on either Amphidia or Earth and yet it fit him in some strange way as if confirming his place and power. The only time the boy wore anything else was in firefight and then he wore flight jumpsuits reminiscent of Elektra's orphan days. If he didn't share physical similarities with Brede, it would be impossible to recognize them as related. Zander's hair, like Brede's, in perpetual box braids pulled back, stuck out at more extreme angles from his head, emphasizing the severity of his personality. Apparently the Amphidian genetic strand stacked up a little higher in Zander. At times Brede wondered if it ever came to confrontation which would prove the stronger of them.

****

"How dare you?" She asked Alekzander in a furious whisper. "How dare you say that to him?"

"Elektra what the hell are you talking about?" He stood inspecting the docking bay where the Scythe emerged perched atop a pedestal that stopped once it reached ground level. 'I have things to do."

"Like hurting a child?"

"What?" He gave her a dark, impatient scowl.

"Why did you hurt Arrian's feelings?"

"I have no fucking idea what you are talking about."

"Don't lie to me Alekzander."

"I have never fucking lied to you and you fucking well know it. I've always told you the truth whether you liked it or not."

"And that's exactly what you've done to my little boy. I found him hysterical. He was crying because he thinks you don't want him."

"I *don't* want him."

"You are the bastard here Alekzander. You're the fucking bastard," she walked away, head down, fighting tears.

Brede watched her go perplexed. What had he done now

to make her crazy? He hadn't even spoken to the boy. He puffed out a sigh, momentarily regretting she'd ever come back to him, remembering all the opportunities to kill her he'd never taken advantage of. He sighed again and turned back to the Scythe. It was so much easier before she grew up.

****

"Did you ever have a girlfriend Alekzander?" she sat beside him on the curb, both doing nothing. Brede was in a congenial mood for once; so much he tolerated even her.

"Yes."

"I never had a boyfriend."

"You're too young to have a boyfriend."

"I could be a good girlfriend...if I had a boyfriend." She glanced up into the late afternoon sunlight, painfully bright and hot but not stifling. Then she moved a small loose cobblestone with a too-big-for-her-foot boot.

"You don't even know what it means to be a girlfriend."

"I could still be a good one. How old do I have to be?" She paused a moment, moving the stone another inch.

"I don't know. Maybe eighteen or nineteen, maybe seventeen,"

"Do you have a girlfriend Alekzander? I mean, like right now?"

He eyed her unable to decide whether to laugh or insult her.

"Not exactly," he hedged.

"But do you have someone that you like?"

"Um, sort of,"

"Who is it?" Her eyes rounded with expectation.

"Someone you don't know."

"Oh."

He watched her deflate, a discouraged expression twisting her mouth sideways.

"Do you have someone you like Elektra?"

"Yes. I do. He's very handsome and very nice to me. He never says mean things to me or about me to other people." At the end her chin jutted out and her lips pursed.

He always knew when she lied to him. She inhaled before every phrase.

"No you don't."
"I do!"
"No you don't."
"Yes I do!"
"Who is it?"
"I—well, I don't know if I should tell you. I know he likes me but he might get mad if I do."
"You're making this up."
"I am not. His name is…is…Husayn. That's his name."
"How old is he?"
"Um, I think maybe…seventeen. Yes I think seventeen."
"And how old are you?"
"Thirteen, I think."
"How come I've never seen you with him? Come to think of it I've never even seen him. He doesn't exist does he?"
She snorted in frustration.
"Shut up Alekzander. You don't know anything."
"I know everything. And I know enough about you."
"No you don't! You don't know anything about me! If you did you'd know who I lo—" she stopped and swallowed hard. "You don't know anything at all. You're stupid. I'm leaving." She jumped up and huffed away, pride hurt and determined to ignore his laughter following her.

****

Earth brought back so many memories for him that he almost dreaded returning to it. His recent explosion of emotions included guilt and he'd done a lot to feel guilty about on this planet. Still he promised Zander the Menkare as a gift and now he needed to make good on it. They walked toward the old bay where he once stowed the Scythe, his personal ship, and he stopped before it fearing the past it dredged up. Currently his craft sat in a public dock parked for the moment he hoped would be short.

"What is this Father?"

"It's where I used to dock the Scythe between jobs or…other things. Just a docking bay I bought a long time ago that's all."

Before Zander could question further, Brede walked away. Zander waited a moment and then hurried to catch up with him. Brede watched him from the corner of his eye. The fact that his son, grown tall now stood almost as tall as him, surprised Brede. He didn't notice it on Amphidia, everyone stood tall there, taller than any of Earth's humans and now for the first time Zander's height was discernible.

"Come on. We need to get to the courts for the transfer to you."

In the handful of years he'd been off Earth, the population of New Cairo quadrupled. People arrived there in droves, refugees from other city-states that floundered economically and civilly. Streets once crowded now stood impassable with throngs of humanity and varieties of races. Animals no longer roamed free with shepherds to corral them but now stood crammed into hastily constructed pens of limestone and sand. Their cries filled the souk fighting for supremacy with the screech and whine of air craft that once buzzed the bazaars and tight crooked streets of the city, but now were forced to hover several meters above them. The presses of people trampled the dust of the city, packing it down and compressing it, resulting in humidity levels dangerous to what was left of the ancient structures and statues. To combat the disintegration of the buildings and tombs, New Cairo placed enormous Plexiglas/Midinium structures over them, temperature and humidity controlled to protect their integrity. From a distance they appeared as glass boxes protecting priceless jewels and indeed they were jewels unique and irreplaceable. Brede inhaled the odors of animals mixed with spiced meat and the reek of human sweat permeating the atmosphere along with the unpleasant scent of pollution that always accompanied it, irritating him. He shoved through the crowds, Zander at his heels and stopped before the massive tower building that housed the government and courts. Zander skimmed the kiosks that listed the floors and guided Brede into one of the hundreds of elevators constantly in motion up and down every other minute. The courts changed location and updated their ponderous legal processes, manned now by android clerks to handle the hundreds of millions of minor legal transactions.

Brede stood before an android now, one this time instead of the nine humans who decided the fate of Elektra years before. With an immense effort he shoved back the memories of that earlier court appearance and focused on the procedures at hand. The android focused its blinking eyes at him.

"You are Alekzander Brede?" The nasal twang of mechanical voice rang over them.

"I am."

"We see that you are the sole owner of the historical property known in the city as 'the Menkare'." You have input that you are here today to transfer title of said property to one Zander Brede is this correct?"

"Yes."

"What is the reason for this transfer?"

"He is my son. It is part of his inheritance."

"If necessary are you willing to submit to DNA identification?"

"Yes."

"Are you the aforementioned Zander Brede?" The electronic eyes focused on him.

"Yes." Zander didn't smile.

"Are you also willing to submit to DNA identification?"

"Yes."

"Please wait until computations end." The machine's lights dimmed a moment and an icon of the court's legal insignia popped out and hovered in front of its face. "We have confirmed you are legal owner of said property and as such can transfer ownership now. Please place your hands on the signature stations and the transaction will complete. Place your hands now."

They pressed their hands simultaneously on the screens.

"Transaction concluded. Thank you for your

cooperation."

That was it. Zander now owned the historic if fairly trashed Menkare pyramid with its entire two and a half floors. It might be historic but apparently not enough for the government of New Cairo to place a Plexi-dome over it. For Zander that was a good thing; he'd be able to do what he wanted with it without interference from any governmental historic society.

They stood again in the bedroom on the second floor, this time Zander gazed out the window as if he sought something below. He turned back to Brede.

"You said my mother never lived here. Where did she live?"

"In two places: in the slum known as Garbage City and then the City of the Dead—a cemetery,"

"*What?*" For one instant Zander's face registered surprise then disgust. "Why the hell would she live there?"

Again his son's precociousness struck Brede.

"She was an orphan. Her family abandoned her in front of Garbage City and they took her in, in a manner of speaking. Later she got into a fistfight and they kicked her out. She had nothing, no money, and the only place left for her to go was a City of the Dead and find an empty tomb to inhabit. That's what she did."

"You never told me this. Why?"

"I never thought it mattered…and at one time…I didn't want you to know. I didn't want you to know anything about her or to remember anything about her."

"Because of her background?"

"No Zander. It had nothing to do with that. I had other reasons, not good ones. I was wrong about them; wrong to do that to you both."

"But you should have at least told me about her history."

"Why? It doesn't make a difference."

"It does to me."

Brede blinked and frowned.

"Why?" he repeated. 'It wasn't her fault. She survived

and amazingly at that. I didn't help her out much. I was wrong about that too. It—we had an unusual relationship. I didn't care what anyone else thought. But still…I could have been kinder to her. I could have made her life a little easier and I didn't. In fact I enjoyed making her suffer at least emotionally. I was very cruel to her most of the time. I thought it was fun. I didn't realize—" He stopped, trying to curb the flood of confession flowing out of him. "After you were born I still hurt her and in worse ways." He turned toward the window himself unable to staunch the rush. "I used to watch her steal her breakfast lunch and dinner from this god damned window." He snorted. "It never occurred to me that I could buy it for her."

"She *stole*? She was a *thief*?" Zander said.

'Not by choice—"

"My mother was a thief," Zander said angry. He paused a moment then asked, "What else was she?"

"What the fuck is that question supposed to mean?" They stared at each other.

"Just what I said" Zander didn't flinch. "What else was she?"

"Nothing," Brede shrugged. "Just an orphan nobody wanted that's all."

"A nothing; a nobody. Just a god damned thief that's all."

Something rang in Brede's head.

"That thief? A nothing? A nobody? That's who you're pining over?"

He closed his eyes and shook his head involuntarily.
"No."

"What?" Zander continued staring at him.

"Nothing," Brede opened his eyes realizing he'd spoken aloud. "I just remembered something that's all." He walked to his son. "And I also remember that your mother did everything and anything to get to you—including killing people. I don't want you referring to her with that attitude again. Do you understand me Zander? Do you?" He stuck his face into the boy's and poked a finger into his son's chest.

"I see. It's alright for you to abuse her but not me. I guess it's because you have sex with her—"

Brede saw nothing but purple for a moment. When he did focus again Zander lay spread-eagle on the floor. The quiet in his own voice unnerved even him.

"I will kill you if you ever say anything remotely like that again boy."

"Right," Zander snarled. He stood up, shrugged and walked around the perimeter of the room. "As I said when I first saw this place, I want it and everything in it." He looked at Brede one more time. "I'll start drawing up plans when we get home. They'll be extensive."

Brede watched his first-born son inspect the entire property with the attitude of a lord inspecting his manor. He wondered if he carried the same attitude at that age. He knew he certainly didn't carry it toward his own mother. But then his mother wasn't an orphan nobody wanted. Brede shook himself to kill the last thought and followed Zander down the stone steps and back out to the street.

CHAPTER FOURTEEN

"How's Zander?" Colin sat across the table sipping his contraband coffee and watching Elektra do the same. He'd brought it to her from Earth's blackest of black markets—it was the best—the kind without the contraband tobacco. Somewhere in her childhood she'd acquired a taste for it.

"He's fine. You know, you don't have to constantly check on him. He's completely healthy and doing very well."

"I feel…obligated. Okay not so much obligated as concerned. I never told Alekzander but I was secretly thrilled to learn I had a nephew and even more thrilled when he came back to life." He laughed. 'He's so much like my brother was at that age.'

"You should tell him. He'd like that I think." Elektra set her cup down. "You know he's a lot different from how he was before he thought he'd lost Zander. He's changed a lot."

"You sound sad about that."

"I am in a way I guess. Our relationship has changed and I think I miss the old one. At least I knew where we stood with each other."

"Traumatic experiences usually do change people and almost losing Zander was pretty traumatic. I'm not surprised Alekzander changed. I should think it would have brought you together."

"In some ways it has but in others…" Elektra shrugged. "I don't know. It's like our whole relationship somehow skewed sideways, at least to me. He just shows so much emotion. That's something he never did in all the time I've known him. Sometimes I don't know how to react around him. It's not like it was before all of this. We had patterns. He was mean to me and I couldn't lie to him. Not physically," she added when Colin sat up. "But just…sort of cruel, he hurt my feelings most of the time but I knew where we drew the lines. I was a little kid and I worshipped him and it was like he punished me for it."

"You probably made him feel emotion too and that's how he reacted to it. He is half human you know. Amphidians are not known for their emotionalism," Colin laughed. He stood to leave. "Aside from anger; I can imagine the conflict he went through. Bye Sweetheart. You've been better to him than he deserves and I think Alekzander finally realizes that." He pecked her on the cheek and she walked to the door with him.

"Thank you, Colin. You've made me feel better at least."

"That's what brothers-in-law do." He dropped another peck on her hair.

She watched him walk to his own ship and then closed the door, thinking. She had no idea how to have an adult relationship with Alekzander.

****

Zander stopped mid-sentence and his head snapped around listening. Before Brede could react he shoved his father aside flinging him into a side street where he landed against a wall. Zander then pulled a weapon and shot through the window of a revamped Cadillac Annihilator, killing the passenger who held his own weapon out and shredding the entire side of the vehicle. The unknown enemy never got to pull the trigger. Brede pushed himself up from the wall and walked frowning to his son.

"Where did you get that gun?"

"What? No congratulation for being accurate?" He grinned at Brede.

"Where the hell did you get it?"

"I—borrowed it."

"From me?"

"If you must know yes," Zander said. "I had a—a suspicion that something might happen and I knew you'd never let me use it if I asked."

"So you just took it?"

"Yes goddamn it! And it's a good thing too. Otherwise we'd both be lying dead across the road." Zander slammed the gun into a hip holster and resumed walking down the main street where people slowly began to fill the area they'd deserted screaming when the firefight began. The scene brought back so many memories that for a moment Brede hesitated before catching up with his son.

"Don't do it again." He said.

Zander continued walking. He glanced sideways at Brede.

"Why are you so pissed off? From the time I was a child this is what you taught me, that weakness is death. Yet when I put it into practice you get angry. I find that hypocritical Father."

Brede found himself with nothing to say for once. His son only acted on what he'd drilled into the boy's brain and rescued both of them. He himself had taught Zander how to fight, and that aggressiveness was a personality trait of Amphidians and it *was* now hypocritical to go against his own teachings.

"I wanted you to survive," he said to Zander when he did catch up with him. "I wanted you to be hard, tough, to survive no matter what you had to do but—"

"You were wrong about that too." Zander finished the sentence for him. "You say that an awful lot these days Father. It's quite different from what you said when I was a child."

"When you were a child things were different. I was

different."

"So what the hell is it that you want me to be?" Zander stopped walking and looked Brede. "Nothing I do pleases you. I've finally decided to be who I want to be and that you will just have to go to hell."

Brede squelched the desire to punch his son again. Zander resumed walking toward the docking bay where the Scythe now sat, and Brede hurried to keep up with him. He halted mid-stride as he watched his son board the ship. During the entire conversation the fact that Zander had just killed someone never arose…as if it didn't matter to the boy one whit.

****

"Leave me alone." Zander did not look away from his work, staring at the turning holograph hovering before his face.

"No, I want to stay here. I want to play wif you," Arrian said, pressing against him.

"I don't play with babies. In fact, I don't play at all. I never have."

"If you don't play with me I'n going to tell Mama."

"You know what? Go right ahead. You know what she'll do? She'll slap you hard for tattling."

"No she won't!"

"Yes she will."

Arrian pursed his lips angrily. He debated whether to abandon Zander or risk physical punishment. He made a decision.

"No Mama won't." he said. "Mama never hits me."

"Well, have you ever tattled before"

"I doan know if I did it. But my Mama never hits me."

"*Our* mother. And if you tattle she'll get mad." Zander shot a quick glance at Arrian. "Do you want to find out if she will or not? I wouldn't. And stop touching my things! If I tattle on you, you'll be the one getting in trouble."

Arrian was no longer listening. He stood transfixed after

discovering that he could stick a finger into the holograph creating lines and began scrawling across the blueprints randomly. Zander lost it. He jumped up, disconnecting the images and knocking keyboard to the floor.

"Stop it!" he thundered lifting Arrian off his feet. "You've destroyed everything! Now I'll have to start again." He held Arrian up to face him and shook the little boy until his teeth clattered. "If you ever do this again, I will kill you." He added in a low voice. "Do you understand brother? I will kill you." He dropped Arrian to the floor in a lump and stamped from the room. Arrian cried yet again, this time curling himself into a ball beside the broken keyboard. He cried as though his heart was breaking and indeed he thought it was; the one person he wanted most to emulate thrust him away with a warning not to bother his older brother again. Arrian stopped sobbing and sat up.

Brother! Zander called him brother!

****

"I can get there by myself." Zander stood again before his father, arms folded. "I've flown hundreds of times over millions of light miles and I don't need you to monitor me."

"We were just there. Why the hell do you need to go back?"

"My *brother*—the mongrel—destroyed my plans. I need to go back and re-image them. I won't be gone long."

Normally Brede would have denied him the trip alone but mention of the boy Elektra insisted was his struck the chord of anger and he looked up at Zander from where he knelt wrestling a baby water devil from the small stream outside the property. He grunted and stood up, holding it down with a boot.

"I hate these fucking things. I'm doing my part to make them extinct on this planet." He commented and looked at his son again. "Alright, go ahead. The Scythe is prepped to launch."

"That's another thing I want to talk to you about. I need

my own ship."

"No you don't."

"I'm old enough to be a pilot you know. We'll talk about it again when I return." Zander turned and walked back inside the walls of the house.

Brede closed his eyes and shook his head. He seriously considered getting a hormonal implant for his son.

****

She couldn't find it. Elektra scoured the entire property growing more and more frantic as she failed to locate the object. She stopped in the center of the huge courtyard the house surrounded and stood perplexed as Brede walked toward her, glancing at the Scythe emerging from its underground docking bay. Its hover rotors began to spin preparing for launch sequence. He watched it lift off and finally turned to her.

"Elektra, I think I need to speak with you."

"Where could I have put it?" She gazed down at the ground pressing two fingers against her lips.

"Put what? We need to talk Elektra."

"It has to be here somewhere. I just need to think—"

"*Elektra!*""

She blinked and looked up at him.

"What did you say Alekzander?"

"I said I need to talk to you." He waited for her eyes to fully focus on him. *"Now,"*

"Oh, alright."

"What the hell is wrong with you? Come *on*," he grasped her upper arm and led her back into the house.

"I misplaced something and I can't find it or remember where I put it."

"Forget that. Come with me."

She followed him into their private suite and sat down on a stone settee looking up and waiting for him to speak. She tapped a foot on the floor, impatient to return to her search. Brede stood before her, hesitating.

"I think we have a problem."

"What? What kind of problem Alekzander?"

"With our son."

Her brows drew down in slight disbelief and she waited for him to explain.

"He's—" Brede inhaled a frustrated breath. 'He's getting an attitude.'

'Oh, is that all?" Elektra smiled. "He's at the age for it Alekzander. It happens to everyone—well everyone human or part human. It'll last a year or so and then he'll mature—"

"You haven't noticed anything different?" Brede's expression changed to concerned.

"Like what? He's a teenager. It'll pass Alekzander.' She repeated and snorted out a small laugh. 'Don't you remember how I was at that age? You used to make fun of the little trinkets I loved so much."

Brede did remember. Just one of the many things he did on Earth to be ashamed of; for an instant he wondered if she still had the little compact world and her precious HoloLocket: the two things she ever owned. Elektra stood and placed a hand on his forearm.

'You okay now?" she looked up into his eyes. "No more parental paranoia?"

"Listen," Brede said. "If he ever gets…disrespectful toward you do two things: one, find me so I can kick the shit out of him and two, remember what you just said." He gazed back into her eyes. Elektra shook her head pursing her lips as if he spoke something absurd.

"He's my son Alekzander. He loves me. He might get a little difficult as you say but I'm sure he wouldn't mean anything really. I remember what it was like to be all hormonal. It's not something you can control—unless you want to implant a regulator into him. I've heard they work better now than they used to; of course I never had any way to get one—I had to suffer through it!" She laughed again and Brede forced himself not to flinch at the memory. She tucked her arm into his and led him back to the living quarters.

****

"You let him go *alone*?" Once again Elektra stood before Brede aghast and furious. "Anything could happen to him! Do you want to lose him *again*?"

"He needs to grow up. He's almost a man. You cannot keep him a child forever."

"He *is* a child Alekzander. You should have gone with him!"

"We cannot live in fear Elektra. If he is to survive he needs to experience things on his own. If you keep coddling him he'll never survive. I am not happy about this either but he has to be a man."

"Man," Elektra said with bitterness. "Men have never done anything but abuse me. I'd rather he stay a child."

"He would have to die to accomplish that. Do not wish it upon him."

Her face blanched white and she swallowed with difficulty unable to speak. Brede walked to her. He grasped her upper arms gently and pulled her to him.

"And I haven't told you the worst part," he smiled, "He wants his own ship."

She couldn't help it; she burst into laughter and then shook her head.

"I can't help it Alekzander," she said sobering. "He's my baby—my first-born. I can't stop worrying about him. Especially after what happened—"

"I told you I'm not happy about it either but he needs to prove something to himself. He needs to prove to himself he's a man. If he doesn't he'll end up frustrated and unhappy forever and then we *will* have to worry. He'll be fine. He's been flying since he was six or seven; since I made him take over the Scythe by himself. It terrified him enough to make him a good pilot—" he stopped when he saw her expression. "Oops. Something a woman shouldn't know about."

"I've done things that any man would be afraid to do, including killing more than a few of them. Sometimes I think you still see me as a little girl."

"Alright, a *mother* shouldn't know about," he amended. He smiled again. "And it would be nice to see you as a little girl again. Before all of this happened."

"Nice? For you—it wasn't that much fun for me. I had to steal everything I had—even my clothes and shoes, not to mention food. And when I wasn't doing that I was scheming up ways to make you notice me, mostly by lying. I thought if I made up stories about myself it would make me seem important, maybe enough to make you like me. But you saw through every one of them. And you didn't mind exposing them either. I just wanted you to like me so badly, especially as a girl." She stopped and looked away for a moment, fighting off tears. When she got control of her voice she continued. "Honestly Alekzander there were days I actually believed that if I got run down by an Annihilator you wouldn't even notice."

"I'd have noticed."

"I didn't think so. And…it just got worse as I got older." She swallowed again. "I wanted you so badly I didn't know what to do. So when I heard you'd been hired for some job for Narita I decided to stow away and surprise you. I thought that if I could just sleep with you that you would want me too; that you would have to see how much I—" Elektra stopped and they gazed into each other's eyes, remembering a similar conversation. She shook her head and looked down. "I was stupid. You never wanted me. You were so surprised when I jumped ship and went back to New Cairo—you couldn't figure out why I wanted to leave. I couldn't deal with it—that you didn't even know *why* I wanted off the Scythe—I didn't want to face it anymore but I had to. I realized that no matter what I did, how hard I tried you would never want me." She looked up and gave him a crooked laugh. "You never mentioned it again. I knew you forgot all about it. For you it never happened. Then, when Zander was born, I was so happy—happier than I'd ever been in my miserable life. Not only did I finally have someone that actually loved and needed me, I had a little version of you too. When you came back and took him—"

"Elektra—"

"I'm sorry." She shook her head one last time mostly for herself. "This is all in the past. It's history Alekzander. None of it matters anymore. I'm just glad that he's alright." She tried to pull her arms from his grasp. "I need to stop talking and thinking about it. It brings up bad memories and besides I'm not trying to dump guilt on your head by confessing now. You never owed me anything." Elektra's face grew grim and she managed to wriggle out of his hands. "I don't know how to do this Alekzander." She turned away from him but he wrapped his arms around her shoulders from behind.

"Do what?"

"Have a—an adult relationship with you. We never had that type of relationship so I'm not very good at it. I don't even know that we have a relationship at all now." Elektra paused. "Let me go. I need to look for something." She pulled away and walked out the door.

CHAPTER FIFTEEN

He entered orbit at night, dropping down into the atmosphere where he dipped and dived between the high building towers and other space craft in search of a general docking bay without success. In the night the stars and the blinking space craft appeared interchangeable; the only way to distinguish them was their movement or lack of it. The ships moved and the stars didn't; the craft kept the sky busy and alive as they landed and launched by the thousands. He buzzed the night streets of New Cairo before remembering his father still owned the small bay on the ground and headed toward it. Maneuvering it inside proved easy; he'd piloted the Scythe so many times he barely thought about it.

Zander hesitated a moment in the still unfamiliar environment of New Cairo. A desire to see where his mother lived struck him and he headed on foot for the souk Brede took him to, hoping he could find information without attracting too much attention. He couldn't. Not dressed as he was; the formal old-fashioned clothing with spiked out box braids. Standing head and shoulders above everyone else didn't help either.

Halfway through the marketplace, lit with warm, rare electric lights strung overhead and real candles still made by the poorest workers the merchants could hire, Zander stopped at a random booth selling rugs and textiles. He waited politely until the young woman finished a transaction and turned to him.

"Yes, what do you want?" she asked in thick accent eyeing him with suspicion.

"I need some information actually.' He leaned over the table. "I need to know where the City of the Dead is—"

He didn't get further. Her eyes widened in terror and she backed away from him and into the interior of the room behind the booth. A moment later an older man emerged wearing an angry expression.

"What is it that you want?" he asked.

"The City of the Dead—"

"No one visits the Cities of the Dead except those who live there. What do you want with it in the night?"

"I want to find..." Zander hesitated thinking how to explain. "Someone I know used to live there. I want to see it for myself."

"Pah!" the man turned his chin a little and spit. "Only trouble comes from the corrupt dead. You would be wise to leave the dead to their own."

Zander pressed down a frustrated response.

"So you won't tell me where it is?"

"No one here will tell you. Now go. The souk is ended for the night. Good bye." The man reached up and began yanking the tent cloth from its poles. He called over his shoulder in a language Zander didn't understand and the girl appeared again, skittish when she looked at him, hoisting armfuls of material and carrying them back and forth into the building. With every trip she stared at him longer, not so skittish but curious and intrigued until she finally ventured a tiny smile at him. Zander blinked at her then ignored her, glancing about the rest of the marketplace street where merchants were indeed rolling up their booths, pointedly ignoring him and he realized the man spoke the truth. He knew he could get no information from them.

Fine then damn you all! There are faster and easier ways to find the cemeteries. I'm wasting time thinking you backward fools wouldn't have superstitions about everything. I'll pull it up on the tracker in the morning.

He spun and walked out of the souk and headed toward the Menkare on foot, a twenty minute walk. He could sleep in it for the night and locate the cemetery in the morning. He would be safe enough until dawn, patting the weapon he'd secretly purloined from his father. His reactions surpassed Brede's by three times the speed and five times the accuracy and he knew it; hours of practicing made it so. He smiled to himself as he climbed the stairs that led from the inner courtyard up along the wall to the upper floor of the Menkare where the bedrooms stood. He waved the LEDs into life but they gave off only faint light.

She sat in the center of the old bed smiling, waiting for him. The moonlight beaming in from the blasted away ceiling made a halo around her head.

Zander stopped mid-step.

"What the hell are you doing here?"

****

"What is this?" Brede sat down at the table and looked at Colin. "You've gone foppish on me again. I thought you were over that," He gave his brother a sardonic grin.

"What? Oh, the jewels? What the hell am I supposed to do with them? I'm still the overseer of Thebes Two. I have to act the part."

"I don't think you're acting."

"I am. What do you think I should do with them?"

"Sell them. Build a home here. I don't know. Make up your damned mind—are you staying on Earth or coming back here?"

"I see no reason to have to choose Alekzander. I have the best of both worlds so to speak."

"Agh! You are a fop. Besides what constitutes wealth on Earth doesn't here. Power—physical power—is what counts here."

"Yes, well…" Colin leaned back in his own chair, twisting a ring on his finger.

"You're not still blaming me for the past are you? Get over that please."

"I was thinking of the future Alekzander. About Zander actually—no hear me out. Elektra told me to tell you this so I am. I never told you but I am very happy to have a nephew and happier that he's now alive and healthy. I know you gave him the Menkare but I don't know if he plans to or you plan to let him live there."

"What are you saying Colin?"

"As I have no children I could help him…"

"I'm sorry about that too—"

"It doesn't matter now. I'd still like to help him."

"Do what? I doubt my son has any political ambitions…at least not right now." Brede said.

"Well, no not necessarily. But you know, just…generally. I like the boy. He's so much like you at that age."

"I don't know whether to thank you or shoot you for that remark."

"I mean it as a compliment."

"Again I don't know which to do. I don't know if I want him like me."

"He's already there in case you hadn't noticed."

"Unfortunately I have. I've been doing a lot of thinking lately and it hasn't been an enjoyable experience."

"Yes I know. Elektra told me."

Brede narrowed his eyes at his brother.

"Elektra? Why would you and she be discussing me?"

"We're not conspiring against you Brother. She's noticed your change and I don't think she's too happy about it herself."

"And she told you this?"

"Yes. I think that neither one of you knows how to deal with a real relationship. It's as if you're searching but you can't find one another."

"Mm," Brede rubbed his hand over his chin. He gazed at

nothing in particular. Perhaps Colin was right for once. He looked at his brother. "You know I thought about asking—" Brede cut himself off.

"Asking?" Colin leaned forward.

"Nothing, it's an idiotic idea, very idiotic," he added.

"Well it's up to you whatever the hell it is. I've got to go. I'm making a trip to Earth myself. Perhaps I'll run into Zander while we're both there." Colin stood and stuck out a ringed hand to Brede. Brede took it, grasping his brother's forearm as well.

"Take care of yourself Colin."

"Oh, I will." He gave Brede a grim smile. "I always do."

****

"What does it matter how I got it? I got it that's what counts." Zander stood across from Brede and crossed his arms over his chest.

"No that is not what counts. What counts is that I never gave you permission to buy your own ship and that I want to know how you paid for it."

"You know, I've passed all the requirements and am fully authorized to pilot. I'm nearly fourteen years old Father."

"You still—"

"It's done Father. I have a ship, it's paid for and it has a name."

"Where did you get the money Zander?"

"I didn't do anything illegal if that's what you're thinking. I told you it doesn't matter. It is done." He spun and walked out of the room, leaving Brede watching him. Brede walked to the window and gazed out at the ship Zander registered under the name of The Tryad. It was a damned expensive one; one that a fourteen year old with no job should not own. It outdid the Scythe in levels of luxury by hundreds and possessed tremendous power with three monstrous fuel cells at each of its three angles: one in front two at each point in the back. What the hell Zander did to pay for it or get money to pay for it Brede couldn't imagine. Who, other than

Elektra, would give in and help the spoiled son purchase his own ship? Elektra would cave immediately but she didn't have money of her own...did she?

Brede left the hangar and prowled the house for her. If Elektra aided their son in some way, he'd make sure she'd both regret it and never do it again. He found her in the far wing of the fortress, the one used only by her and the bastard she birthed.

"Leave brat." He didn't look at Arrian but the boy ran from the room immediately.

"Do you have to treat him like that Alekzander?" Elektra sighed and rose from her chair.

"I treat him as what he is. However that is no matter now. I want to speak to you about Zander."

"What is it now?"

"He has a ship of his own. I want to know how he got it."

"I thought *you* gave him the money for it!"

They stared at one another.

"Well, then how the hell did he get it?" Elektra finally broke the silence. She frowned in anger.

"I don't know and he refuses to tell me. I thought perhaps he'd somehow talked you into it."

"I'm stupid but I'm not crazy Alekzander."

"Yes, well, that's always been debatable." He walked to the window and gazed down at the ship ignoring whatever response she gave. "How the hell did he get it?" he asked himself narrowing his eyes. He rubbed his chin between his thumb and finger. Elektra moved beside him and pressed herself against his back.

"Want *me* to find out?" She gave him her old lopsided grin.

"Eh, I doubt you can get it from him if I can't. I—"

"You threaten him with physical violence. I don't. I'm his mother I can get it out of him." She wrapped her arms around him.

"Alright," Brede sighed. He doubted anyone could get

anything out of their son that he didn't want out. "Go and try."

"Hah! You forget Alekzander getting things out of people was how I survived on Earth!"

"How could I? You never let me forget. Besides, you weren't as good as you thought you know."

"Oh! I deal with you later!"

Elektra let go and walked out of the room. Brede did not turn around. Whatever Zander was doing, if it wasn't technically illegal it was shady as hell. But what the *hell* was it?

****

"Hey that's some impressive transportation," Elektra found her son tweaking something on the Tryad. He didn't turn around when he spoke.

"Did *he* send you?" He asked.

"Yes, but that's not the only reason I'm here. I wanted to see it too. Now that I have, it is pretty impressive Zander. It's funny," she walked under the front of the ship running a hand along it.

"What's funny Mother?"

Elektra laughed a little.

"It's funny how time is Zander. I remember when you were a baby. I wasn't sure I'd ever see you old enough to drive your own ship."

"Pilot is the word Mother, not drive." He finally stopped and eyed her evenly. "Besides you weren't around most of the time when I was learning."

Elektra stopped.

"I—that wasn't my decision Zander,"

"Doesn't matter," he said. "It's fact. You weren't there."

"So you're angry at me? I told you I had no choice."

"That's what Father keeps saying."

"What?"

"That you had no choice. Apparently, you never had any choice for anything that you did or didn't do," he put his hands on his hips and his face hardened. "You had no choice but to live in filth and squalor. You had no choice but to live in a cemetery. You had no choice in being a thief and a liar and a cheat. Having no choice must have made it all easy for you." He continued glaring at her.

Her eyes widened with tears. She looked down for a moment and then up at Zander.

"Look, I understand that you're resentful. And I know we've never talked about this. I should have known to do it earlier but I was just so glad to have you back from—" she stopped and looked away again. "I guess I didn't want to deal with anything negative—"

"We don't have to talk about it now either Mother," Zander said and moved toward a power cell on the ship. "It doesn't matter. I know what I need to know about you and the past cannot be changed. It just might have been nice to know what my mother was; at least what you'll admit to," he busied himself inspecting the cell. "It also might have been nice to know that I was a bastard and still would be had not my father acknowledged me formally and publicly. It might have been nice to know that my mother was a whore—"

He didn't get any further. Elektra grasped his shoulder, spun him around and slapped him with her left hand. He hit the side of the ship and dropped to the ground on his back. Elektra gasped and dropped beside him on her knees.

"Oh God, I'm so sorry Zander! I'm so sorry! I didn't mean to hurt you, I just—I'm so sorry!" She burst into tears and touched his face with the same hand she'd struck him. He jerked away from her and scrambled to his feet.

"Don't touch me. I can see why you and Father stay together. You're both violent when someone speaks the truth." He rubbed his jaw, now rapidly bruising.

"No! No, it isn't true Zander! I never—I didn't plan for you—"

"Ah, I see. Now I'm just an unfortunate mistake that you managed to twist to your advantage."

"No!" She walked around again to face him. "I—I'm not saying this right! You were never a mistake Zander—

never. I loved the second I knew about you. Your father didn't know about you until he kill—until he came to look for me. He took you away from me. I couldn't do anything about it. I even took you and hid you but he found us—I went to prison—I did anything I had to, to get to you—"

"Stop lying Mother. I know that's hard for you since it's what you do best or second best—"

Again he got no further. From behind Brede picked him up off the ground and pressed his head against a rotor blade.

"I thought I told you not to do that," he said through gritted teeth.

"Go ahead. Kill me." Zander's expression didn't change.

'Don't tempt me boy."

"Alekzander! Stop it! *Stop it!*" Elektra thrust an arm between them. "He doesn't understand! He doesn't understand how it was for me—for us—"

"No. He doesn't. He's a spoiled fucking brat who's never had to sweat for one fucking thing in his fucking life. I want you off this property by tonight. You take your shit and get the fuck off this planet. I don't want to see you again—"

"No!" Elektra wiggled herself between them and stared into Brede's eyes. "Alekzander, I told you, he's young and he's hormonal and rebellious that's all this is. And it's true, I did hit him. I'm sorry my baby," she turned to Zander who remained expressionless. "I'm so sorry. Alekzander, please stop it. I can't live through losing him again, I can't."

"No woman." Brede picked her up and set her down a foot or two away from them then turned back to his son. *"She—"* He pointed at Elektra. "Is the only reason you are still breathing. You think you are a man? You don't even know what that means. You can return once you learn—if you learn. Once you stand on your own. Until that time comes stay off my fucking planet."

"You think I can't?" Zander's voice changed to a rebellious little boy for an instant. Then he shrugged his clothes to compose himself. "I can Father. I assure you of that. The Tryad completes everything I need to survive. I don't need you—either of you. Goodbye." He walked into the house leaving his parents to gaze after him.

"Where will he go Alekzander?" Elektra asked face pale. 'What if he doesn't come back? This is all my fault—I shouldn't have asked about the ship—I shouldn't have hit him but—"

"You should have hit him a long time ago. Shit *I* should have hit him for that matter. In fact, I did. Guess it wasn't hard enough. He'll be back, I promise you that Elektra. To spite us if nothing else," he walked a pace past her then paused, a hand out to her. "Come. He'll be back." Brede took her hand, ignoring its trembling and chill. He hoped he was right.

CHAPTER SIXTEEN

"I'm raising my percentage of the profits thirty percent." Zander sat on the old throne-like chair on the dais of the main room of the Menkare his chin resting on his hand. He stared at his employees without expression.

"You cannot do that!" One of them exclaimed. "We barely make a living as it is! To take thirty percent more will ruin us!"

"I can and I will. I am sure if you work hard, hard enough that is, you'll make a nice profit and still make my share easily."

'But Sir you cannot do this! We work hard—so hard—for not only ourselves and our families but you too—"

"Don't bother being sycophants. I know that you skim from the top of the profits so do not take me for a fool by including me as part of your pitiful lives. Do your children not work to help you?"

"Our children are in school, what there is left of it. They cannot work—"

"Yes they can. If I make petition to the government they will allow your children to work to assist you. They will just have to study a bit more than they probably do now. Either way, you will make your money and mine. There is no more discussion. It is done." He glared at them until they backed away one by one, expressions of fear covering their faces.

He did not see them congregate between the mechanical camels that he owned as they worked for him in the New Cairo tourist trade, speaking as they readied the machines to carry tourists over the desert to the pyramids and Sphinx. He at least was not that tyrannical—yet.

"He will destroy us!" one of them whispered to the others.

"Why would he do that? He won't do the work himself." Another said.

A third man spoke.

"Because hiring robotic tour guides will give him all the profits, not just sixty percent, that's why!"

"He wouldn't! He can't! Only we can curry the favor of the tourists. They won't want to be spoken to by voices that have no life in them."

"He has as little life in him as do they!" Yet another man spoke and the others laughed darkly in agreement. "He has as much emotion as this droid. He is as cold as Akbar here!" He touched the rigid nose of the dead camel.

"He already has many enemies for such a young man. He should take care he does not collect more," the only man who had not spoken said. "If he does not want to die a young man."

All nodded in agreement and then keyed their phony camels into life with the keyboards hidden under the saddles and howdahs. The mechanical animals beeped and buzzed and squealed into life, shaking their heads, jangling sounds coming from both their speaker accoutrements outside and their sound effects on the inside. They snorted out stench-filled chemical breaths and snot and chewed invisible cud that could be spat out at unsuspecting tourists to give them an authentic thrill of ancient Egypt.

Inside the Menkare, Zander dispensed thinking about his employees and the business he ran competently. A different business occupied him now.

"I see you are conducting your enterprise well, Prince."

She gave him a small smile.

"I detest when you call me that. It sounds demeaning."

"Everyone else considers it a term of endearment, my prince."

"I do not. My name is Zander. You could try that."

"I shall call you what I like. I have the right. Besides, if you cared for me you would want me to."

"I do care for you."

"Well then, show me."

****

"Colin?" Elektra's voice was barely a whisper though he could see her with crystal clarity.

"What's up honey?"

"I need a favor from you. A big one."

"Elektra just name it."

"I—I want you to keep an eye on Zander."

"Okay but it will be a little difficult from here."

"No. He's there on Earth." She made a small frustrated sound. 'He and Alekzander got into a fight after I hit him—"

"You hit Alekzander? Good for you!"

"No! I hit Zander. We were arguing and he said something and I just lost my temper. Alekzander went berserk and kicked him out of the property and off the planet. I haven't heard from Zander in almost a year. I don't know where he is or how he's doing. I'm going crazy over this. Would you help me?"

"You could just contact him and ask."

"No, he was angry too—at both of us. I don't think he'd talk to me. I just need to know he's alright, that's all."

"What about my brother?"

"*No!* Alekzander can't know about this. He wants me to ignore it all. He says that Zander will learn about life and come crawling back. But I can't—I can't. Please Colin, please?"

"Alright Sweetheart, I'll take care of it. Do you know where he might be staying?" He watched her bite her lip.

"He—Alekzander gave him the Menkare in New Cairo. Do you know where that's at?"

"Yes. I'll find him don't worry. I'll call you when I—"

"No! I'll call you. If you call here too often Alekzander will be suspicious."

"We're not doing anything wrong."

"I know but you know him Colin. Everything has to be his way. And right now his way is to abandon Zander to force him to live on his own and grow up."

"Okay, don't worry. Give me a few days and call me back. Good enough?"

"Yes, of course. I can't ever thank you enough Colin."

"Nothing to thank me for Elektra, I'll talk to you soon. Bye sweetie."

Colin watched the screen image fade, Elektra's face drawn tight with worry. He wished he could kick both Alekzander's and his nephew's asses. He flipped on the com and called his personal staff to the top floor of the building.

****

Brede found it harder than Elektra knew to ignore the absence of his son. Still he'd be damned before he caved first. He walked the house restlessly, trailed at times by Arrian who followed him closely thinking himself unobserved. The boy was about as artful at that as Elektra had been: neither was as good as they liked to believe. He resisted turning and growling at the child, for some reason finding it humorous. When he stopped at the quad so did Arrian. Brede paused a moment, thinking of Zander and forcing himself to remember that his son needed to grow up and learn some humility—not that he himself ever learned it—but Zander needed to badly.

"Where is my brover? Did him run away from home?"

Brede blinked and turned to face the little boy, surprised by his boldness.

God he's so like Elektra.

"No. He did not run away. I sent him away."

"Why? Him is my brover and him is your son too. Why did you send him away? Was him bad?"

"Well...yes. He was behaving very badly and I told him to...go away until he learned some respect for his mother."

Arrian's eyes widened in shock.

"Him was bad for my mother?"

"Yes. He was very bad. He made your mother cry. I told him to leave until he learns what it means to be a man."

"Him said that I an a baby and that I an not a man." His chin stuck out like Elektra's.

A hard laugh escaped Brede.

"Yes, well right now you're more of a man than he is."

Arrian's eyes grew wider.

"I an a man?"

"Right now yes."

They locked eyes a moment and Brede waited for the question. Before the boy could ask it he changed his mind.

"You ask too many questions brat. Get out of my sight. And you'd better be good to your mother."

"I an a man and I *an* good to my Mommy!" Arrian squeaked breaking into a run in the opposite direction.

When I am a man I will not make my Mommy cry.

You will Zander.

I won't ever! I'm not like you. I'm not mean.

You are like me regardless. Whether you like it or not. And one day you will find that you have another side, like me, that is different from a man. A side that likes to hurt just because he can do it.

"Damn you Zander." Brede shook off the memory and walked back inside. "God damn you...and me."

****

Colin flipped on the Comcast screen and gave Elektra a smile.

"You're early."

"I waited nearly three weeks. Did you find out anything?"

"He's living at the Menkare and doing fairly well. He's not sick or in trouble. In fact I think he has a job."

"Zander has a *job*? What kind of job?"

Your son's running the god damned fake camel tourist racket.

"I think it's something with tourism, I'm not really sure. I need a little more time if that's okay Elektra."

"Of course it is Colin! I'm just so glad to hear he's alright," her shoulders dropped as she sighed.

"Look I'm going to try and contact him just to be sure everything is kosher to use an ancient phrase so give me another month or so before you contact me again okay?"

"Yes I will. You'll let me know if he needs anything."

"Yes. Are you or Alekzander giving him money?"

"No, I don't have any and I'm sure Alekzander isn't giving him a credit. Why do you ask?"

"I just want to know where he stands when I talk to him, that's all. I don't want to insult him or hurt his pride. He's still just a teenager," Colin held in his own sigh.

A teenager with a massive fucking ego and tight ass personality.

"Oh, right. Thanks so very much for being so good Colin. Like I said, I can never repay you."

"And like I've said, there is no need. He's my relative too you know. He's my nephew. This is what I'm supposed to do. I'll talk to you later Elektra. Hey," Colin waited until she sat back down at her own comscreen. "Is that new?"

"What? This?" Elektra's eyes widened and she glanced down at her clothes. "Yes. Alekzander insisted," she laughed. "He says since I don't live in a cemetery anymore I shouldn't dress like it!"

Ouch. What a crappy hand you were dealt Elektra. And what a son of a bitch you love.

"Very nice Sweetheart," he told her. "You look beautiful. Alekzander is an idiot if he doesn't say the same thing."

"You're very sweet to me Colin. I'm glad you are in my—our—life. I'll call you in two months is that okay?"

"Perfect. See you then. Take care of yourself."

He sat back and stared at the blank screen for a moment,

chin on hand. So, if neither Alekzander nor Elektra was giving him money, where was Zander getting it? What or *who* was he doing to be able to buy into or buy out the extremely corrupt tourist racket in New Cairo? Colin unlike Elektra was not blind where the boy was concerned. His nephew might be young but he was shrewder than most adults including his mother who hustled to stay alive on the streets of the city. But he was still a kid and like most kids—human kids—he still wasn't mature enough to resist entanglement either personal or professional. Colin's own minions brought back what they gleaned from the outside of Menkare along with the information that the place was locked down tighter than the New Cairo mint. No one went in and no one left most of the time; those rare times someone did, it was with the utmost care for privacy and anyone tempted to spill any secrets was dealt with summarily. Colin debated whether to demand an audience at the Menkare for a few moments then made a decision. He shook his head over the situation then headed toward his own bed and whatever woman from his harem decided to join him there.

****

"It's about damned time," was all Alekzander said when Elektra paraded her new clothes before him.

"Don't you like them?" she asked stopping movement.

"I prefer you without clothing. But anything is better than that jumpsuit or those grey skirt things."

"Well I couldn't afford anything else back then if you don't remember!" she snapped and stomped from the room.

Alekzander pressed his thumb and finger into his eyelids.

"Woman, if I didn't—agh!" he made fake fists and then stood up. He followed her and found her pulling off the new shoes she'd bought as well.

"Elektra I'm sor—"

"It's alright Alekzander." She refused to look at him. "Here! You can take your damned clothes!" She flung a shoe toward him, missing his head by a centimeter. He ducked reflexively and then walked toward her. The only other time she'd been this angry was when she'd abandoned him after their fateful first sexual contact. He didn't know if he hated or loved that memory.

"I said or tried to say I'm sorry. I didn't mean to insult you. I'm just—well I guess I'm trying to make up for the past. I want you to feel happy here. I want you to forget Cairo and understand that you don't have to live like that anymore that's all. I thought you might like to have new things to do so. You said that you don't know how to have an adult relationship with me. Well, I'm no good at having a relationship at all."

"No," she hobbled toward him with one shoe still on and flung her arms around him. "It's me. I don't know why I'm acting this way. I am happy here Alekzander. Really I am. You know it's funny but Colin said something a while ago about you realizing your emotions. I think maybe he's right."

Without warning he grasped her shoulders and held her away to look at her.

"Why are you constantly talking to my brother? Your relationship is with me not him."

"It was a long time ago Alekzander. We were talking about you and me—"

"*Why?* Your fucking relationship is with *me*! If you want to talk about it you'll talk to me. Do you understand Elektra?"

"Well, yes I do but—"

"No more. I won't tolerate it. *Do you understand me Elektra?*"

"But what if—" She stopped mid-sentence at his expression. "Alright, I understand."

"Good goddamn it. Put your fucking shoe back on." He spun and walked out of the room.

****

"Zander?" Colin did his best to appear surprised. In reality he placed surveillance around every inch of the Menkare that he could get close to as well as mini-satellites that hovered just inside Earth orbit eyeing ship activity though there was little of it. He watched his nephew's face register real surprise.

"Colin? What are you doing in New Cairo? Normally you spend most of the time in Thebes Two."

"I had some minor business to take care of here. Now that it's concluded I'm about to enjoy lunch. Why don't you join me?" He held out an expansive arm.

"I really shouldn't. I've got—"

"Come on! I'll pay and you can suggest somewhere since as you say I'm rarely here. Come on, talk to your old uncle," Colin repeated before Zander could hesitate further.

"Well."

"Come on." Colin said for the third time. "I haven't seen you in ages!" He placed an arm around the boy's shoulder. Zander breathed out a deep sigh.

"Alright Uncle," he said. "What are you in the mood for?" Zander shot a glance at someone Colin didn't see. "There's the souk," he suggested.

"Anywhere more private?"

"There are restaurants downtown but they're expensive."

"When has that ever been my concern Zander?"

"It's your money."

An hour later they sat in a private booth lit in blue and purple chromalights sipping excellent espresso. Colin set his cup down and leaned back against his seat. He spread his arms over the back of it and gave Zander an earnest gaze.

"What are you doing here? Visiting?"

Zander barked out a hard laugh reminiscent of Alekzander's.

"Hardly Uncle. I live here now, full time."

"Why? Why not stay with your parents? You're barely eighteen."

"It was...*time* to go. Besides my father gave me the piece of property I live in now. It's not as if I'm homeless." He laughed again this time grimly.

"What are you doing for money? Is your father helping out?"

Zander snorted, humor gone.

"Him? No. I make my own money. I don't need him." For a brief moment Zander's expression changed to a resentful teenager.

"I can see that. But what are you doing?"

"I'm learning about running a business."

"What business?"

"Just business, that's all. Why are you asking?" Zander paused. "Did *he* send you?"

"No." Colin said truthfully. He knew his nephew wouldn't think of Elektra. "I'm asking because I can help you if you need it."

"In terms of what?"

"Well, if you need a job or..." He leaned toward Zander. "I mean, I *am* the Overlord of Thebes. If you like I can help you if you have any interest in politics—ah—" he held a hand up when Zander moved to protest. "You might not be interested right now, but think about it. I can practically pave your way with gold Zander. In fact I can offer you a position right now."

Zander looked at him with an expression that told Colin his nephew thought him hopelessly out of touch. At last he sat back himself.

"Thank you Colin. It's very kind of you but I prefer to work independently."

"So does your father."

The boy shot him a look of hatred and then said stiffly. "I am *not* my father."

"Yes, I can see that as well Zander. That's why I thought you might be interested in politics or government. Plus, I'm curious as to what business you're learning and how you came to have enough seed money to start one."

"I—met someone on the way back from the souk. A business mentor who thought I had potential."

"So you have a business relationship? I trust you know enough not to mix business and pleasure Zander."

"Really Uncle, do you think I'm an idiot? I know what

I'm doing." Zander sat up and waved a hand over the holosign for the table to be cleared. A droid waiter hummed toward them and Colin pressed his palm against the sig station. Clearly the lunch was over.

"Alright then nephew. But keep in mind I am here should you ever need anything. All you have to do is call. And you might show a bit of respect for your uncle by reciprocating with dinner at the Menkare at some point," Colin grinned. Zander responded with a silent wan smile. "I have faith in you Zander," he added. "I know you're not foolish. You're just young and need a little more experience that's all. I know you can do things on your own and I know you'll do the right thing. Oh, by the way, you might call your mother. She's probably hysterical over you by now."

"Right. My mother."

Colin experienced an inner thrill of apprehension at Zander's tone. Apprehension over what he didn't know. He looked away from Zander's curled lip and shook himself down internally and held out a hand to the boy.

"Take care of yourself Zander."

"Yes. I will. Thank you for lunch Uncle." Zander pumped his hand twice and turned away toward the numerous elevators that constantly shot up and down in the building. He did not look back.

****

After the lunch with Zander, Colin found himself disconcerted. Something was definitely going on with his nephew but what it might be he had no idea. Someone backed the boy financially and Colin planned on finding out whom even if he had to do it himself. He convened his employees and servants and grilled them before making the decision.

"I need to know every single person that lives or works or is in contact with my nephew and whoever is living there with him."

"We would like to know that very information

ourselves," they told him. "When he leaves his ship emerges from somewhere beneath the Menkare —he has revamped the entire building—only the façade' is left and most of the interior décor."

"And you have no idea who is feeding him money?"

"No idea whatsoever."

"You must know who works there and comes and goes," Colin insisted. "You should have ingratiated yourselves by now."

"We have tried. Their loyalty is bought with fear, not affection." Another man said.

"Could they recognize you?" He asked them.

"We have all tried to get in; most likely they could recognize us easily."

"Then I will proceed from here myself. Thank you."

Once they left, Colin walked to his window that looked out over Thebes Two and watched the buildings standing at terrifying heights over the city. He wished he'd thought about sending in women first; they could more easily blend with the staff and if needed could zero in on Zander himself…assuming his nephew preferred women. Colin smirked. If Zander continued as the incarnation of his father, he would prefer them a little too much. And that could be downfall of them both.

****

Zander inspected a mech-camel as it stood inanimate. He flipped open the lock on the jaw and pulled it down to see the tubing that provided stinking fake phlegm to spray on unsuspecting tourists. Yellowed with age and wear from the desert dust but still functional, he tugged them and then thrust his hand up behind the machine's eyes to where the brain sat. He pressed the reset and the animal's head jerked up and down, jangling the shiny false jewels hanging from its forehead. Zander removed his hand and walked to the side of the beast, unzipping the thick synthetic fur beneath the braided rugs with synthasilk tassels in dusty gold and lapis colors. The material and metal ribs parted and he inspected the containers holding liters of the chemicals that fed the mechcamels their scents & mucus via the tubes. Lastly, he walked around the back of the animal, grasping and feeling its tail then dropping it to continue to the other side. Without warning he put a boot into a stirrup and hoisted himself up on the seat.

"Well, it's uncomfortable enough," he commented to the tourist guide who watched him with nervous eyes. "That should cut down on time and provide extra for more rides. *What?*"

"The mechanical animals are old. They begin to creak loudly with unnatural sounds that make the tourists suspicious," the old brown man said.

"What do you want *me* to do about it?" Zander stared at him, wondering if the man knew his mother before he was born.

"Perhaps upgrades on some of the older ones' systems…or perhaps some new mechcamels for us to work—"

"I am not made of money. You will work these mechanical camels until they fall apart and truly need replacing. It is up to you to distract the tourists with banter, or historical information or even music if need be—must I instruct you in *everything?*" Zander swung the same long leg back over the saddle horn and jumped down from the beast. "Tell the others. *I* will decide when it is time to replace these machines, not any of you." He adjusted his collar and vest and walked away, already concerned with other things. The camel guide stared after him with an expression of frustrated fury. Once back inside the Menkare, Zander gazed out the window where Brede once stood but not staring at the same scene. His father watched his mother; he watched his workers with a hawk's eye but not without concern. She walked behind him and rested her chin on his shoulder. She nuzzled his neck a little.

"What are you looking at?"

"My camel guides. I sometimes wonder if I shouldn't give them a bit more to work with; if that might make things run more smoothly for everyone," He said but didn't respond to her touch.

"Have I taught you nothing? Perhaps you need to return to the souk as a reminder of how business *should* work."

"You know, when I first visited the souk on my own I met a shy young girl there."

"That shy young girl is gone. It is doubtful she will ever return my Prince."

"One day I will make you stop calling me that. It is annoying if not disrespectful."

"I am only teasing, well, only half teasing."

Zander sighed.

"And I am only half teasing when I say that I might try to find that shy girl again—" His sentence ended as he heard shouts and saw a figure race down the cobbled road followed close by another in the darkening evening. They tussled a moment and then the first shot away at top speed leaving the other to curse in the shadows. "Huh." Zander snorted. "Thieves, they never change. Just like my mother—"

"Your mother," she said. "You have little respect for her. Nor should you from what I know of her."

"You know nothing."

"I know enough and more than enough through you. Forget mothers and thieves for the night. Your workday is ended but you still have work this night." She grasped his hand and led him toward the bed that his father occupied once as well.

****

"Elektra?"

"Hi Colin! How is—everything?" She glanced over her shoulder and then inched closer to the screen.

"Everything's okay. Has Zander called you?"

"No why?"

"Hm, I suggested it to him—don't worry—" he said

when her face changed to fear. "I just suggested it. He has no idea we're communicating."

"Oh! That's good. If he or Alekzander found out…"

"They won't. Besides I told you we're not doing anything wrong whatsoever. If anyone's doing anything wrong it's—never mind. Anyway I've offered to help him any way I can but your son is very…I'll say stubborn so you don't get pissed at me. But he seems okay. I just want to make sure he's not into something that's over his head. I'll contact you again as soon as I can. Talk to you later, Sweetie."

"Goodbye Colin. I'll wait for your call."

The last image he saw was someone dark standing behind her.

****

Elektra snapped off the comscreen and rose to walk away.

"Who were you talking to?"

She blinked several times and then cleared her throat.

"Just—just Colin Alekzander," she said. "Just Colin."

"Why?"

"We were just…catching up with each other. That's all."

"Catching up," Brede frowned at her. "You spoke to him two days ago. What could you have to catch up on?"

"I asked him to—"

"What are you hatching with my brother bitch?" He grabbed her hair and pulled her head back. "What trouble are you plotting for me now?" He shook her hard enough to make her teeth rattle.

"Alekzander, stop hurting me!"

"I'll kill you. What are you hatching Elektra?"

"Nothing!" she squeaked. "Nothing Alekzander I swear! Like Colin says, we're not doing anything wrong!"

"That tells me you *are* doing something wrong. Now what is it?" He loosed his grip a bit.

"We're not doing anything wrong Alekzander." She repeated, pursing her lips like a child.

"I'll judge that." He moved toward her, furious again. "What—are—you—doing—with—my—brother?" He repeated, hissing through his teeth. "If you are sleeping with him or planning to I will kill you Elektra. You know that."

"Let me go Alekzander."

"Not until—"Brede stopped and shoved her back from himself. "What are you doing with him?" His voice dropped to quiet and a rush of his old icy fury flushed through him. Elektra did not know how close to death she stood.

"I—I'm afraid of what you'll do if I tell you."

"You'd better be more afraid if you don't tell me."

Elektra inhaled and then sighed.

"Okay. Okay. I asked him to do me a favor."

Brede remained unblinking. She continued.

"I asked him to..." she swallowed. "I asked him to keep an eye on Zander. That's all I swear Alekzander. I swear that's all we're doing. He's keeping tabs on Zander and keeping me updated. That's why we're always talking. I know you didn't want me to contact Zander but I had to know he's alright. I had to know." Her voice trailed off and she squeezed her eyes shut waiting for the violent response. Brede burst into laughter. She opened her eyes and stared at him.

"What? What are you laughing about?"

"I'm laughing at my own stupidity. I should have thought of that myself! What an idiot I am!"

CHAPTER SEVENTEEN

"Hello."

Brede spun around, unhappily surprised. He stared at the little boy as if he wore horns.

"Don't sneak up behind people boy. It could get you killed. If I'd had my gun you'd already be dead."

"Okay." Arrian said, unconcerned. He walked around the Scythe toward Brede. "What are you doing?"

"What does it look like I'm doing?"

"Playing."

Brede snorted.

"Hardly boy," he shook his head, trying not to smile.

"Then what are you doing?"

"Working."

"Working?" Arrian stopped and looked at him. "Do you has a job?"

"Some people would say no," again Brede forced the smile from his face.

"Why?"

"Because…they're idiots that's why,"

"What is a idiot?"

"Someone stupid."

"Why is they stupid?"

"They just are," Brede answered with frustration. "Shouldn't you be with your mother?"

"Uh uh," the little boy walked further around the ship to where Brede knelt, struggling to grind a rotor. He sat down on the ground. "I am sad," he informed Brede.

"Sad?" Brede's brows drew down. "Why would you be sad?"

"Cause Zander is gone. I doan have nobody to play with," he gave Brede a mournful gaze and a slow shake of his head. "Is you sad that Zander is gone?"

Damn kid, you can draw a bead on me...just like your mother does.

"Well, sort of," he held up the rotor blade in front of his face and inspected the razor sharp edge. "But I thought you and Zander didn't play. I thought you didn't like each other."

"I play while him does stuff. He gets mad at me but I like him. He is my brother." Arrian paused and Brede knew the question would arise again. He waited. "He says you doan want me cause I am a baby and cause I have many fathers." Arrian paused again. "My Mama says I am your son. She says me and Zander are brothers." A beat passed between them. "Am I your son too?"

Brede lowered the blade and frowned for a long moment undecided how to respond. If he upset the child he would never hear the end of it from Elektra. He gazed at Arrian. It wasn't the boy's fault his genetics were hopelessly coagulated. Children did not choose the circumstances of their birth. Elektra didn't. He didn't. And now this boy didn't. And if, as Elektra insisted, he had initiated the pregnancy then Arrian was his son like it or not. He stared into eyes like his own—not human. Unless Elektra had engaged in some sex orgy with a random group of aliens all of the men she'd slept with were human. Though, as he'd told her, his DNA ran in her now too. Either way this boy was his son. Brede continued staring at the child, still not sure what to say. Did he dare acknowledge the boy? Did he refuse to acknowledge his second son? What would happen legally if he did either? He knew how Elektra would react but what about his oldest son? Things were strained enough between the two of them and it might drive Brede and his firstborn permanently apart if Zander perceived any acknowledgement as a revenge move.

"Arrian," Brede said at length. It was the first time he'd ever said the boy's name. "You're a little too young for us to be talking about this. Besides, I need to speak with your mother first. You need to wait for a while before we do. Can you understand that?"

Arrian stared back at him, eyes unnerving Brede by reminding him of Zander. Then the child nodded.

"Then after you talk to my Mama will you tell me yes or no?"

"I don't know Arrian. It's complicated—that means there's a lot to talk and think about. And I don't know the answer at least not right now. It may take a very long time years maybe. I don't know. Do you think you can wait that long?"

If he expected impatience he got none. As if the little boy possessed an extra sentience he nodded again, more solemnly.

"Yes. I will wait."

Brede hid a shiver. The voice also resounded with Zander's seriousness and precocity.

"Then you *are* being a man about this. Now, shouldn't you go and find Elektra? Why don't you ask her when the hell dinner will be ready?"

Arrian jumped to his feet, a little boy once more.

"Okay! And I will come back and tell you!"

He ran toward the house with the speed only children achieve and disappeared inside it. Brede closed his eyes.

Elektra what have you gotten us into now? Won't you ever grow up and think things through?

He shook his head for the millionth time. She would never change, never. She'd burst back into his carefully built life, saving their son but changing all of their lives permanently, dangerously. Brede planned, built, and decided the life for himself and his son without her and when that fell apart she'd appeared unexpectedly with the shock of a second son to rearrange everything and make him think in planes unknown. And she'd done it all with the annoying spontaneity of a fifteen year old girl. He hoped he could refrain from screaming at her when they had the upcoming discussion he'd promised Arrian. He hoped even more fervently that he could refrain from killing her.

****

"Jesus *Christ*!" Colin ducked reflexively as the Tryad boomed over his head and out of orbit. Not one of his spies told him his nephew's ship was the equivalent of an old Earth muscle car. He'd been standing outside the Menkare on a nearby major street and the sound of the engines nearly knocked him against a wall.

"Where the hell did you get *that*, boy?" He eyed the space, heat waves still hovering as the Tryad shot through. "Now I *know* there's something wrong here." Colin walked toward the entrance of the Menkare and waited for the scanner to identify him. Gone were the guards who stood at attention to prevent physical entry where it was not wanted.

"What is your business with the Menkare?" The small box on the door beeped into life.

"I am a relative of the owner here, Zander Brede."

The scanner sped a red line across its tiny monitor and then stopped.

"What is your name and relationship?"

"Colin Factor, Overlord Thebes Two. Paternal uncle."

Again the tiny red line grew along the mini-screen then stopped.

"You are not on the list to be admitted Mr. Factor. Would you like to leave a message?"

"No. I want to come inside and speak with my nephew. This is official government business."

"That information will be taken into consideration at the earliest possible moment. At this time permission to enter is denied. Please leave your contact information. Thank you."

"No. I'll come back."

"Thank you Sir."

He walked back to his own ship, an unnamed government vehicle, and got inside.

"Thebes Two," he told it, eyeing the Menkare as the car sped back toward his home.

****

"Mama!" Arrian shot into the house like spitfire from a gun. "Mister Alekzander Brede wants to eat something!"

"What?" Elektra walked out of the suite and stood in the hallway frowning at her second son. "He said that to you?"

"Yes!" Arrian's voice squeaked high. "He said ask your mama when the hell dinner is ready!"

"He *said* that to you?" she repeated unable to believe it.

"Yes!" the boy squeaked again. "We were talking and he said that."

"Talking? You and Alekzander were talking. About what?"

"We were talking about Zander and me and him."

"You're not making this up?" Elektra hated to doubt him but the chances of that reality were slim.

"*No* Mama! We were talking. We were talking about being sad Zander is gone. We were talking about if I am his son."

"Honey, are you sure? You weren't taking a nap, right? You weren't dreaming? You feel okay?"

Arrian sighed as if he was nineteen instead of nine.

"No Mama. He said to ask you when the hell dinner is ready! We were talking."

Elektra pulled the boy to her and sat down on a large chair against the wall.

"Okay. Arrian, I want you to tell me everything that he said to you. Everything, okay?"

"Okay. He said he was working and people are idiots. Then I said I was sad Zander was gone cause I doan have no one to play with. Then I asked him if I was his son too and that me and Zander are brothers." He inhaled before every sentence.

"*You asked him that?*" she whispered. Elektra took a breath. "What did he say?"

"Well, he said that he didn't know and that he and you would talk and then he would tell me yes or no."

"*What?*" She placed a hand over her mouth. "Was he angry?"

"No Mama, he was nice to me. He said I was being a man for waiting for him to tell me."

"I can't believe this. You're not playing are you Arrian?"

"No! I said I would come back and tell him when the hell dinner is ready!"

"Well, that sounds like him. I'll go and tell him—"

"*No Mama!*" This time Arrian squealed outright. "No! I am going to tell him! *I am!*" He pointed at his chest.

"Alright Arrian, can I come with you?"

"Okay but *I* am going to tell him."

"Okay. Let's go." Elektra rose and grasped the boy's hand but he yanked it away. They walked down the long dark hallway toward the quad area. She stopped at the doorway and leaned against it, arms folded.

"My mama says that dinner will be ready…" Arrian glanced at her.

"Ten minutes," she said quietly.

"In ten minutes. *That's when the hell dinner will be ready!*"

Elektra clapped a hand over her mouth to squelch laughter.

Alekzander shoved the rotor blade back into place on the Scythe and glared at her.

"What the hell is so funny? It's a perfectly rational question."

"He's your son Alekzander. He even swears like you!"

"That doesn't make him my son. Besides, he picked that up just now."

"From *you*," she pointed out. "He doesn't seem to have any problem using it correctly either. If that doesn't make him your son, nothing will." Elektra shook her head.

"Boy, go into the house and let your mother and I talk." Arrian nodded and ran back into the hallway.

"Yes," Elektra said when he was out of sight. "What is this about whether he's your son and missing Zander? You spoke to Arrian about that?"

"What could I do? He bearded the old water dragon in his own pond. The question was coming at some point or another and he braved me by asking directly."

"What did you tell him? He says you told him you would talk to me and then give him an answer."

"That I did. I told him it was complicated and asked if he minded waiting years if need be. He eyed me coldly and said he would wait. I was impressed."

"You called him a man?"

"Yes."

"Alekzander you are wonderful!" She ran to him and threw her arms around him. "You made him the happiest little boy on this planet or on Earth! That's his dream you know, to be a man like you and Zander."

"Elektra, it's not that easy regardless what you think. There are and will be ramifications if I acknowledge him as my son, not to mention how Zander will react. God knows what he'll do if he thinks I'm doing it as retaliation. Even if he doesn't think that's the reason, he still might react unpleasantly."

"Zander jealous?" Elektra's eyes widened. "I don't think so. I think he loves lording it over Arrian that he's the older brother. Making it official might help their relationship."

"Nothing will help Zander's relationship with anyone. Colin thinks he's like me but I think he's worse."

"You were pretty badass at times Alekzander," she reminded him. "You killed a few people you know."

"It was a job Elektra. I didn't do it because I hated other living beings."

"You still did it."

"Yes, and look what it got me; my son killed. If you hadn't arrived with your little voodoo kit—"

"It wasn't a voodoo kit," she sighed. "It was the ankh thing from the Beket-Re vessel. I didn't know how it worked and I still don't. In fact, I can't even find it now."

"Good. Be done with that thing. I'm sorry I ever heard of it."

"That thing saved your son and brought him back. You should be concerned with putting it somewhere safe. What if we needed it again?"

"I don't want to talk about—fuck I don't even want to *think* about needing it. Let it stay lost Elektra."

"Alekzander—"

"No. You and I have to talk about Arrian. I have to think about and consider all the consequences of naming him my son. We'll talk about it tonight, after dinner. I assume he's joining us," Brede gave her a dry expression.

"Well, you practically invited him Alekzander," she laughed again and let go of him to walk back into the house, still shaking her head.

****

"I am so excited!" the woman sat beside Zander, sliding a hand up his thigh as he powered the Tryad out of Earth's orbit. "Taking me to see your mother! How did you know I wanted that for my birthday?"

"I know a lot about you," He kept his eyes on the dashboard.

"You think you do," her eyes slid toward him. "What if she doesn't approve of me?"

"Then that will be her problem won't it?"

"I doubt that she will."

"Again, it's her problem. Besides, she's no one to be judging anyone. She's just a...no one." Zander gave her a grim smile. "Unlike you."

"Then why are we going?"

"Don't you want to go?"

"I do Prince. You know that. It's my present, remember?"

"I'm piloting aren't I?"

"Agh, you're incorrigible! How long will it take to land? I need to make myself presentable."

"You are always presentable. That is why I love you."

She gave him a small, smug smile and rose, knowing that he'd never used that word before to her or anyone else. She'd finally made a crack in his armor; the first of many to come.

****

Arrian kept up a flood of conversation, only stopping to suck in large breaths to continue babbling. Even Elektra looked bleary eyed after thirty minutes. He finally had a captive audience and wasn't about to let it go.

"Does he do this all the time?" Brede asked her as he watched Arrian describe something by waving his fork in the air.

"You'd know that if you ever spent three minutes with him."

"If the answer is yes, I don't think I can."

"You've never spoken a word to him except 'get out' what do you expect? He has no one else but me and Zander."

"And Zander barely speaks at all…except to order everyone about."

Elektra didn't answer him but gazed down at her plate.

"Elektra, I know you miss him--"

"It's my fault. I shouldn't have lost my temper. I should have tried to talk to him earlier, when he was younger. But I didn't know how much he resented me."

"That was not your fault. It was my fault entirely. But still Elektra, he has no reason to resent you. He needs to grow up. He needs to have his ass kicked. I should have done it myself but I was afraid that I would kill him. He's too much like me."

"What if I never see him again? What if he never comes back?"

"You'll see him again I assure you of that. He'll be back. Forget that for now Elektra. There's something else I want to talk to you about. I've been thinking—"

He got no further. The house shook and the power grids flickered from a rumbling boom. Both jumped to standing and Elektra grasped Arrian's hand by instinct and held him close to her as she followed Brede to the launch pad. They watched the Tryad hover and then drift down to a soft landing. It docked easily and the pedestal lowered down into the underground bays. Elektra turned to Arrian and pointed to the house. "Go to your room," she said. "You can come out later."

"Is it Zander?"

"I'm sure it is but you need to let Mommy and Daddy talk to him first okay? I promise you can come out later." He frowned and sauntered away, stopping every few seconds to inspect the floor, a speck on the wall, anything to delay removing himself from the area.

"Arrian," Brede's voice warned him but he did not look at the boy who broke into a run toward his room at his name. "How the hell did you raise Zander for the first five years?" He added with a glance at Elektra.

"Mother?" Zander's own voice prevented her from answering. "Father?" Still in his formal dress he walked toward them. "I hope you don't mind our paying an unannounced visit." He kept his tone carefully neutral.

"Zander—"Elektra moved but stopped when Brede held an arm out toward her.

"Our?" He eyed his son.

"Well, yes. I've brought someone along. It's her birthday and I promised I'd bring her here to see you."

"Her?" Even Elektra frowned.

"Yes," Zander stopped and half-turned, holding out his own arm to beckon someone.

Alekzander Brede's face had never paled in his life. It did so now out of sheer astonishment.

"Well, well, well. I see you've made good use of my money, Alekzander."

"*Narita?*"

She shoved her way past Zander and stood before Brede. She gave him an ugly red smile.

"You're dead."

"I *was* dead. But now I'm alive."

"How..." Elektra moved to Brede's side.

"Remember this little trinket?" Narita pulled the ankh from somewhere and held it up. "I thank you Elektra for finding it and making it possible for Zander to give it to me. As for how, well, when you dumped me out in open space Alekzander, someone happened by who...managed to work some science magic...and here I am! Seems you only shot out my heart, something completely replaceable. Next time aim for something they can't regenerate in a lab." She glared at Elektra. "I see you've been enjoying my money as well, thief. But then what could I expect from someone like you? I hope you'll enjoy returning to the streets as much as you've enjoyed all this."

"You know them?" Zander managed staring at her as if she was a poisonous insect.

"Yes. I know them extremely well, especially your father. I shared the same bed with him as with you."

A strangling sound emerged from Elektra.

"You stay away from my son."

Brede reached out to grasp her but she wrenched her arm away and moved toward Narita who laughed.

"I have to say, that in this case, the son is better than the father!"

"Remember *this*?" Elektra held up her left hand, the torn flesh and red ball still exposed.

She reached out, clutching Narita's throat cutting off her breathing and laughter. She squeezed slowly tightening her grip. Narita's eyes bulged and she struggled for air making hideous gurgling sounds. "You—stay—away—from—my—son—*bitch!*"

"Elektra," Brede said but did not move.

"Mother! *Mother!*" Zander shoved between them, panicked. "You're killing her! Stop it! You'll kill her! Stop it!

Mother!"

A quick burst of fire jerked Elektra back and she looked down at a smoking hole in her chest. Her hands dropped and she looked back up at Zander whose gun dangled in his hand. They stared at each other and Elektra reached to touch his face with her right hand before she staggered back a few feet farther and dropped to the floor, dragging in breaths.

Only Narita retained presence of mind. She laughed again, loud and vulgar and hard, hands on hips, her permanent stance. She continued laughing until her eyes spewed forward out of her head like eggs scrambling and she dropped to the floor herself jerking as her body died once again.

"Well, well, well. I guess you were right brother." Colin mocked her then lowered his own gun. "I wish I'd listened to you a lot earlier."

He reached out and held Zander back as Brede blinked into reality and knelt beside Elektra. He lifted her in his arms, unable to speak.

"Alekzander," Elektra said. "I never told you." Her eyes fluttered shut then opened again. "Alekzander, I…"

"No!" Brede found his voice and lifted her higher. "No, wait Elektra! Wait, please," He held her head with one hand and patted his chest down seeking something. "Please, wait," he told her again, finding what he wanted. He pulled something out and took her limp hand gently. He slid a ring of Amphidyte on her finger and cradled her hand against his face.

How long he held her and rocked them both Brede had no idea. Time lost meaning, everything lost meaning; everything but the fact that Elektra was gone and that it was too late. Too late to do anything, say anything. Even the frozen emptiness he'd felt over Zander was gone; in its place numbing blankness. Thoughts refused to form even when his son dropped to his knees and half crawled toward Elektra's body. The teen reached out and touched her hair gently.

"Mommy? I'm sorry I hurt you Mommy. I'm sorry I

made you cry. I'm sorry, I'm so sorry." He looked at Brede eyes wide and crazed. "I killed my Mommy."

Still Brede could do nothing. Colin stepped toward them and jerked Zander to his feet.

"Come on," he said.

"But my Mommy…"

"It's too late to do anything about that now Zander. You need to be away from this. Come." He ignored the teen's weak protests and pushed him through the doorway, pausing to glance at Brede and then shook his head.

What a starcluster fuck.

****

Meaning ended and time stopped for Alekzander Brede. It mattered not that his son had regressed back into the insane safety of childhood or that his brother killed the woman he loved to save them both. Nothing mattered other than the fact that his most inconceivable fear became concrete hard reality and that he'd waited too long. Too long to tell Elektra he loved her, too long to put the ring on her, too long to stop her from being killed when he could have easily done so. All that mattered was that she lay dead in his arms and all that was left for him now was to rock her endlessly, pointlessly until he died too. Whatever happened would have to take care of itself because he couldn't. He couldn't do anything but hold Elektra and rock her without thought. So deep in sorrow he never saw the hand that reached out slowly and wrapped itself around the forgotten ankh, the life-giver and perhaps the only future left for any of them.

THE END

ABOUT THE AUTHOR

After an extended detour through the entertainment industry, P.I. Barrington has returned to writing fiction. Among her experience are radio air talent and the music industry. She lives in Los Angeles.

Her work includes:

Future Imperfect Trilogy (Crucifying Angel, Miraculous Deception, Final Deceit)
Inamorata Crossing/Borealis 1: A Space Opera
Isadora DayStar
The Button Hollow Chronicles: The Leaf Peeper Murders
Free stories on ReadWave.com & Wattpad.com

She can be contacted via email:
pibarrington@dslextreme.com or pibarrington@yahoo.com
and welcomes readers to do so!
Her blog: http://www.pibarrington.wordpress.com